WILD WOMAN OF THE ICE!

Hunched on all fours, hands bent into claws, gape stretched wide, eyes-flat green encircled by white and encircling two tiny pits, she swayed. Inhuman, her noise ripped down his backbone. He edged away, hand on dagger hilt. "Donya," he stammered, "what's wrong, be calm, take care." The cabin bulkhead stopped him.

"Rra-a-ao-o!" she screamed, and sprang.

He saw her fly at him, crooked fingers, distorted bleach-white face, teeth ready to be fangs. His knife jumped forth. Before he could stab, she struck. . . .

Tor books by Poul Anderson

Alight in the Void
The Armies of Elfand
The Boat of a Million Years
The Dancer from Atlantis
The Day of Their Return
Explorations
Harvest of Stars
Hoka! (with Gordon R. Dickson)
A Knight of Ghosts and Shadows
Kinship with the Stars
The Long Night
The Longest Voyage
Maurai and Kith
A Midsummer Tempest
No Truce with Kings
Past Times
The Saturn Game
The Shield of Time
Tales of the Flying Mountains
The Time Patrol
There Will be Time

The Winter
of the
World

Poul Anderson

A TOM DOHERTY ASSOCIATES BOOK
NEW YORK

This is a work of fiction. All the characters and events portrayed in this book are fictitious or used fictitiously, and any resemblance to real people or events is purely coincidental.

THE WINTER OF THE WORLD

Copyright © 1976 by Poul Anderson

Cover art by Paul Lehr

A Tor Book
Published by Tom Doherty Associates, Inc.
175 Fifth Avenue
New York, N.Y. 10010

Tor® is a registered trademark of Tom Doherty Associates, Inc.

ISBN: 0-812-52311-3

First Tor edition: February 1995

Printed in the United States of America

0 9 8 7 6 5 4 3 2 1

To
George Scithers
in memory of many a pleasant journey on the
Terminus, Owlswick, & Ft. Mudge Electrick
Street Railway

CHAPTER

1

Once during the Ice Age, three men came riding to Owlhaunt, where Donya of Hervar had her wintergarth. This was on the Stallion River, northwest of the outpost Fuld by four days' travel which the wayfarer from Arvanneth found hard.

The sun had entered the Elk last month and now was aloft longer than a night lasted. Nevertheless, earth still was white; the old stiff snow creaked beneath hoofs. A wind, cutting across level evening light, carried a feel of tundras beyond the horizon and glacial cliffs beyond those.

The country hereabouts came nearer being taiga, though: rolling, mostly open, lean blue shadows tucked in it everywhere, but spiked with groves, darkling pine, birch on whose twigs only icicles grew as yet, shivery willow. Its sky shaded from violet to the east, where early stars blinked forth, across a pale zenith to green

around a disc the color of blood. Crows cawed overhead, nestbound. Far above them, a hawk at hover
caught glow on its wings. Quail scattered to right and
left of the riders, as if on wheels. A pheasant flew in
splendor from a blackberry thicket. On a ridge that
bounded the view south, several hundred big game animals pawed after moss and remnant grass: prairie deer,
horse, moonhorn cattle, dwarf bison mingled together.
From time to time, unseen, a wild hound bayed and a
coyote yelped answer. It was a rich land the Hervar kith
held.

Two of the men belonged in it, Rogaviki born. Theirs
were the shoulderbreadth, ranginess, and height of that
race—the stirrups hung low on their shaggy little
ponies—as well as the fair skin, long head, face wide
and shortnosed and strong in the cheekbones, slant in
the eyes. They happened to be clad much alike, too,
fringed buckskin shirts and trousers ornamented with
dyed porcupine quills, soft half-boots, hooded woolen
cloaks. Each bore two knives, a massive cutting tool
and a slim missile; boar spear, hatchet, bow, quiver, and
lasso were at their saddles. Zhano's hair was ruddy and
he wore it in braids coiled above his nape; Kyrian's was
brown, cut along the jawline. At their ages, seventeen
and eighteen, neither could grow a real beard, so both
went clean-shaven. Zhano was the eldest child of
Donya, Kyrian her youngest husband.

The third was Casiru, former thief, swindler, and cut-
throat, presently vicechief of the Rattlebone Brotherhood and hence a director of thieves, swindlers, and
cutthroats. He had the amber complexion and black eyes
common in Arvanneth, but not the handsomeness. At
fifty, he was small, scrawny, sharp-featured. The hair
trimmed above his ears and the beard and mustache
trimmed to points had long since gone wispy-gray. A

few snag teeth clattered in the cold. His sober-hued elegance of tunic, hose, and shoes was adequate for the South, but not here. He huddled in a borrowed mantle and cursed drearily. The scabbard of his rapier stuck out from beneath like a frozen tail.

Because Zhano and Kyrian were supposed to conduct him to Owlhaunt as fast as might be—after an express courier brought word to Donya that he was aboard a coach for Fuld—they had not hunted their food along the way, but loaded meat, mead, and dried fruit on a packbeast. A second carried a tent, since it was not to be awaited that a city man could simply spread his bedroll out for the night. A third had Casiru's belongings. A fourth, unladen, relieved the rest and was a spare in case of accidents. Otherwise they took no remounts. It was not to be expected either that a city man could travel at the pace of Rogaviki in a hurry.

Thrice this day they had glimpsed the smoke from a homestead, and Casiru asked if that might be their goal. His guides said no. Talk came hard when he had scant knowledge of their language or they of his. Mostly it struggled in Rahídian, a tongue he spoke fluently and they had learned well enough for trade or combat. They managed to explain that those places housed members of Donya's Fellowship—the best translation of *gorozdy* they could arrive at—which was the biggest such informal association of several families to be found in Hervar. Casiru thought of it as hers because he gathered that, in some fashion he didn't quite understand, she led it.

Finally the riders topped a certain crest. Zhano pointed. "There!" he grinned, thumped heels on his mustang, and yelled his way down at a gallop. Kyrian trotted after, leading guest and packhorses.

Casiru strained his gaze ahead. Twilight already filled

the hollow. The hill he was on curved and swelled around on his right until it bulked as a huge rough wall on the north. No doubt it was the graveyard of an ancient town—yes, he thought that among trees and bushes he could make out scars of excavation. To west and south the land lay more flat; but the Stallion River slanted across, thick growth of evergreens along its banks forming a windbreak. From the ridge Casiru looked over the iron-gray frozen stream to mile upon mile of snow tinged pink by the sun as it sank. Further down, his vision was hemmed in. However, the cursed whining wolfwind was likewise blocked, and the end of his journey in sight.

Birches sheltered the buildings. These outlined a broad quadrangle which had been cobbled. Casiru believed he could identify shed, smokehouse, workshop, and stable, kennels, mews for the three kinds of animals the Rogaviki tamed. They were of undressed timber, sod-roofed, but well made. The dwelling filled an entire side of the court, long and wide though standing less high. This was because it was mainly underground, its carpentered walls a mere clerestory. Smoke rose from two of the several chimneys. On the south side, big, flat, black behind glass, tilted a sunpower collector made in Arvanneth. At the middle of the yard reared a skeletal windmill from some manufactury in Rahíd.

Hounds roared forth to greet or challenge. They resembled their savage kin, tall, gaunt, gray. Breath exploded white from their fangs and frosted their muzzles. Zhano quieted them. A door opened in a dormer jutting from the house. Black against yellow light, a man bade the newcomers welcome.

He led them down a ladder to a vestry, and thence to the principal chamber. Wood floors, carpeted with hides or imported fabrics, kept feet warm. Interior partitions were movable, grotesquely carved, gaudily painted. In the largest room, weapons blinked bright on white-washed earthen walls, amidst stylized murals of creatures, plants, and natural forces. Shelves held hundreds of books; heat came from a Rahídian stove whose tiles were delicately figured; Southland oil lamps shone from a dozen brackets. Among bundles of fruits and greens hung on the rafters were flower sachets to sweeten the air. As the travelers entered, a girl put aside a crook-backed stringed instrument on which she had been accompanying a song. Her last notes seemed to linger for a space, less wild than wistful.

Folk sat crosslegged on ledges running around the floor, or on cushions by a low table. Present were Donya's six children, ranging from Zhano to three-year-old Valdevanya; Zhano's wife, staying here while he was away since thus far he was her sole husband; two of Donya's men, counting Kyrian, the other two being off on expeditions of their own; four unwedded kins-women, aged, middle-aged, young, half-grown; and Donya herself. Faces and bodies declared that all belonged to the Rogaviki. Else they showed little in common—certainly not dress or hair style, save that in this warmth they went either scantily clad or nude.

Donya sprang from the platform where she had lain sprawled on a bearskin, to seize both Casiru's hands. On her way, she quickly and passionately embraced Kyrian. "Welcome, friend." Her husky voice stumbled a bit over the Southland words. "*Eyach*, wait!" she laughed. "Your pardon. I am out of practice." Crossing wrists on bosom, bowing deep, she uttered a polite formula of the city. "O guest, may God the Indweller shine forth between us."

Half a smile twisted Casiru's lips. "Scarcely when it's

me," he said. "Have you forgotten in these past three years?"

For a moment she grew grave, and picked her way phrase by phrase. "I remember . . . you are a rascal, yes . . . yet trustworthy when you have reason to be. . . . And why have you come this far . . . jouncing over ruts on a coach . . . rather than comfortable on a packet boat . . . unless you need us . . . and we, maybe, need you?"

Her regard of him was a steady searching. His of her was a probing, which touched her in passage around and around the room; but it had a thief's intensity.

She'd not changed much since she visited Arvanneth and they met. At thirty-five, she remained straight, her movements flowed and strength pounced in her grip. He could well see that, since tonight she wore a cloth kilt for its pockets, a necklace of shells and teeth, and a good deal of skin paint in red and blue loops. She was fuller-figured than most Rogaviki women, but muscles underlay each curve. Her breasts swelled milk-heavy; a mother among the Northfolk often gave suck for years after she gave birth, not just to her latest child but to siblings, or the children of friends, or even an adult who might want refreshment. Her countenance was striking, the oblique eyes gray-green, nostrils flared, mouth broad above a square chin. Wavy yellow-brown hair fell to her shoulders, clasped by a beaded headband. At this end of the dark season her color was luminous white; a few freckles crossed the blunt nose like ghosts of summer's gold.

"Come, sit, be at ease," she invited. To her youngsters of intermediate age and to the spinsters she said a few words. They left. Obviously she had requested them to unload Casiru's baggage and prepare food. But despite what study of Rogavikian he had done on his journey—and a Knife Brother in polyglot Arvanneth was a quick study, or he went under—he could not follow what she said. The same held true later on, whenever remarks passed between members of the family. At most, he caught single words here and there. He had heard of each kin-group evolving its own traditions, its very dialect; but the reality upset him.

After all, when they met in the Southland city, he had taken her for a barbarian: intelligent, delightful company (in spite of refusing him her body, no matter how lickerish a reputation her people bore), but still the naïve daughter of primitive hunters. Arvanneth, ancientest metropolis in the known world, was the labyrinth where subtleties and secrets dwelt. This man-empty North had no right to them!

Accustomed to chairs, Casiru perched on the rim of a ledge, feet on floor. Donya smiled and put pillows behind him so he could sit back. She settled at his right. Yven, her first husband, took the left side. He was a couple of years her senior, leathery, eyes pale blue, close-cropped hair and beard streaked white through their sorrel. A tunic of foreign linen left bare a great scar on his thigh, where a bull he was hunting had gored him.

Unoccupied members of the household disposed themselves on the rug. Their direct gaze betrayed interest, but they were as aloof, as reserved, as every civilized visitor had reported. . . . No, wait, Zhano and his girl-wife had gone out, arms around waists. . . . Donya's six-year-old Lukeva brought glass goblets of hot mead on a tray. Casiru gratefully took one, warmed his palms on it, inhaled the fragrance, leaned his aches and saddle sores back into softness.

"Would you rest a night before we talk about why you came?" Yven asked in surprisingly good Rahídian. Maybe he made a trading trip yearly or biennially, southwest to the Khadrahad Valley, Casiru thought; or maybe he had mastered the language for war purposes—Donya had described how members of her kith joined in helping repel the Imperial invasion a decade ago, herself among them—or maybe both—"We will eat soon, and you can go straight after to your bed."

"Well, we'd best not confer at length before tomorrow," Casiru said. He drank a mouthful, dry and herbal-pungent. "But a general idea—How have you fared here? What news?"

"None for our folk as a whole," Donya answered. She interlarded her hesitant Arvannethan with occasional Rahídian, and frequently stopped to translate for the rest. "The seasons run their course. Among us, Valdevanya is new, not that you ever saw any of my family before. Likewise Kyrian. We married last winter solstice. Two years past, my third husband died, drowned fishing when his skiff capsized and he struck his head against it."

"I regret," Casiru murmured.

"We miss him," Yven said.

"Yes." Donya let her sigh fade away, reached down to rumple Kyrian's hair, and smiled at Yven across Casiru's breast. "Folk lose, folk win; in the end, we give back to the land what it lent us. How has your life gone?"

The city man shrugged. "Up and down, in and out, round and round, as ever. Until this fall, when Arvanneth was conquered."

Donya leaned on an elbow, waiting. Fingers tightened about her goblet and a ripple ran beneath lamplit skin. Through windows gone dark came a lonesome hooting.

"I would not think, from what I know of your kind, Casiru, that you suffered any real change," said Yven slowly. "How many different masters has Arvanneth had, through how many thousands of years? And each believed he owned it, until time blew him away, and Arvanneth abided."

Casiru coughed out a chuckle. "And the Lairs were never touched, eh? My sort continued like the rats. Correct, more or less. Yet . . . when ferrets come, woe betide the rats. I fear this is what's happened."

He hunched forward. "Listen, I pray you. What have you heard in Hervar, farther north than navigation goes on the Jugular River? That the Empire of Rahíd marched eastward along the shores of the Dolphin Gulf, captured Arvanneth, and occupies it. You think: What's that to you? The Southrons will still want metal. The trade will go on. Your kiths will wander free throughout their lands.

"But I tell you, Donya, everybody among the Northfolk, this is not the same as before. The Empire fell apart three hundred years ago. Its rebuilders are the Barommians, warriors from the highlands to the south of it. Their might and ambition are what menace us, you and me alike.

"I own I expected no harm from the conquest. Rather, pickings should be fine for us Brothers while the turmoil lasted. But it's been different. Ferrets indeed have been loosed in our tunnels. Growing desperate, I booked a seat on the first post coach of this year, under a false name. At the Agameh hostel I found a Rogaviki courier and paid him to bring you, my lady, a letter that said I was coming. Zhano and Kyrian kindly met me in Fuld. And here I am."

He stopped for breath and drank deep. The mead began buzzing in his weary head, as if the bees of a long-gone summer awoke to clover meadows.

"Then . . . you believe . . . the Barommian lords of Rahíd mean to invade us next?" Yven inquired.

"I am sure," Casiru replied.

Donya tossed back her cougar-hued locks. "Our oldest tales remember no time when Southrons did not want our country for plowland and pasture," she said. "Whenever they tried, they got ruin. In my lifespan, we fought them on the Dusty Plains till they slunk back to their Khadrahad River; and they had Barommian leadership then too. If they cannot learn, well, let them troop through the Jugular Valley. The buzzards will be glad."

"I tell you, this captain who took Arvanneth is like none ever before him," Casiru pleaded. "I understand you can't act on my naked word. But come see, listen, feel, think for yourselves."

Donya's eyes kindled. She had lived quietly of late, compared to her earlier farings. "Maybe," she said low. "We will talk further."

They did, throughout the following month. Messengers brought heads of household from widely about, some even from kiths whose territories lay beyond Hervar. They listened intently, conferred earnestly, agreed that in this business they and the Brotherhoods had a shared interest. Meanwhile Casiru enjoyed lavish material hospitality. Several unmarried women sought him in private, driven by a curiosity which was soon quenched. Yet no matter the politeness accorded him, he never saw below the surface of any person. Nor did he find any hope of mobilizing the Rogaviki. That concept did not exist for them. His attempted explanations glided straight off.

When the ice melted on the Jugular and the first boat from Arvanneth docked at Fuld, he took a berth home on it. Donya promised she would investigate his warnings further. But a year went past before she seriously did.

CHAPTER
2

Tornado alive, Josserek Derrain burst from his prison cabin. Behind him, Second Mate Rigdel Gairloch sprawled bloody-faced. His sheath knife gleamed in Josserek's grasp.

Sailors at work around *Skonnamor* saw the huge man come bounding, and yelled. Three of them moved to stop him. He left the deck in a leap. His right foot smote a belly. The sailor fell backward and lay clawing for breath. With his own weapon, Josserek blocked a thrust, while he stiff-armed the companion. He reached the starboard rail, snatched a belaying pin from a rack, whirled, and laid it across the scalp of a fourth shipmate who was almost upon him. A final spring, and he went overboard.

His dive crashed water aloft and shocked back through his bones. When he opened his eyes, yellow-green murk enclosed him. He could just make out a shimmer on the surface, and the freighter's dim hull. Tucking blade under belt, he strove deeper into chill and heaviness. *Pass below her keel*— he scraped against barnacles; a trace of blood trailed after—*port side, wharf*—

When his lungs felt about to erupt and darkness thundered in his skull, he sought upward again. Barely did he let nose and mouth poke forth, and he struggled not to gasp. The air was full of harbor smells, salt, smoke, tar, fish. He heard soles thump swiftly on planks, angry shouts, alarmed gulls. He was beneath the dock where *Skannamor* lay, far back in a cave of shadow which it made. Pilings and a clutter of moored boats gave added concealment. *Thus far we're on course,* he thought.

For a while, then, he let himself float and rest, holding onto a painter. The racket ended overhead. No crewman had really cared to hunt the escaped mutineer: a dangerous quarry. The officers must regret losing him, since to take him back for trial and punishment in Eaching would have set an example. However, tracking him was now a job for local patrollers. If they failed, it was not too important. An outlaw alien, Josserek had no place to go but the underworld, and probably could not prosper there. Likeliest his gullet-slit corpse would soon be found in an alley or on an ebb tide. If his ship had not already departed, that might prove a healthier lesson than his sentence to a labor gang.

Still, chances were the Barommians would do their best to catch him. As soon as the commandant here got word, he'd set the Watch out searching. Possibly he'd not be content with native police, but order some of his soldiers to the task as well. Authorities never welcomed the idea of a violent man at large in their jurisdictions. Besides, it'd be a goodwill gesture; and the gods knew

how strained relations had grown between Killimaraich
and Rahíd.

Therefore, son, we'd better make Arvanneth, and fast.

Josserek poised peering and thinking. He'd been confined to a spare compartment in the after deckhouse,
tethered to a staple, since before his ship entered the
Dolphin Gulf. Through the portholes he'd barely gotten
glimpses as she reached Newkeep and was warped into
her berth. This refuge was little better.

Skonnamor blocked most of his view. She was a big
vessel, a four-master with a powerful auxiliary to
drive a screw propeller, meant for months-long jour-
neys. Her trip here had exceeded the usual. As a rule,
merchantmen between Killimaraich and Rahíd simply
crossed the Mother Ocean to one of the Empire's west
coast harbors. But then, Arvanneth had not been in
the Empire till a year and a half ago. Rather than risk
Damnation Straits, Captain Bahin had navigated his
command south of Orenstane, then west over the Feline Ocean till he rounded Eflis, and finally northwest
across the Rampant to his goal. He brought hides,
wool, and pickled meat, always in demand, especially
so in the aftermath of war. (*Why* didn't the barbarians
who roamed northern Andalin take advantage of the
market? Travellers said that earth shook beneath the
mass of the wild herds yonder.) But, while lengthy,
his voyage was not extraordinary by standards of the
Seafolk.

Josserek's glance sought past bow and stern, right and
left and behind. Docks and warehouses lined this mouth
of the Jugular River. Many were in use, and more craft
rode out at anchor. *Skonnamor* was the only real blue-
water ship. The rest were coastal schooners and luggers,
fishing smacks that never went outside the Gulf, clumsy
steamboats that plied upstream. Inshore, Newkeep

raised walls, towers, battlements. The light of a newly risen sun glowed on lichenous brick, flashed off high windows, gave back red and gold from the Imperial standard which flew above.

Scant information. Josserek must rely on memory of maps and books and sailors' tales. Despite its name, as commonly translated by the Seafolk, Newkeep was over three thousand years old. Before, Arvanneth had been its own port; but the retreat of the sea, the ever deeper channeling of the river, the silting of the delta, had finally made that impossible. Now the Ancient of Ancients lay almost a hundred miles inland.

Now? Whole civilizations had lived, and died, and from their ashes engendered new, while that "now" lasted.

Josserek shook his wet head. Time to stop gathering moonbeams.

The hunters would expect him to seek a hiding place in Newkeep. Small and engirdled, it didn't offer much. Arvanneth had more holes and burrows than a hull the teredos had been at, as well as an estimated half million people among whom to vanish. Not to speak of—Let that wait. First he must get there, undetected. Later he'd see about surviving there.

A throb in air and water reached his senses, grew, brought him alert. Yes, his chance, better than many he'd taken in his thirty-two tumultuous years. A tug was bound his way, hauling three barges. It was a side-wheeler; to judge by the smoke from the tall stack, its engine ate wood. Those things meant it was built in these parts. Short of timber on their plains, the Rahídians had mostly burned oil in their comparatively few machines, till the Barommian conquerors reserved that precious stuff for military and naval use. Today the Empire copied the alcohol and methane motors of the Seafolk. . . . The barges carried barrels that smelled like fish, and assorted boxes of goods which must be from the coastwise trade, unloaded here for transshipment to the queen city.

Josserek struck out on an interception course. His crawl kept most of him submerged, unlikely to be noticed amidst the trash bobbing about. As the tug threshed nigh, he went altogether below, let it pass, rose by the rearmost barge on the side opposite his ship. Freeboard was a bare two feet. He reached, caught hold of a lashing on deck, let himself trail. The water gurgled around him, cold when the heat of escape had died away. Sharktoothed cold.

He risked chinning himself sufficiently high for a peek. A couple of pikemen lounged by a shack on the forward barge, guards against bandits. They weren't looking aft, and nobody else was outside. Josserek came aboard in a swift slither.

Three crates made a wall to hide him, a niche for comfort. And, yes, he could pull a flemished line in there to sit on, pleasanter than planks. He noticed his fingers snap. That was a habit he'd picked up in his wanderings, a gambler's gesture of thanks to the elves when they made dice fall right. Superstition? Maybe, maybe not. Josserek had no formal faith. His nation's cult of gods forever at strife—not good against evil, but simply opposed, like summer and winter—seemed reasonable to him; however, he hadn't made a sacrifice since boyhood.

He removed his garments and spread them to dry. Except that he was barefoot, they were too characteristic of eastern Orenstane for him to display hereabouts, a male's loose blouse and bell-bottomed trousers, colorfully woven. From an ankle hung the stump of the cord which had restrained him. Seated

among the crates, he cut it away. A chance-found rag
made a loincloth; it would be stupid to shock people.
Thereafter, senses fine-tuned, he let his thews ease
off.

He was a big man, even among his home folk: six
and a quarter feet in height, broad to match. His features
were craggy, gray-eyed, curve-nosed. By choice he went
clean-shaven, but during his confinement had grown a
beard which partly hid the scar seaming his left cheek.
Black hair was bobbed just under his earlobes, which
carried small brass rings. A snake coiled around an anchor was tattooed on the thick right forearm, an orca on
the left. Where clothes had shielded his skin, it was pale
brown; like most Killimaraichans, he had among his ancestors some people of that country's tributaries in western Orenstane. The weathered parts of him were much
darker.

*We'll pass plenty of crews today who'll spy us,
Josserek, me bucko,* he thought, *and we can hardly pre-
tend we're a short, slim, saffron-colored Arvannethan—or
a stocky, red, nearly whiskerless Barommian—can we?
But we might well be taken for a Rahídian by whoever
doesn't squint too close; and the bulk of the Imperial
army is Rahídian by descent; and maybe it's not strange
that, say, an Imperial soldier would commandeer a ride,
and be so boorish as to relax semi-naked in public after
a swim. Hey?* He lounged back as if he owned the whole
rig. To the occasional stare he did draw, he returned a
cheery wave of his hand.

Water traffic wasn't as dense as at a major port of
Seafolk. But it was more than he had expected. Conquest didn't seem to have damaged commerce for very
long. Rather, the Barommian overlords were encouraging new activity in the stagnant old city-state.

Early on, Josserek saw a barge train come down-stream laden with slabs and rails of rusty iron. That would be metal the Northfolk supplied in return for manufactured goods and such luxuries as spices. But this consignment was scarcely for Rahíd, whose dealers had always bought their share from Guildsmen in Arvanneth and transported it home overland. If any-thing, dominion here would reinforce their style of op-erating. They were landlubbers at heart, reluctant to trust valuable freight to the sea.

Barommians, horsemen and mountaineers from the bleak country south of Rahíd, had had no maritime in-terests at all . . . till they overran and reunified the Em-pire. Now—Hm. Josserek scratched in his beard, which itched as it dried. They were stimulating the expansion of Imperial enterprise beyond the Gulf, among the is-landers of the Hurricane Sea and the forest folk along the Tuocar coast. And *that* forbode trouble, because traders from Killimaraich and allied realms in the Mother Ocean had developed a strong interest of their own in those same regions.

Well, we knew this already, he thought. *Yon outbound iron cargo is a symptom, not a surprise.* He was never-theless fascinated. Nowhere else did excavation yield metal in as prime a condition. What fabulous ruins did the barbarians mine?

Other craft included rowboats, log rafts, a patrol gal-ley whose fighting men gave him a sharp second look but didn't question him. When the gilt-arabesqued many-oared yacht of what seemed to be an aristocratic lady, or a favorite concubine, passed by in music and perfume, he got a stare more appraising. Twice, in stretches of reed and gray-behung cypress, a canoe glided from a creek, manned by a short-legged grass-skirted savage from the Swamps of Unvar. Elsewhere the land lay flat, ditched, cultivated in great plantations belonging to the city's Lords. At this springtide it was delicately green, save where orchards flamed and snowed. It smelled of growth. Occasionally it smelled stronger, when he passed a clutch of workers' huts and henyards behind a rickety wharf.

At sunset the tug wheezed to a halt for the night. Men came from below to set out anchors and riding lights. Josserek was ready for this. He slipped into the water and swam ashore, his clothes on his head. Somebody called through swift-falling dusk, "Hoai, what's that?" but another voice answered, "An alligator, I think, in-migrated early this year." Brush concealed his re-entry onto land; the bank was steep and overgrown. Not far inward from the top, he found a highway and struck off along it, *pad-pad* on paving blocks where uncounted generations of feet had worn faint channels. He was soon dry again, and dressed himself. Stars bloomed big and soft, but tendrils of fog which sneaked forth across the plowland were nastily chill.

Emptiness growled in his guts. He could ignore that. However, he'd better start thinking how he, a wanted man with not a bronze in his pocket, might get through the next few days. First came a swifter means of reaching town.

When he was fifteen years old, Josserek had been sentenced to a labor gang for assault on a naval officer who taunted him in his raggedness. The gang went to a sheep ranch in central Orenstane. After two years he escaped, wandered starving, eventually reached the coast and got a berth on a tramp ship whose master was too short of crew to quiz him. Later he had done many different things. But he remembered the ways of horses.

The one he lifted was too good for the ramshackle barn that held it, on the edge of the next hamlet he came to: a spirited gelding which whickered softly as he led it out, danced around him while he put on the bridle he had also found in the dark, and carried him bareback at a fine, ringing clip. No doubt the plantation owner had left it to be pastured on fresh grass after winter's hay. Josserek regretted that at first he'd had to kill a noisy dog, drag the carcass off, and wait while an aroused tenant decided there had been a false alarm and went back to sleep. Had the mongrel been a pet of whatever children lived in that hovel?

Toward morning he reached Arvanneth.

Towers climbed gaunt or squat, bulbous or jagged, the mingled works of more centuries than history had counted, up from among crowded walls, roofs steep or flat, lanes full of night, till they loomed athwart fading stars. Mostly the city was blackness and silence; a few places there glimmered a lamp or prowled a whisper. The water around sheened oily and rank. Eras past, Arvanneth had been circled by a bight of the Jugular, and the moatlike remnant of this was still called the Lagoon. But now the river ran no closer than five miles. Canals crossed the land in between. A single causeway ran from the end of the Grand East Highroad. Josserek saw how lanterns burned on posts along it, and a fortified checkpoint scowled at its end. He decided he'd better abandon his mount. The ferry service which at dawn would leave the inn at this terminus of the Newkeep road was not for a pauper like him, either. Yet he dared not swim. The wizards of a vanished glory time had bred strange and gluttonous creatures to inhabit those depths . . . or disease brewed in filth might be a worse danger.

A skiff was chained near the ferry. Josserek whittled links and lock free of bollard and stempost both, because the metal ought to fetch a good price in Thieves' Market. Oars were absent, but he found he could pry a board loose from the half-rotted dock and paddle across with that.

He didn't go directly over. There lay Treasure Notch, where rivercraft and warehouses must have better guard than here. Instead, he circled left. His plank worked slowly and tiringly. But he was soon too caught by everything he saw, as false dawn turned sky and waters pallid, to notice his body much.

He passed New Canal, which divided a forested game preserve and the grounds of a moldering mansion; more estates, some of which kept their elaborately trimmed gardens; Royal Canal, where traffic already stirred; West Canal, its especially high-arched bridge, the road that paralleled it; and further on, the Westreach, weeds, bushes, bog, scrub oak, pine running on toward unseen Unvar. Opposite, the canals continued from the Lagoon into the city. At each entrance hulked walls, turrets, portcullis: Seagate, the Grand Bastion, the Little Bastion. Cannon, catapults, helmets, spearheads caught light and sparked. Imperial banners drooped in damp hushed air.

Sunrise had unfurled when he decided he'd come far enough. By all accounts, this part of town held the Lairs, where honest folk did not go if they could help it. He might be safe on the north side—the Hollow Houses district was said to be almost wholly abandoned—but what would he eat there? He pushed to a small pier. Stone, it had not decayed like the ferry slip, though iron cleats and mooring rings were long gone and the building behind it gaped vacant. Josserek stood for a moment in his boat, wondering if he should secure it somehow: might get a price for it too. No, likeliest it would disappear the instant he left. Let it drift free. Hope the owner could reclaim it.

He jumped ashore. "Stand quiet," said a voice. "Drop that chain. Don't bring your hands anywhere near your knife."

Very carefully he obeyed, before he turned to meet the three men who had taken him.

CHAPTER

3

Here snowfall of winter had given way to rain, or to fog
that sneaked through twisty streets, turned walls to
shadows and folk to phantoms. Almost since the day
when his army rafted over the water, hewed over the
causeway, raised its standards in triumph above antiquity and the slain, Sidír had longed elsewhere. He
thought less of lacquered splendor and Imperial court
ceremony in Naís—though there Nedayin, his young
wife bestowed on him out of old Rahídian nobility,
dwelt with the one thin child of theirs who lived—than
of Zangazeng the Black, where Ang the wife of his
youth abode with her sturdy brood of six, in sight of
white-crowned volcanoes; and mainly he remembered
the high country around that town, Haamandur itself,
pastureland of horses, Barommian encampments where
firelight and merriment twinkled under diamond-
brilliant stars, herds guarded by cowboys or shepherd-

esses who were alike armed and fearless, a windy gallop
to the music of hounds till wild boar or stag stood at
bay and he laid hand on spear. In Arvanneth he often
wryly recalled a saying of his mountaineer kin: "The
bobcat has captured the cage."

This morning had been clear, but about noon clouds
massed and moved on a wind that blew off the Swamps
of Unvar and smelled of them. Now heaven hung low
and leaden, gloom walled the west and rolled ever
closer, lightning winked, thunder grumbled. Despite
broad windows, the Moon Chamber had already gone
nighted in its corners, and elsewhere the phases painted
in silver upon violet shimmered only dully. Rather than
freshening air, the oncoming storm prophesied summer's dank warmth.

Sidír leaned forward. His fingers tightened around the
carven water moccasins along his chair arms. "Do I understand you, your Wisdom?" he asked. In months of
viceroyalty, his Arvannethan had become fluent; but it
was still roughened by the Barommian accent he could
never quite get out of his Rahídian either. "The Council
would naysay this next Imperial enterprise?"

I hope that struck the right note, he thought. *Not
overharsh—I could sweep the whole weird theocracy
aside with a few beheading strokes, except that I need,
the Empire needs its cooperation. At the same time, I
must keep it reminded who's master. Should I have spoken softer? These people are so cursed alien!*

Ercer en-Havan gave him a look he couldn't read, sullen or sly or half afraid or scornful or what? The
Wiseman was middle-aged, his forked beard dark but
wrinkles deep in the yellowish face, around delicate nose
and mouth, forming a network across hands whose rose-
painted fingernails he bridged point to point. The robe of
his order, Gray, swathed him from curl-toed shoes to

thrown-back hood. On his chain of office hung a smoke crystal sphere engraved with a global map so old that a naked eye could see how, later, Ice had waxed and oceans waned. He was Holy Councilor for the World.

Sidír thought of him in prosiac Barommian, as the city-state's head of civil affairs. That made Ercer the last of the lords spiritual who had anything real to do. As for the Holy Councilor of the Godhood, religious matters in Arvanneth had long ceased to be much more than intrigues between Temples. The mass of the population was sunken in superstition and corruptions of faith, or in unbelief, or in the worship of strange gods. As for the Holy Councilor of the Woe, conquest by the Empire had removed his responsibility for military business and left him simply a courtesy title.

Presiding over this triumvirate, the Grand Wiseman of the Council was a figurehead. His predecessor had led resistance to the Imperials, but conveniently died in honorable detention soon after they entered. Sidír had never asked for details, nor perhaps had Yurussun Soth-Zora. A hint, dropped to Rahídian subordinates who were skilled in such things, would have sufficed. The city abbots had elected as their new head of state that harmless dodderer whom the conquerors tactfully suggested.

Thus Ercer en-Havan was the logical spokesman for the former rulers of Arvanneth. Doubtless he called secret meetings of his colleagues which debated what united front they should present to the foreign overlords. And this past year and a half he had done well by the native upper class. His blend of respectfulness, sound advice, and hauteur too subtle ever to be called arrogance, had won concession after concession.

Today's word, though, was astounding.

"The Captain General knows we would never presume to question an edict from the Glorious Throne." His voice slithered like a snake across the silken carpet. "Yet—forgive a search for elucidation—is his proposed campaign the direct will of the Emperor, or is it an . . . executive decision . . . made by lower and conceivably fallible officials—say, on the provincial level?"

Sidír barked a laugh. "You ask, Ercer, if I alone order it. Or if not, how high are the heads over which you must appeal to get it countermanded?"

"No, no! God, Who is in all things and above all things, give His grace to my truthtelling. The Captain General and—" tiniest hesitation, barest flick of lidded eye across Yurussun—"the Imperial Voice, between them represent the Glorious Throne. Their mutual will is not to be gainsaid. But they have shown themselves to be of that intelligence which is ready to hear counsel: counsel which, may I dare remind them, comes from those whose forebears also had . . . experience in empire."

Yurussun sat unstirring, countenance and body alike. Perhaps, as a Philosopher trained, he meditated on the Nine Correct Principles, off which an infinitely more gross insult than Ercer's ought to glide. Having given his co-governor several seconds in which to respond, Sidír made answer:

"Well, your Wisdom, I will confirm what you have reckoned out. The Northlands are next. Or I might say they were always first. No slur intended, Arvanneth is a rare jewel on the Emperor's brow, but from a strategic viewpoint this territory is more a way station than a goal in itself." He gestured outward. "Half a continent yonder!"

"We know." In that phrase did Ercer again recall to them how many centuries his chroniclers had watched peoples wash to and fro across the world. "Ever has Rahíd desired those plains for its farmers. Lately Baromm has reached the edge of them, and desires grazing for its flocks. The Divine Mandate has passed to the descendants of Skeyrad, making conquest no mere decision, but a destiny. Yes. However, may I in my ignorance ask why the Imperial forces do not simply move straight north from the Khadrahad Valley?"

"Because that was tried again and again, including under the present dynasty some ten years back, and never worked . . . as a scholar should know." Sidír suppressed his irritation. "A drive up the Jugular, now, can split the barbarians in two, cut off their metal supply and foreign trade, provide us strong bases in fertile country from which we can reduce them in detail. Later, when they're weakened, will come the direct push out of Rahíd."

Ercer maintained a waiting silence. Sidír's fingertips drummed on his chair arm, until it burst from him: "Look here! Let me give you a speech, starting with the obvious. That's sometimes harder to see than the esoteric is.

"Of your three levels of dominance in Arvanneth, naturally your secular Lords are embittered. We've pushed them down to being plantation owners with pedigrees nobody will care about next generation; for *we* will raise and command the rural levies. When we open the Northlands to settlement, your old noble families will get competition in food and cotton marts. No wonder they complain, conspire, and squirm.

"But why do you in the Temples join them? You must likewise have listened to the Guilds. You know how on the whole, more and more, your merchants are glad of the Empire. It's breaking the crust of law and custom that bound them. It's widening and making safer their trade. As they win money, they win power. They don't mind in the least if that's at the expense of a class which sneered at them aforetime.

"They are the future. You can be too. The Council, the Orders that elect it and staff its offices, the Temples that nurture the Orders—all the Wise can play a high part in the Empire. A higher part in fact, if not in name, than what you had before—" Sidír checked himself from using a Barommian expression: "when you were chief ghosts in a graveyard." Rather, he finished, "But for that, you must change with the times. Live and prosper with the Guilds, not crumble away with the Lords."

"It is not always well to change with the times, Captain General," Ercer said slowly. "Those nations which did it too readily are gone and forgotten. Arvanneth has abided." His tone became practical. "Yes, we have heard out various Guildsmen. Some do fear trouble. For instance, their metal trade with the Rogaviki is immemorial. Institutions have evolved around it. To break those arrangements and agreements will dispossess many, and stop the flow."

"For a while," Sidír snapped. "You've heard how we're working on means, like subsidies, for preventing undue distress. And soon we'll start the flow afresh, beyond what those scattered barbarians ever cared to bring you. Most merchants grow content after I explain."

Ercer's regard changed somehow. Was it even a little frightened? His speech dropped until the wind beyond the panes well-nigh drowned it. "Do you truly propose . . . going the whole way . . . to Unknown Roong?"

"Maybe. My plans are still on the forge, being reshaped as I get information." Sidír leaned back. "In due course, yes, Roong will absolutely be the Emperor's. Just when or how is a matter for his servants to determine. My basic scheme, a campaign through the Jugular

Valley, has been approved. I have broad discretion. I could actually decide it's unfeasible. So, your Wisdom, you may present whatever arguments you want, to me."

Ercer paused before he said, "The Captain General is a sagacious man, ready to hear the very humblest." His failure to include Yurussun did not escape Sidír. The Rahídian kept impassive. "Let me say merely this. His plan is bold, worthy of his grandsires whose valor brought oneness and peace back to the Empire. Yet . . . conceivably too bold? We Wise oppose nothing in principle. Nevertheless, having been made subjects of the Glorious Throne, we share a right and duty to advise wherever we can. And what we say is, you should not attempt further expansion this year. Nor the next, nor the next. The Northlands have waited a long while; they can wait a while more. Ancient, intricate Arvanneth is what needs continued attention. Soldiers alone cannot hold it; statecraft is required. In due respect, I remind the Captain General how many, many potentates throughout these thousands of years believed they had made Arvanneth theirs."

"You fear, if I take most of my forces north—what? Rebellion? Who would be so crazy, knowing I would return to punish them?"

"And the Orders will, of course, lay ban and curse on whoever speaks sedition. But . . . the Seafolk have numerous ships in nearby waters."

"Merchantmen, explorers, making trouble for ours among the islands, quarrels that sometimes lead to fights—yes, I know. However, I know too that they can't by themselves take any defended place hereabouts; and they have no allies ashore. Besides, the Seniory of Killimaraich is not composed of fools. If anything, Eaching tries to restrain the lesser Seafolk nations, lest a war with the Empire be provoked. They don't feel ready for one . . . yet."

"If your army should suffer disaster, though—Captain General, Roong is not called Unknown for nothing. We in Arvanneth, whose dominion once reached there, we ourselves have scant records left of it, besides myths and mysteries."

"You've never thought of returning. Nor, pardon my bluntness, are your scholars interested in acquiring new knowledge. I am. It goes well." Sidír drew breath. "I told you, maybe I won't strike all the way to Roong this year. I am not as rash as you seem to think. I'll not risk my men, my own Bright Lances, for vanity's sake."

Ercer gave him a close look. "But you do intend to risk yourself," he murmured. "Can I persuade you, at the minimum, not to do that? Send your army if you must. But you stay here. Continue your work among us."

Taken aback, Sidír exclaimed, "What? You want to keep me, whose horse left red tracks up the stairs of your Crown Temple?"

"You govern sternly but justly. Why, alone the criminals whom you have hunted down and executed put us in your debt."

"I do not govern by myself." Sidír spoke with sharpness, for he thought Ercer's baiting of Yurussun had better cease. "My task is military. Well, Arvanneth and its hinterland are pacified. My duty reaches elsewhere. Civil government lies with my viceregal colleague, the Imperial Voice."

"True." Millennia of an ingrown, stratified society had taught Ercer an urbanity which could scoff. "Still, two such great men would not be coequal were their tasks not intertwined. Let me list how much remains to be done by the Captain General in person."

For the first moment since he had ceremoniously greeted the Councilor, Yurussun took a part. Beneath softness, his tone crackled: "Your Wisdom, I assume you would go into endless detail. I fear we have no time for that today. Other people expect to see us. And in any event, such things are best submitted first as written reports, facts and figures which we can study at length. If you will do that, your Wisdom, we will receive you here for further discussion when circumstances permit."

Hatred smoldered in Ercer's gaze. He dropped lids over it, touched forehead to fingertips in deference, and said, "I realize the Captain General and his colleague are busy. I will prepare the letter the Voice demands, as fast as scribes can take dictation. Perhaps my next interview should be with the Captain General only. There is no reason for me to trouble the august Voice, whom indeed I did not anticipate finding here. May God reveal us truth."

Rituals of good-bye followed. At last a nacre-covered door swung shut, and Arvanneth's masters were alone in the Moon Chamber.

Sidír could sit no longer. He sprang erect, prowled among furnishings, back and forth before a marble hearth, until he crossed the floor to stand at a window, thumbs hooked in belt. This room was on the fourth story of the Golin Palace and the window was large. Thus he saw widely over the city he had conquered.

On his left he glimpsed the Gardens of Elzia, surrounding Lake Narmu where the waterways met. On his right he spied similarly a bit of the arches carrying the Patrician Bridge (for courtiers five thousand years dust) from this building, above the New and Royal Canals and the common life of the metropolis, to the Grand Arena. Ahead he viewed a plaza surrounded by marble façades which remained impressive though time had blurred their columns and blotted their friezes. It had likewise, even in this wet climate, put a purple iridescence in the glass through which he looked, so that he saw the world strangely hued.

Otherwise it was a world of ordinary bustle. Several major streets emptied into the square. Beyond the enclosing public structures reached plain, flat-roofed shops and tenements, generally of brown brick. In front of them huddled booths where ragged folk sold tawdry wares. Between them passed humans, sparrows, pigeons, now and then a gaunt dog or laden wagon.

No soldiers were in sight, apart from an occasional native militiaman whose striped kilt, below a green tunic, identified his unit. Sidír was careful to keep his army as inconspicuous as possible. Male civilians wore their tunics longer, to the knees. A majority had shed the hose, boots, and cowled cloaks of winter, and bore sandals on their feet, knitted caps on their heads. The long-tressed women wore brief, provocative versions of the same. Materials were gaudy and a great deal of cheap jewelry glittered. Exceptions were the old, who muffled themselves in drab clothes and dignity, and monks and nuns of the four Orders of Wisdom, Red, White, Gray, Black.

They were a short and slender race, these Arvannethans, dark-haired, dark-eyed, amber-skinned, fine-featured. Their movements were usually quick and graceful, their gestures lively. The weight of a civilization millennia petrified did not burden the chaotic, mostly illiterate mass of its Low. Sidír could just catch the marketplace noise, footfall, hoof-clatter, talk, laughter, a reed flute played for a dancer, the groan of an ox-cart wheel. He could imagine smoke, incense, dung, dream weed, a vendor's roasting ears of corn, sweat, perfume, like a shimmer across the odors from canals and swamps. But thunder and wind were overriding these, and people thinned out beneath the lightning. A few raindrops blew past, scouts for storm.

He grew aware that Yurussun had joined him, and turned. "Well," he asked, "what do you think about our visitor?" Immediately he realized that, though he spoke Rahídian, he had allowed Barommian brusqueness to shape it. *The Devil Mare kick me for a fool!* he thought. *I don't want him insulted any more this day. He and I have enough trouble working together as it is.*

Expressionless, the other replied, "Ever oftener, I believe we are mistaken in trying to conciliate those so-called Wise." No matter how levelly he spoke, his blunt phrasing came as a shock.

"What would you do instead?" Sidír challenged.

"That was a rhetorical question, Captain General. You know. Dissolve the Council, discharge its underlings, rule Arvanneth directly. Put the Temple leaders in preventive detention. Watch their lower ranks, and punish every least recalcitrance promptly and mercilessly. Prepare the stage for an eventual confiscation of the Temples' wealth. It is enormous. The Imperial treasury can well use it."

"Hai, I thought I scented such ideas burrowing in you. No. We'd need a swarm of imported administrators, who'd not just arrive ignorant about governing this country but would find bedlam. Not to speak of ten or twenty regiments tied down to control resentment. It'd delay conquering the Northlands for years."

"Ercer was right about that much. The conquest has waited. It can wait."

"It will not." Sadír tried to speak mildly. "Yurussun, you don't sound like a disciple of the Tolan Philosophy. Quite aside from practical politics, you should be the first to preserve the world's most venerable society."

"Venerable no longer." Anger broke loose. "Dead. Nothing but dry bones. Let us give them decent burial and forget them."

"Ah-h-h," Sidír breathed. "I see what flogs you."

They stood confronted.

Yurussun Soth-Zora was the taller despite age having stooped him, thinned hair and limbs, whitened the beard that fell over his breast, turned a fair skin into brown-spotted parchment. The Rahídian features jutted prominent as ever, and behind gold-rimmed spectacles his eyes were still like polished lapis lazuli. He wore the flat black cap of a graduate Philosopher, upon it the silver badge of his Zabeth; a green robe with ivory buttons; red sash and slippers; purse for writing materials. His serpent-headed staff was a sign of respect-worthy years rather than a support.

Sidír, son of Raël of Clan Chalif, had more height and less breadth than usual among Barommians. (But then, a grandmother of his was Rahídian, taken for a concubine when Skeyrad's hordes first overran her land. Not until later did the horsemen from Haamandur cease thinking of the Empire as booty and begin thinking of it as heritage.) He was thickly muscled, however, and at forty-five had lost no springiness. His legs were straight, not bowed, because he had spent only part of his boyhood in the ancestral uplands; the rest of it, he was getting a civilized education. His beardless hatchet face was red-bronze, eyes narrow and dark, midnight hair streaked by meteors. He cut it short in the Rahídian style. At his right hip was the emblem of his Imperial authority, a dagger in a crystal sheath to show its damascened blade, which dated from the second of the Three Radiant Dynasties, twenty centuries past. But around his neck twined, in gold because he could afford that, the Torque of Manhood, which none save adult male Barommians might bear. And he wore close-fitting shirt and trousers of course blue cloth, tooled leather boots, horsehide bolero—nomad's garb.

"I do," he said. "Shall I tell you, Yurussun?" *For best I speak plainly now, before strife worsens between us.* "You knew from chronicles how Arvanneth first brought civilization to Rahíd. But such a long, long time had passed. Arvanneth was a shell already when the Ayan Imperium flourished along the Khadrahad. Your race saw itself as the flower of the ages. Then you came here and found a city that was great before the Ice moved south, and remembered that greatness, and scorned your nation for a pack of yokels who, luckily, would soon break back down into savagery as so many before them have done. You must live with this, day by day, month by month. In buildings and books everywhere around you, in the very real learning of the Wise, you saw it wasn't an altogether empty boast. Yes . . . Ercer and the rest soon discovered how to taunt you."

Yurussun flushed. "What of you, Captain General?"

"Oh, I grew up being looked on as a monkey from the wilds. I'm used to it. Anybody else is welcome to claim yesteryear for his, if tomorrow be mine. I think the Arvannethans and I get along pretty well, same as do they and the Northfolk, who have no pretensions to culture either. But the Northfolk and the parvenu Barommians are going to fight. And as for the Arvannethans and Rahídians—"

His hand shot forth to grasp the old man's staff. He shook it very slightly. "Yurussun," he said, "I honor you . . . maybe the more, when at last you've shown some warmth in your blood. I need your help, academic knowledge and governmental experience both. But you'll give them to me the way I want, or I'll find somebody else. We are not truly equal. Never forget: the

Emperor wears Rahídian robes and quotes Rahídian classics and is high priest of the Rahídian God; but he remains a grandson of Skeyrad, who'll hearken to a clan chief from Haamandur before a prince from Naís."

The scholar dropped composure across himself like a visor. "Captain General," he said low, "the Fourth Lesser Precept of Tola states: 'When a seed of anger falls, water it not nor warm it, but bare it to heaven and depart.' Let us go our separate ways to our separate tasks, and each tonight meditate on how the other serves the Glorious Throne as honestly as human frailty permits. Then tomorrow evening let us dine privately together."

"That would be well, Imperial Voice," Sidír agreed with less restraint. They exchanged bows. Yurussun shuffled out.

Sidír spent a while more by the window. Rainfall came in a rush. Murk flashed and banged. *Am I ashamed?* he wondered. *Sometimes one like him holds up a mirror which my brashest words cannot fog. One like Nedayin—*

His junior wife was frail and timid. Her dowry and the alliance with a noble Rahídian house were useful to him but not necessary. Yet in her presence he often felt as he did at court functions, taught how to behave but not bred to it. With Ang in Haamandur he knew ease, laughter, frank lust—No. Not really. Her world was the uplands, the gossip and songs and sagas of herders; in Zangazeng, though it was a small town, she longed for their tents. Therefore on his visits he soon wearied of her. . . . Concubines, whores, chance-met tusslemates had never been more than bodies.

Startled: *What in the Witch's name got me thinking about that? Why this awe of the Empire, anyhow?*

His Rahídian part replied, in Barommian words: *Well,*

it is civilization. Arvanneth possesses older things, but they're preserved the way a desert-dried mummy is. Age isn't enough. There has to be life. And that abides in the Empire. Counterpoint: *It was dying off, torn between war lords, till we Barommians brought our sharp medicine. Today—today Rahíd owes us its life. Then why are we shy of it? Why these daydreams about becoming complete Rahídians? My father was wise, who gave me half my youth in school but half in Haamandur.*

Though since then I've never been wholehearted.

Lightning seared, thunder bawled, rain blurred the glass and chill crept from it.

Are the Seafolk? They have a civilization too, including better machines than ours. But they're a mad scramble of nations. Killimaraich in half of Orenstane, a dozen tributary kingdoms in the other half, a hundred or more independent islands and archipelagos, Omniscience alone knows how many separate races and mixes, hardly a thing holding them together except trade, and that apt to break in a quarrel. How lonely do men among them get?

Sidír lifted his head and cast out the self-pity which for an instant had brushed soggy fingers across him. *They're not truly civilized. A rabble. Never mind their engineering tricks. We'll take those over when we decide to. Here are my people. My* people. *An Empire of hardworking hardy peasants; merchants and artisans who know their places too; aristocrats born and raised in a beautiful tradition; the Zabeths, the societies that organize lives and give everybody something close and beloved to belong to—all this, brought under the guardianship of disciplined warriors—my Empire is civilized in a way that yonder freebooters can never know.*

His musings had lasted a minute or two. He put them aside when a gongbeat requested admittance. "Enter," he called. A boy belonging to the majordomo asked if Guildsman Ponsario en-Ostral should be ushered in according to his appointment. "Yes, yes," Sidír growled. "But first I want light here." Slaves who had been expecting this command scuttled in with tapers and kindled gas lamps whose reflectors turned the room mellow.

Sidír kept his feet till they were gone and the door had opened for his next visitor and shut again. He didn't know why the merchant had, this morning, sent an urgent request for audience. The reason must be valid. The effete gourmand that Ponsario showed the world was a mask. Sidír's back and belly tautened slightly in anticipation of trouble. The feeling was quasi-pleasant. He was sick of misunderstandings, cross-conflicts, intrigues, formalities, delays. He and Ponsario had a plain common cause. They were as mutually alien as eagle and peccary; should need or advantage dictate, either would cheerfully flay the other; but meanwhile they came near being friends.

The newcomer gave him the three bows due a prince, to which rank—long extinct in Arvanneth—Yurussun had decreed an Imperial viceroy was equivalent. He intoned in return, "The Captain General of the Divine Majesty receives you." Solemn farces: for lack of which, or occasionally because of which, men died and nations burned.

"At ease," added Sidír. "Would you like refreshment, tea, coffee, chocolate?"

"Thank you, sir, I'd prefer mulled wine, but since you don't drink during working hours, I'll settle for this, by your leave." Ponsario took forth a rosewood cigar case. "Would you like one?" He demonstrated homage in camaraderie by using the second most deferential of the five second-person pronouns in his language.

(Rahídian was content with three.) "Freshly arrived from Mandano."

Sidír shook his head. "Wasted on me." He smoked a pipe, but with deliberate infrequency. A soldier was unwise if he got addicted to a scarce, expensive drug. He sat down, shank over thigh, and gestured that Ponsario might do likewise.

The Guildsman squeezed into a chair. He was ridiculously fat. Short legs and flat face betrayed a tinge of swampman blood. Balding in middle age, he dyed hair and beard. Gold stars were painted on his nails. Furs sleekened his embroidered tunic. Gems glistened on his fingers. He made a production of clipping his cigar, snapping a coil-spring flint-and-steel lighter to a sulfur-tipped splint, lighting the tobacco and inhaling till blue fragrance awoke.

"Well?" Sidír demanded.

"I know you're busy, sir," Ponsario commenced. "And truth to tell, I hesitated about whether to come straight here or approach a lower official—or nobody. The matter looks trivial on the surface, an incident, ditchwater dreary. And yet—" He dropped the stick in a porcelain ashtray held by a mahogany dragon. "Seafolk ships are sailing halfway 'round the globe from the Mother Ocean, more each year . . . sailing to northeastern Tuocar and the islands of the Hurricane Sea. Why?"

"For profit, I suppose, which you'd prefer to rake in yourself," Sidír said dryly.

"Indeed, sir? Would normal merchant adventurers plod around Eflis or dare Damnation Straits? If nothing else, the two great countercurrents in the Rampant Ocean make for a number of icebergs right along the equator there. Why risk that crossing, not to mention time spent in passage? The Seafolk have more rewarding territory nearer home—besides the islands, the whole litto-

ral of Owang along the Mother and Feline Oceans, the
whole west coasts of Andalin and Tuocar where those
aren't under the Ice. What gain in faring beyond?"

"Well, no doubt some expeditions are covertly subsi-
dized," answered Sidír. "I don't imagine the Seafolk
generally, and Killimaraich in particular, like the prospect of Rahíd taking over all Andalin and then, maybe,
expanding south into Tuocar. Apart from restricting
their traffic, we'd become a power in the Mother Ocean
ourselves." An impatient hand chopped air. "We've
been over this ground before, Ponsario. Why did you
come today?"

"Ah, yes, sir, yes, I am grown long-winded in my
dotage." The merchant gusted a sigh. "Well, then.
Lately the *Skonnamor*, a freighter out of Eaching,
docked at Newkeep, and my factor negotiated for part
of the cargo. They had a mutineer confined aboard. Yesterday he escaped. The Watch threw out a net. Your
Barommian commandant down there has done a grand
job of reorganizing the Watch, grand. He dispatched a
pair of fast riders to check northward, just in case the
fugitive had headed that way. You see, the fellow's said
to be dangerous, and Lieutenant Mimorai didn't want to
neglect any chances. He was right. The men got report
of a horse stolen from Lord Doligu, and later of its being found astray by the Lagoon. Also, a skiff disap-
peared from the ferry terminal at Nightshield Inn. And
nobody found spoor of the chap in Newkeep, though
that shouldn't have been hard to do. Seems probable he
made for Arvanneth itself, no?"

"Gr'm. What of that?"

"Not what I'd expect him to do, sir. Lieutenant
Mimorai saw no special significance either. But my factor did. Being desirous of keeping *Skonnamor*'s captain
happy, he'd used his connections to follow the reports

of the Watchmen. When he learned this morning where the runaway had likeliest gone, he got permission to use the telegraph. Marvelous innovation you've got there, sir, marvelous. As soon as the military messenger brought me his words, I arranged this conference with you."

"Get to the point. Why?"

"Please remember, sir, I've admitted my fears may be unwarranted. Insubordination is not uncommon on Killimaraichan merchantmen. Their commerce is expanding so fast, you see, they must engage whatever crews they can. Toughs from their own cities; natives of far-flung islands, mostly isolated and primitive, from Eoa to Almerik. Those foreigners get infected by the Killimaraichan individualism. But they don't lose their foreignness on that account. Rather, they tend to exaggerate it, self-assertion, do you see? Friction develops on long, hard, dangerous voyages, tempers flare, fights erupt, officers who impose discipline and punishment become hated—and always the temptation is to form a cabal, seize the ship, depart for tropical waters, seek wealth on one's own."

Sidír resigned himself. Ponsario was embarked on a lecture, and that was that. Maybe it served a real purpose. He, the Barommian, had had little to do with Seafolk. Rehearsing certain facts about them might help his thinking.

The Guildsman blew a smoke ring. "This escaped mutineer, sir, Josserek Derrain his name is, he doesn't fit such a pattern. My factor discussed him at length with the captain, whom my factor deems honest as far as this affair goes. Josserek was a good hand. Then suddenly he provoked a brawl. When the second mate intervened to restore order, Josserek attacked him, till overpowered by several men. Assault on a ship's officer is a grave crime in Killimaraich. Nevertheless the second mate visited him a few times in his confinement, trying to gain his confidence and learn what had caused his lunatic behavior. At Newkeep, Josserek got a chance to knock the mate out and break free.

"Now does it strike you as entirely plausible, sir, that a madman who, allegedly, has never been here before, would run for distant Arvanneth rather than nearby Newkeep, and succeed? On the other side of the coin, is it plausible that a sane man would go amok in the first place, or afterward seek the Lairs?" Ponsario squinted through the haze he had made. "Unless he had a plan from the beginning."

"Hunh," Sidír grunted. "What does the second mate have to say?"

"He *says* the blow he took left him weak, dazed, with gaps in his memory. I know no way to disprove that, short of carrying him off the ship and into a torture chamber. Which could have repercussions."

"Torture takes too long anyway, and the results are too unreliable," Sidír said. "Besides—you suggest this, m-m, this Josserek is an agent of the Seniory? Nonsense. What could he spy on? How could he report back?"

"As for the second item, sir, haven't you heard about wireless telegraphy? A recent Killimaraichan invention. We in the Guilds know little more than the fact that it exists. But surely a number of those, ah, explorers snooping around south of the Dolphin Gulf, surely they carry wireless telegraphs as well as cannon and catapults. An apparatus may have been smuggled into Arvanneth."

"Yes, I've heard.—Why, though? What in the name of the Nine Devils could a foreign agent do in the Lairs, besides get a knife in his gut?"

Ponsario stroked his beard. "Sir, this incident crystal-lized a decision I've long had a-cook, to warn you of the possibility the Northfolk are more sophisticatedly aware of your intentions than is proper for barbarians."

"What has that to do—Oh, never mind. Go on."

The cigar end waxed and waned. "I admit indications are faint, much is hypothetical. The new order which the Empire brought has disrupted the old clandestine coop-eration of Guilds and Brotherhoods. But I can still bribe or trick a bit of news from somebody in the Lairs. I've reason to believe that, about a year ago, a gang chief visited the Rogaviki . . . with what result is uncertain. Since Seafolk call at Newkeep several times annually, he could have contacted them too. Many Killimaraichan mercantile officers are naval reservists. Given ships here and there around the world, able to relay messages to Eaching, the Seniory could well send a man to use this liaison. It would be a mission whose probability of payoff was low, but whose risk was equally low, to ev-erybody save the agent. And should there be a payoff . . . well, Seafolk and Northfolk are natural allies against the Empire."

"But why an elaborate rigmarole about—Hai, yes." Sidír nodded. "Any Killimaraichan who entered Arvan-neth on shore leave, we'd keep an eye on, and if he van-ished, we'd get suspicious. But a loose hotspur is nothing to us."

"The deception should have succeeded," Ponsario said. "It was happenstance that I, almost the sole person likely to wonder, heard of the business. That ship could as well have brought spices from Innisla, or copra from Tolomo, or ornamental building material from the Coral Range of eastern Orenstane—" he rolled the list of mer-chandise lovingly off his tongue and seemed reluctant to stop at Sidír's frown—"or something else for which another Guild than mine has the lawful dealership. My esteemed competitors are too obsessed by their immediate interests in this time of upheaval, to think beyond, to reconstruct a pattern. . . . Well. Possibly the pattern is a fantasy of mine. But since I would sooner or later, in all events, have told you my suspicions concerning the Northfolk, and since this just might be an opportunity to confirm those—" He let his words trail off.

And curry favor. Sidír's thought was not contemptuous. He no more despised a merchant for being a merchant than a dog for being a dog. "Perhaps," he said. "Next tell me how. You know what scant results I've gotten from raiding the Lairs. A gaggle of wretches for the executioner's table. Didn't even close down Thieves' Market, only made it movable. Where in that warren could your beast be?"

"I can offer you a good guess, Captain General," Ponsario said. "At the headquarters of—" Thunder trampled the name underfoot.

CHAPTER

4

A latch outside clicked back. The door opened. "Hold where you are," said the man of the Lairs. He and his companion, two of the three who had captured Josserek at dawn, were skinny, pockmarked, scarred; but they walked like cats. Their tunics and sandals were of good quality, their hair and beards neat. Besides their knives, the first bore a pistol which must have been taken from an Imperial officer, or likelier his corpse. A firearm was too rare and valuable a thing for nearly all soldiers, let alone criminals. Evidently the head of the organization trusted this man. And evidently it had itself a certain standard.

Carefully slow, Josserek turned from the window through whose bars he had been watching dusk seep in among rainspears. Unglazed, it let chill, humidity, alley stench into the bare and tiny room where he had spent this day. Lamplight from the hall threw shadows grotesque across clay floor and peeling plaster.

"Why are you nervous?" he asked. His Arvannethan was fluent. "What trouble could I make if I wanted to?"

"We may find that out," said the gunman. "Come along. In front of me."

Josserek obeyed. It thrilled in him that his wait might be at an end, his hunt begun. He felt no fear. His captors had treated him fairly well. They had disarmed him, of course, and locked him in here. But they explained that Casiru was absent, who must decide about him. Meanwhile they left him bread, cheese, water, a bucket, and his thoughts. As often before, he'd whiled away hours among memories. A shully like him had many colorful ones.

Past the hall he entered a room which didn't fit the mean exterior or filthy neighborhood of this house. A plush carpet caressed his feet, hangings of purple and red glowed between lamps, furnishings were elaborately carved wood with ivory and nacre inlays, a censer burned sandalwood. The man seated there had the taste to wear a somber-hued silken tunic and scant jewelry. Display wouldn't have fitted a body marked by starvation early in life, dwarfish, rat-faced, well-nigh toothless. But between thin gray hair and thin gray beard, his eyes were luminous.

The guards took chairs in corners. "Greeting," said he in the middle. His voice rustled. "I am Casiru, vicechief of the Rattlebone Brotherhood. You—?"

"Josserek Derrain, from Killimaraich."

"Ah, yes. Will you sit?"

The big man did. The small man took from containers on a stand a cigarette and a smoldering punkstick to light it. He didn't offer Josserek any. His gaze analyzed.

The half-prisoner shifted about, crossing arms and

legs. "Pardon my appearance," he said. "And my smell." His skin longed for a bath, a razor, a change of clothes. "First I was busy, then I was drydocked."

Casiru nodded. "Indeed. Will you tell me your story?"

"I already told your men, but—Yes, sir. I shipped as an able-bodied seaman on *Skonnamor*, from Eaching to here by way of Fortress Cape, southern tip of Eflis, I mean. You know? While we watered there, I got in a fight over a local woman with a crewmate. Beat him flat. Afterward he and his cousins set out to make life hard for me, three black bastards from Iki. In the Hurricane Sea, things came to a head. I'd made ready. I was going to take them, finish them off or teach them a lesson, end the whole string of garbage. Rigdel Gairloch, second mate, tried to stop me. They claim I attacked him. Muck! He'd thrown a cord around my neck and was tightening it, and the last Ikian on his feet was dancing around, about to open me up. I *had* to break loose, and did. Gairloch got a little damaged. Then everybody jumped me."

"How did you escape?"

"Well, Gairloch's not too bad a dingo. He knew I hadn't decked him for fun, and wasn't sure but what there might be, uh, excuses for me. Maybe I just deserved five years in a labor gang, not ten. He'd come and question me. I was tethered in a spare cabin. Yesterday he got in reach. I saw he was relaxed, and hit him, took his knife, cut myself free, burst loose. Five years breaking rock or cleaning fish for some damned greasy contract buyer is still too much." Josserek described his journey. "Your lads saw me land and brought me here."

Casiru blew smoke and nodded anew. *I'll bet he's already had my story pretty well checked out,* Josserek thought. "They would simply have relieved you of what you carried and let you go," Casiru said, "but you told them you wanted work in the Lairs."

"What else can I do? Sir."

Casiru stroked his whiskers. His tone grew pensive. "It isn't as easy to become a Knife Brother as to become a bravo in a slum elsewhere. If nothing else, we have our past to maintain, which no mere brute can do. Men built Arvanneth before the Ice came. In days when they could fly, when myth says they went to the moon (and myth may not be lying), in those days—ten thousand years ago?—under whatever name, already Arvanneth was. Everything here is time-hallowed, all usages have prevailed for uncounted centuries. Yes, in the Lairs too. This particular Brotherhood, for example, was founded when the Ayan Imperium ruled in Rahíd. It has outlived that civilization, and it will outlive the successor civilization which today, for a moment, bestrides these parts. We do not lightly admit strangers to our secrets. How do we know you are not a spy for a rival Brotherhood or for the Imperial viceroy who is so eager to exterminate us?"

Josserek quirked a smile. "Sir, I'm not exactly inconspicuous among your people. You'd know if I'd been around. As for serving Rahíd, didn't I arrive on a ship from Killimaraich?"

"How do you come to speak our language, then?"

"Well, I'd been as far as the Hurricane Sea earlier. Was on the beach on Mandano several years back, after jumping ship because of, uh, personal problems. You probably know the Dramsters' Guild has a factor there who deals with the rum distilleries. He gave me a drayman's job. I stayed for more than a year, became his transport supervisor, but that meant learning Arvannethan. I've always been good at languages. Faring between the Mother Ocean islands, it's a talent worth

developing. After I left Mandano, I met a woman of
your folk, she'd gotten in trouble and gone off with a
sea captain from Eaching, he abandoned her there, we
lived together a while and talked her talk—No matter."
*Especially since every bit is a lie. Almost every bit. I am
good at languages. A plausible yarn though. Better be.
Mulwen Roa and I worked hard on it.*

"M-m-m—What do you think you can do among
us?"

"Practically anything. I've been a sailor, longshoreman, hunter, fisher, miner, field hand, timber cruiser,
carpenter, mason, shepherd, animal trainer, mercenary
soldier—" Josserek called a halt. *True, if incomplete.*

Casiru studied him, in a silence which deepened till
the rain on nighted windowpanes rushed loud. Finally:
"We shall see," the leader said. "Consider yourself my
guest . . . provided you do not leave these premises
without permission and an escort. Do you understand?
We will discuss things further, beginning at supper in an
hour's time." He addressed a guard: "Secor, show
Josserek to my bathroom." To the companion: "Aranno,
find . . . m-m . . . Ori and send her to meet him there
and tend him. And have someone lay out clean clothes
and what else he will need, in the Manatee Room."

"You are very kind, sir," Josserek said.

Casiru chuckled. "Perhaps. It will depend on you."

*A corpse in the Lairs is nothing except food for stray
dogs. On the way from the pier this morning, I saw a little naked child at play in the street. He was rolling a
human skull around.*

Turned amiable, Secor guided the foreigner through
oak-paneled corridors. In the bathroom, two sunken tubs
waited steaming full. Ori proved young and pretty. She
slipped off her own brief garment when Josserek was in
the first tub, scrubbed him clean, shaved him efficiently,

then gave him a manicure and sang to him while he lounged in the perfumed water of the second tub. His reaction didn't embarrass her. It had been long since his ship left Eflis. When he emerged and she started toweling him, his hands roved. "Please, sir," she whispered. "Casiru would not like your being late. I will be in your bed tonight if you wish."

"I sure do!" Josserek stopped, stared down at the slight body, the almost childish face caught between raven braids, let her go and asked slowly, "Are you a slave?"

"I am a Lily Sister."

"What?"

"You haven't heard, sir?"

"I'm a stranger in the city, remember."

"We . . . our lines . . . are bred for looks—have been, oh, for always." Ori crouched to rub his feet dry. "I am a cull," she said humbly. "Casiru's agent got me cheap. But I will try to please you."

Above her back, Josserek grimaced.

I should be used to slavery. The gods bear witness I've seen it aplenty. Even in Killimaraich, where they brag they don't have it, they're a free people, even there they not only keep labor gangs—well, I suppose you must get some value out of convicts—but the waterfronts are full of crimps. He sighed. *What I can't get used to is the way most slaves accept it.*

The Manatee Room was less pretentious than its name; somebody had once painted a sea cow on a wall. It was adequate, however. Several tunics hung in a closet for him to choose from, plus a cloak and two pairs of sandals. He removed the robe Ori had given him before they left the bath—Arvannethans had a nudity taboo, which fact reminded him of her lowly status—and clad himself. The garments fitted. "Did you expect company my size?" he laughed.

"We sometimes entertain Rahídians, sir. Or Northfolk— Oh!" Appalled, she laid fingers across her lips. Josserek curbed response; but his pulse leaped.

A purse, attached to his snakeskin belt, chinked. He inspected the contents: coins, lead and bronze, stamped with incantations in the spidery Arvannethan alphabet. From what he'd heard about price levels, he judged he could live ten days on the sum if he wasn't extravagant—and if Casiru let him out, of course. *Bribe? No, far too small. Either goodwill token or sly insult. I can't tell which. Mulwen should have sent a man who knows this race. But, aye, aye, he did say nobody who does has my other qualifications.*

The image of his chief rose before Josserek, Mulwen Roa, himself not from Killimaraich but from Iki near the equator, on which island folk had coal-black skins and snow-white hair and frequently, like him, yellow eyes. But it was Eaching where they sat, in a room whose windows stood open to salt summer air and a view of red tile roofs drooping steeply downhill toward a bay where barks lay at rest and, far, far out amidst blueness, two whales were playing. . . .

No. Don't get wistful. You can't afford to.

Hospitality here included a carafe of wine, cigarettes of both tobacco and dream weed, toiletries, but not knife, scissors, or razor. (Ori said she would barber him.) The containers were wooden. Glass or fired clay could have made a weapon. Doubtless the girl would report daily on everything he said and did. Josserek accepted this. If Casiru really was what he hoped—if, by sheer luck, he'd found those he sought on this first day of his quest—then Casiru did right to be cautious. *Same for me.*

"Will you come dine, sir?" Ori asked.

"Hungry as yonder flipperfoot," Josserek said.

She conducted him to the appropriate chamber, where she departed with a promising smile. Frescos on its walls were long faded to blurs. No one had ventured to restore them. Instead, embroidered draperies hung between many-branched bracketed candelabra. A mosaic floor of peacocks and flamingos remained bright, save for a badly chipped place repaired with red mortar and an inlaid name. Josserek guessed the chipping had happened during a fight, perhaps centuries ago, when a head of the Rattlebones got killed, and was left as a memorial to him. Lace, crystal, porcelain, silver decorated a table where three places had been set. Lighting was ample, savory odors filled warm air, servants moved noiselessly about. But they were all male, black-tunicked, dagger-armed, close-mouthed, stark-faced. And the windows were full of night and flooding, whispery rain.

Casiru entered. Josserek bowed. "Well," said the Arvannethan. "You were certainly keeping a different person beneath that wild man appearance of yours."

"A person who feels a lot better than he did, sir. Uh, we'll have a third?"

"You do not want the Watch to know where you are, Josserek Derrain. You might well kill for the sake of silence about it. I trust you will understand that your fellow guest—a highly honored guest—requires a similar discretion."

"What must I do to prove myself to you, sir?"

"That is what we will seek to discover."

Then she arrived, and Josserek's blood shouted within him.

She was a hand's-breadth less tall than he. In the forests of southern Owang he had seen tigers move as superbly. The fullness of her body had known much

running, riding, swimming, hunting, fighting, and surely
lovemaking. Her eyes, set far apart and obliquely above
high cheekbones, were the hue of winter seas in sunlight. Her amber-colored hair, shoulder-length, was as
carelessly worn as her undecorated, man-style tunic.
She had a knife sheathed at either hip, a heavy one and
a slender one. He saw that they had seen use.

"Donya, of the Hervar kith and country in the Northlands," Casiru said solemnly. In Arvanneth the most re-
spected were named first. "Josserek Derrain from
Killimaraich."

She drew near and they bowed in the manner of the
city, which was alien to them both. Killimaraichans laid
their right hands on each other's shoulders. Rogaviki—
what Rogaviki did was a matter of choice among them,
or of family practice. It was said that they rarely liked
to touch at first meeting. But her head came near
enough his that he believed he caught a hint of sunny
woman-fragrance off her skin. He did see how that skin
was finely lined between yellow hair and black brows,
and at the corners of the eyes. She must be some years
older than him, though else she bore no sign of it.

"Casiru told me a little about you. I hope you will tell
more." She spoke the language rather awkwardly, in a
husky contralto. He couldn't be sure whether her interest was real or feigned. The Rogaviki were also said to
be a very reserved folk.

If she doesn't care, he thought, *let's try if we can
change that. She must be part of what I'm searching for.*

Casiru gestured, servants moved chairs back, the
three sat down. White wine, doubtless chilled in an ice-
house, gurgled into goblets. Josserek raised his. "We
have a custom at home," he said. "When friends meet,
one among them makes a wish for well-being, then the

group drinks together. May I?" Casiru nodded. "To our happiness."

Casiru sipped. Donya did not. She locked her gaze with Josserek's and said, "I do not know that we are friends."

He could only gape. Casiru sniggered.

When the silence had stretched, Josserek floundered, "I hope we're not unfriends, my lady."

"Neither do I know we are such," she replied. "We will find out. But until—" She smiled, astonishingly gentle. "No harm intended. Many Rogaviki would have—drinked?—with you. But in my Fellowship we have a way which is like this, kept for the closest friends."

"I see. And I apologize."

"Apo—?"

"He means he intended no harm either, and regrets if he fretted you," Casiru said.

"Eyach!" Donya murmured. She surveyed Josserek across the table. "Should a rough man have soft manners?"

"I got in trouble," Josserek said, "but that doesn't mean I'm an oaf."

"Casiru told me what you told him. A part. I would like to hear the whole, from the first." A tiny frown, as of puzzlement, touched Donya's forehead. "I cannot grasp how anybody would freely go where terrible might things happen to him."

"We can't all be hunters and metal traders, my lady. I must earn my keep somehow."

"And you are a . . . a sailor, then? I have never met a sailor before."

"M-m-m, a sailor when that's the best work available. What I really am is a shully."

"A what?" Casiru inquired.

"Common word around the Mother Ocean," Josserek said. "We have people, mostly men, who go rootless, wander around from island to island, living by whatever comes to hand and never staying put for long. Some are—worthless, or dangerous, beggars, swindlers, thieves, bandits, murderers, whenever they think it's safe."

Casiru smiled a shade grimly. "That was not the most tactful possible remark in this house," he said. The nearest serving man glided closer.

Josserek's muscles bunched. Donya broke the moment with a whoop of laughter.

Josserek collected his wits. "No offense, sir," he said. "Different practices from ours are, uh, institutionalized in Arvanneth." *Everything is.*

"Ho, what is a shully?" Donya asked, and tossed off her wine.

"An—" *All right, I'll say it. I've got a sudden notion she won't let him tell any of these slinks to knife me.* "An honest migratory worker." He felt tension ease, and smiled into her eyes. "Not necessarily law-abiding. There are too many silly little laws, in the countless silly little nations around Oceania, for us to keep track of. But we have our code. Also, we take pride in being skillful workmen. Not that we're formally organized or anything. We have a king, ceremonies, yearly meetings, but nobody keeps a register of membership, or initiates new chums, none of that nonsense. Word gets around. Everybody soon knows who is and is not a proper shully."

"Not before have I heard aught in the South that sounds so much like home," Donya said.

Turtle soup came.

She was no coquette, flipping her eyelashes to let Josserek expand his ego. She was simply, bluntly interested in his world. He was surprised at how much she already knew about it. But that was book knowledge. He was the first of the Seafolk whom she had ever actually encountered.

If his guess was right, she was the one whose confidence he must win. Casiru was only a means to that end.

(A dangerous means. He too must be attracted, gratified, made an ally of sorts. Especially since it was not yet sure why Donya was his house guest. Asked, she replied, "We are acquainted of old, he, me. I came down to learn what I can about what to expect, now when Rahíd has swallowed Arvanneth." No more. In the Northlands, taciturnity was not rude.)

Josserek found himself telling them about his life, again truthfully if partially.

He was born to the daughter of a dockside innkeeper in Eaching, result of an affair between her and a scion of a noble family. ("We still have a limited monarchy in Killimaraich. It presides over the Seniory—squirearchs and capitalists—and the Advisory—popularly elected by tribes, though these days the tribe you belong to doesn't mean a lot more than a surname.") They might have married, but commercial competition destroyed the father's inheritance, and he died in an accident trying to work as a longshoreman. Josserek's mother and grandfather raised him. He always liked the tough, shrewd old man, but never the stepfather eventually wished on him; that sent him into the street gangs. Long afterward—after his conviction, and flight, and knocking around a quarter of the globe—he returned to the inn for a visit. His grandfather had died. He stayed quite briefly and didn't come back.

"Weren't you wanted as a loose prisoner?" Casiru wondered.

"I'd done a favor for somebody who wangled me a pardon," Josserek said. "But isn't this enough about me?"

"You talk like a more educated man than your career would suggest."

"You'd be surprised how much spare time a soldier of fortune can find, to read or think or listen to intelligent people, if he has a mind to. Like my lady Donya. I'd like to listen to her."

"Another while," she said, and thought for a bit. "Tomorrow? You must want an early bed tonight. And I—" she stirred—"once again I begin feeling penned. I am going away to be alone. Tomorrow let us drift about, we two, Josserek Derrain."

"Wait," Casiru started to object.

A glance from her overrode him. "We will." Unspoken, unmistakable: *I can handle him. If need be, I can kill him.*

—No matter his weeks of singleness, Josserek found Oni curiously insipid. He didn't tell her so. That would have been unfair. She had done her knowing best. Maybe the trouble was that he couldn't imagine ever pitying Donya.

CHAPTER

5

"Once," the woman from Hervar said, "I saw the Glimmerwater. What you call the Mother Ocean. I can never forget."

"How was that?" asked the man from Killimaraich. "I thought your folk were complete inlanders." He called forth maps he had studied. They were damnably vague. Civilization knew little of Andalin outside that southerly stretch occupied by the cultivators of Rahíd and Arvanneth. The east was mostly the Wilderwoods, from the Rampant seaboard to the low Idis Mountains. Thence the plains swept westward which the Rogaviki held, on across the Jugular Valley and beyond to the Tantian Hills, enormous plowlessness bounded northward only by the glacier.

"We go trading and trapping in countries not ours," she told him. "Past the Tantians is a great windy plateau, where little save jackrabbits and coyotes can live, and past them rise the Mooncastle Mountains, in the grip of the Ice. But there are passes, and lower ranges on the far side where beaver, mink, cat abound—and oh, the heights, strength, hugeness, the speaking silences! At night are more stars than is darkness."

Josserek gave her a look which lingered. Was she coming out of her armor at last?

They had left the house this morning, attired to avoid drawing close attention. Conquest had brought many Rahídian civilians here as well as their military. In a robe girded up from his buskins to allow free stride, a kerchief falling from his cap to conceal haircut and earrings, Josserek could be an entrepreneur or functionary from some Imperial town. Her features and fairness made Donya impossible to disguise. But, grinning, she showed (the exact right word) in filmy tunic, jangling bangles of glass and brass, insolently reddened lips. "Certain of our girls who know they will never wed work the Arvannethan posts upriver," she explained. "A few find their way to the city, though they stay not long." She hesitated. "We reckon this an honest trade too, among those a spouseless female can ply. And Southrons can't imagine her, alone, doing anything else."

Apart from that hint of defensiveness, she had given little of herself. Arrogantly she insisted they walk, not south toward the Grand Arena and the better districts, but deasil around the center. Nor had she said many words while they wove through the slime and shrillness of streets, the poor of the Lairs, the Knife Brothers and petty felons who battened off these and recruited from among them, amidst blind brick hulks.

The quarter ended abruptly at the Avenue of Dragons, a thoroughfare between the Old Bastion and the Council House which militia patrols kept safe. Secor and Aranno

had come along, precaution against attack. Here she
sent the men back, in a manner she might have used at
home toward her hounds.

But almost immediately after she and Josserek were
in the Hollow Houses area, she began talking readily,
even eagerly. She asked him about his wanderings, and
then—

"Aye," she said, "I've thrice crossed the Mooncastles.
Not of late. Four living husbands, five living children, a
big wintergarth ... oh, property does catch us by the
ankles, no? And the Fellowship, younger members especially, ask advice or help from me. And there are others
to visit, and our share of the metal trade to manage, and
larger seasonal gatherings of our people, and hunting—
But I was sixteen that first time, one year married to
Yven, with nothing I must guard. We were all young in
our band. We decided we would not spend the summer
running traplines, we would fare on west to find whatever we found. Travelers before us had told the country
beyond the high glaciers had ample game and friendly
natives. We carried gifts to thank for hospitality—
always carry gifts, going outside the last kith territory—
knives and steel needles of our own make, beads and
medallions and cheap pearls from the Arvannethans, a
few ... magnifying? ... lenses from Rahíd. So we took
our bearing on the sunset, and set forth."

She tugged his elbow. He felt warmth and slight cal-
luses. "See, a good place for resting," she suggested.

Rain had made heaven glitter. A few cloud-fluffs
drifted. Light spilled across buildings which breathed
its glow back over the street they enclosed. They were
ruinous: roofless walls, wall-less chimneys, porticos,
colonnades. The ivy had them; poplars, brambles, prim-
roses overran the rubble heaps at their feet; grass was
patiently levering pavement blocks apart; lichen had all

but devoured a monument to an unremembered hero. But the stone showed mellow through greenery, the air held a scent of jasmine, and somewhere in the stillness a mockingbird trilled.

Donya settled herself on a mossy slab, chin on knees, arms around shins. A mile off, through an archway, they could see the black bulk of Dream Abbey, one of the few steads hereabouts where life—of a sort—remained. Closer by hung an oriole's nest.

Josserek joined her, careful not to touch, no matter how the bare, faintly sun-tinged limbs drew at him. "You went as far as the ocean, then," he ventured. "Did you make a profit?"

"Oh, yes." She smiled straight ahead. "I saw surf break in white and green thunder. I swam in it—cold, bitter, but what an embrace! Gulls, sea lions, sea otters. Clams we digged, like funny, burrowing nuts. Out in a boat, dawn hushed and silver, some killer whales swam by. One raised his head over our rail. Maybe he said good morning."

"I wouldn't be surprised," Josserek remarked. "They've found in Killimaraich, the cetaceans—whales, dolphins, do you know?—think and feel about as well as humans."

"Truly?" she exclaimed, delighted.

"Well, so the scientists claim. Could be they're, uh, prejudiced. You see, in the main religion of our country, the whale tribe is sacred. Dolphin's an, uh, incarnation of the life gods, same as Shark is of the death gods— Never mind. I suppose our myth helped get our protection laws passed."

"You forbid slaying?"

"Right. The flesh, oil, baleen are valuable enough that our navy has to keep out quite a patrol. I—" *No. It's too soon to admit how Mulwen Roa found me as a shully, and got me pardoned at home and talked me into the service, first on whale police, then later when I'd learned the organization ropes—* "Twice I've happened to see battles between a cutter and a crew of hunters or smugglers."

"I am glad," she said, turning grave. "You feel you belong in life. I did not know."

Sardonicism touched him: *If we're kind to the whales, my dear, our consciences pester us less about our fellow men. Besides, there's always a demand for convict labor. However, if you want to consider me an idealist, fine.*

"We Rogaviki will not kill game for the market," Donya added. "It would be wrong."

Then, practically: "It would be foolish, too. We live well because we are few and the herds are great. Change that, and we must become farmers." She spat. "Yeow! I've traveled through farmlands of Rahíd. In their way, they are worse than a city."

Hm, Josserek thought. *You may not be impressed by idealism after all. I don't know. You're not like any woman I've ever met before, anywhere in this jumble of a world.* "How?" he asked. "I've heard your people hate being crowded. I guessed that's why you grew chipper after we came into this descrted section. But farms, grazing ranges, plantations?"

"There the whole country is caged," she said.

After a little she went on: "Cities are bad too, but less bad. We can stand having strangers close around us for a while, till their stinks make eating too hard. We cannot—we will not have many strange minds pressing in on us that long. Farmers always do. Here, in town, nearly everybody is only meat on two legs, they to me, I to them. Tol—tolerable." She stretched, tossed her head till the locks flew, and rejoiced. "In these Hollow Houses lives peace."

"My lady," Josserek said, "if I annoy you, please warn me."

"I will. You are good to say it." Calmly: "I might like lying with you."

"Hoy?" he choked, then grabbed. His pulse brawled.

She laughed and fended him off. "Not yet. I am no joy girl handling customers, quick come, quick gone. Casiru and his henchmen crowd me; they question, they try telling me what to do, they want I dine at his table each meal. My loins lose appetite before my belly."

Maybe later, out on your own open plains, Donya? Control returned. *Meanwhile I've got Oni.* It chilled. *Why do you suppose I, a runaway sailor, ever will join you yonder? Or do you?*

"Well . . . I'm flattered nevertheless," he achieved saying.

"We will see, Josserek. Barely have I met you, and know naught real about your kind." Half a minute went by. "Casiru says they care just for money gain. I am not sure, if they protect whales."

That gave a chance to become as impersonal as she seemed to have been right along . . . and, incidentally, show both his nation and himself in a light she should find favorable. "We aren't pure greed," he said, picking his words. "Most of us, I mean. Mainly—in Killimaraich, anyhow—we've cut the individual free. Let him make his own life, sink or swim, inside a pretty loose law. Which is hard on those who can't, I know. But what do you Northfolk do about your losers?"

Donya shrugged. "Most die."

Presently she asked: "Is Casiru right? He says the Seafolk are angry at the Empire over nothing but the—the tar—what do you say?"

"The tariff? Well, yes, in part. Arvanneth never taxed imports much. Now, naturally our companies don't like paying the stiff rates the Empire charges. Plus stronger competition south of the Gulf. But it's their loss. No cause for the rest of us to fight."

"Then why are you—" She broke off.

He counterattacked: "Why are *you* here?"

She sat still, looking away from him. Sunlight flooded. The mockingbird was happy.

"I promised I wouldn't probe," he said. "Yet I can't help wondering."

"No secret," she answered, flat-voiced. "I told you already yesterday. Talk goes about, how the Imperials will invade Rogaviki land out of Arvanneth. Casiru has spies in many places. He warned me it is true. I came to see for myself, so I could tell it at home. Not so much whether they come, but what they fight like, under these new leaders. Their last invasion, they bumbled north from the Khadrahad, mostly infantry. We destroyed them as always we did before. Their Barommian cavalry gave us hard trouble; but it had too little water and forage on the loess plains. We would strike during a dust storm or—The Jugular Valley is different. This army is different too." She sighed. "I have learned scarcely anything. Arvannethans breed no more real soldiers. They do not understand, they cannot describe the thing that rolled over them. Rahídians I met, by myself or when they came to earn a bribe from Casiru, they are witless, ox-obedient rankers. And how can I get near any Barommians?"

"Are you afraid they may succeed against you?"

"Never." She rose in haughtiness. "Come, let us walk on. . . . But we could lose more lives than need be."

He fell in step beside her. Sherds crunched and rattled, brush crackled, down what had been an avenue. "How did you join Casiru?" he inquired. "If I may ask."

"We met several years ago when I came here. Not

whoring," she interjected. "There were things to talk
over. The Metallists' Guild wanted bigger trade with us.
That meant meeting with other Guilds too, because they
supply goods we trade for. Of course, none can speak
for the whole Northfolk. But some of us thought we
might well find out what the merchants wanted, and explain at home. We fared together. Afterward we often
saw the Guildsmen separately. In those days they all had
ties to the Lairs. Through ... Ponsario en-Ostral, he
was ... I met Casiru. I found nothing to talk to Ponsario
about. He wanted us to sell him meat and hides, or at
least supply him more furs; and we would never do that
to the earth. But Casiru and I, we found things in common."

Both of you predators? Josserek wondered. Ashamed:
*No, not you, Donya. You don't hunt human prey. From
what I can learn, your Rogaviki never raid anybody
else, never fight unless attacked and then only as long
as the enemy is on your soil. ... Can that be true? Is
that much innocence possible?*

"He is—he can be—" She searched for words. "Interesting. Amusing."

"He lives off the city," Josserek said, less to moralize
than to explore her. "He takes, never gives."

Donya shrugged again. "That is for the city to worry
about." Then her lucid glance shook him. "If you care,
why did you seek his kind?"

"I'd no choice, had I?" To cover himself, he continued fast: "Actually, I overstated. The Brotherhoods have
had a place in city life. They've controlled crime, kept
it within bounds."

"They drained off less, I think, than any government
does; and as you say, they were of some use." He suspected she spoke in dead earnest, though her tone was

calm, like a naturalist's commenting on the social arrangements of ants.

"Well, anyhow," he persisted, "the way I heard it, they were also undercover allies of the Guilds. The Wise and the Lords tried to hold the Guilds down. The Brotherhoods could supply at need strong-arm men, snoops, burglars, rabblerousers. Their illegal enterprises were handy places for venture capital in a frozen society, while a lawful business could welcome investment from them. That kind of thing. Lately this has changed. The Barommian-Rahídian Empire has a boot on the necks of Wise and Lords, while it attacks crime. And it encourages the merchants. They don't need the Brotherhoods any more. So the Brotherhoods, too, look for new allies."

"Like the Seafolk?" Donya wondered low. When Josserek made no reply: "I'll not chase that question further this day."

She understands as well as I dared hope, sang in him. *Better than Casiru, maybe. Should a barbarian?*

His position spread itself before his mind, more focused and detailed than his map of her Northlands. The man from the Lairs had—reasonably from his own viewpoint, maddeningly from Josserek's—been furtive in speech as well as advent, when last year he sought out a Killimaraichan captain whose ship lay at Newkeep. How could he know that what he said would be transmitted, or whom it would be transmitted to? No consulate for any Oceanian nation existed here, nor permanent residents. The skipper might well hope to gain from blabbing to the Imperials. Quite possibly several commanders had been similarly approached through a period of months, and this just happened to be the one who was in the naval reserve and started a radio message on its way to Intelligence headquarters.

The whisperer from Arvanneth had not even identified the Brotherhood he represented. He had hinted at
much but promised nothing. A potential link to the
Northfolk—who possessed the principal source of metal
in Andalin, and who could not be mere wild plains-
runners, not altogether, since they had century after century chewed up host after host which sought to grab
their hunting grounds from them—the Northfolk, being
threatened themselves, might conceivably prove helpful
to Seafolk who were having their own problems with
this troublesomely reinvigorated Empire—a certain Brotherhood or two would be glad to discuss the arranging
of a liaison, not with chance-met barbarians in their
home country, who probably knew nothing, but with
picked leaders right in the city—for a consideration to
be agreed upon, of course—

"We can't go ahead quite like that," Mulwen Roa decided. *"Those underworlders are thinking like any other
Arvannethans, or most Rahídians, in terms of lifetimes.
Ten years of negotiations are a fingerflick to them. Well,
the Barommians won't wait a lifetime, or ten years, before their next big strike. We'll have to move faster, in
the dark, or lose whatever chance we've got here."* His
grin gibed at himself. *"We'll send in an expendable."*

The arrangement with Rigdel Gairloch was straight-
forward, as things went in Naval Intelligence. Josserek
had not hurt him badly. He alone aboard *Skonnamor*
knew the truth—unless Mulwen Roa had had some talk
with those three sailors from Iki, his own home island—
The fewer who knew, the less likelihood of betrayal:
say, by a man who got to smoking dream weed in a joy
house.

But then Josserek was likewise ignorant. He dared
not blurt forth his mission to the first gang lord he met.
Nor would such a person quickly confide in him. It be-

came a matter of mutual feeling out. For instance, the
more he saw of Casiru, and especially of Donya, the
more he revealed a better vocabulary than a common
salt ought to have. And they in their turn, if they were
what he hoped, studied him and gave him signs. . . .

No hurry. He'd allowed a month or two for finding
his way to whomever it was he wanted. Seemingly he'd
need days. He could therefore ease off and enjoy this
ramble.

As if she had winded his mood, Donya said, "Let us
take pleasure in the now that we have."

They did.

Among the Hollow Houses they found many fragments, odd, charming, pitiful. They even came upon a
small farm in what had been a stadium, and would have
chatted, but the squatters were too timid. Beyond the
northern arm of the Royal Canal, they were back in
well-populated territory. However, this was mostly ec-
clesiastical, abbeys, temples, tombs, slow-paced monks
and nuns, not the raucous life of hucksters and beggars
which bothered Donya. Further on they reached Palace
Row, and strolled along it until they wearied of architec-
ture and turned to intricately connected paths, enigmatic
topiaries, and symbolic flowerbeds in the Gardens of
Elzia. On Lake Narmu they rented a canoe. The price
was exorbitant, but that kept the water from being
beswarmed. Under the arches of the Patrician Bridge
they ate a very late luncheon, steamed catfish and baked
yams bought off pushcarts, and in a drinkery snuggled
into a doorway of the Grand Arena (where no spectacle
had happened for more than a hundred years) they
found cold beer.

It took Josserek an hour to appreciate how compan-
ionable Donya's returned silence was. A woman in
Killimaraich would have chattered, a woman elsewhere

might never have spent a whole day at his side, or might
have imagined a courtship if she did. Donya just didn't
say much about herself, inquire of him, or make devious
comments on the scenes around, Nor, despite her half-
invitation earlier, did he think she was in any way woo-
ing his attentions. She had wanted to judge him, free of
the confinement and distraction in Casiru's place. Later
she merely wanted an afternoon off.

Toward its end they must hurry a bit. The sun was
low, shadows filled streets, the Lairs outdoors were un-
healthy for an attractive woman and unarmed man who
doubtless carried money. Set on by daylight, they could
probably rescue themselves by showing tokens Casiru
had lent them, to prove they were under the protection
of the Rattlebone Brotherhood. That wouldn't work after dark, when no witnesses could identify their assail-
ants for the sake of reward.

Fountain Street was the district boundary: on the
south side, shops and homes whose owners were barri-
cading for the night, on the north side the brick jungle.
Josserek and Donya came down Pelican Lane, which
gave on Fountain Circus, reached its mouth—and re-
coiled. The open space was full of horsemen.

"Barommians," she muttered.

Josserek jerked a nod. The mounts were tall, the riders short and sturdy, copper-skinned, their black hair
cropped in the Rahídian manner but their scanty beards
shaven in highlander wise. They wore boots, spurs,
leather trousers, bullhide corselets and armguards over
rough blue shirts, conical steel helmets. At their saddles
hung small round shields emblazoned with regimental
totems, and some had axes while some had bows and
arrows. Every man bore saber and dirk and held a lance
at rest. A breeze brought the sweet odor of their beasts,

the ring of hoofs shifting about on pavement. Their troop numbered a score.

"What's happening?" Josserek asked, lips to her ear so a stray hair tickled them. His heart thuttered.

"I don't know. A raid on the Lairs? Casiru says they have been made whenever the viceroy learned where important Knife Brothers were holed up."

"M-m-m. Do you think we should scat?"

"Where else can we go? Under the new rule, innkeepers must report foreign guests who can't show entry permits. Any who disobey, likeliest think they will cut your throat, plunder your purse, and for me—" Donya uttered a snarl.

Josserek gathered she had arrived unlawfully. Casiru could arrange that for her, after she sent word she was on her way. No matter now. They retreated back down the lane and crossed the street at a safe point. Scant traffic moved along it, a mule-drawn wagon, a few hasty pedestrians, and none in the Lairs. There everybody was gone to his den. Except that it was less ruinous—but ugly, littered with trash and offal, prowled by curs and alley cats—this might almost have been the Hollow Houses. Echoes flapped among shadows. The chilling air quenched most stenches.

Overtopping the neighbors which jammed against either side, Casiru's dwelling loomed square above the narrow way on which it fronted. "We're home," Josserek called, and sprang forward.

Through twilight he saw the door lie smashed.

A shout. Men who sped from within. Men out of two more buildings. Drawn blades agleam. "Hold where you are!" *When they didn't find us here, they waited.* Clatter of boots on cobblestones. A hard hand clapped around his wrist. A Barommian face behind.

Josserek yanked his arm free, between thumb and fingers. His knee lashed upward. The soldier lurched back, dropped his sword, wailed his pain. Josserek whirled about. He swayed and crouched aside as he did. Steel whistled where he had been. "Take them alive, you scuts!" yclpcd in the tongue of Haamandur. Through him flashed: *That makes things easier for me.* He glimpsed Donya, backed against a wall. Her chance was gone. But these cavalrymen didn't know dirty fighting afoot. Bone crunched, blood squirted beneath the heel of Josserek's hand. The edge of it chopped at a neck. Then he was clear, running on longer legs than theirs, into a murkful maze. Behind him a horn lowed, calling the squad at Fountain Circus. Too late.

Yet where now could a spy from the Seafolk hide?

CHAPTER

6

"No, the Nine Devils take him, Casiru was gone from his house when my men seized it," Sidír rasped.

"Or else he had a tunnel known to himself alone," Ponsario suggested. "They say every fox digs two ways in and out of his den. This fox, moreover, has many earths. I fear your hounds will get no spoor of him for a long while to come."

Sidír squinted at the fat flat face. "Why did you never tell me about Casiru earlier?" he demanded.

Ponsario shifted in his chair, folded hands across belly, glanced around the Moon chamber. Morning brightened it, coffee steamed delicious, windows stood open to mild air and a cheery sound of traffic. But the red man had laid hand on dirk.

"Well, Captain General, you bear a thousand different burdens," Ponsario said. "At your behest I, like colleagues of mine, informed on those Brotherhoods which

most threatened your purposes, such as the Rippers and
their academy for assassins. That was when we had specific information, sir, which was seldom. The Lairs keep
their secrets, especially since the Guilds began getting
alienated from them. But should we trouble you about
every scrap of word which still comes our way?" His
gaze grew pointed. "I believe your distinguished colleague, the Imperial Voice, vetoed proposals to clean out
the Lairs entirely. Besides hurting too many innocent
people, that would create more difficulties than it re-
solved. Drastic changes cannot well be carried out overnight. I am sure the Captain General agrees."

Sidír half laughed. "Also, you'd rather hold something
in reserve, you Guildsmen."

"M-m-m . . . in this instance, sir; may I respectfully
remind you that, precisely because he was left in business, Casiru received foreign agents whom you might
otherwise have had much trouble in identifying and
catching. You did catch them, did you not?"

"One. A female Northlander. The Killimaraichan she
was with, he got away."

"They are definitely of those nations, sir?"

"Yes. No mistaking a Northlander, and the Killimaraichan admitted being such in the hearing of household
members that we did grab and interrogate. He claimed
he was a fugitive, but Casiru showed more interest in
him than that might warrant. As for the woman, there is
no doubt she came down to spy on us."

Ponsario sipped his coffee, obviously relieved that the
talk had veered from accusing him. "In my opinion, sir,
Casiru had no intentions beyond acting as a middleman,
for whatever squeeze he could get. Which would likeliest have been bribes and fees out of all proportion to the
service rendered. What could anybody really accom-
plish? A lone Killimaraichan—well, he is worth capture,

to find out if his superiors have some important scheme. But the odds are, he came on a mere fishing expedition. The Northlander cannot even be called an agent."

"Why not?"

Ponsario raised his brows. "How, sir? You know no ghost of a government has ever existed in that country. A few worried matriarchs—matriarchs only of their homes—may have agreed somebody should go and try to learn about you. At most. The Rogaviki have no state, no tribal structure, no military cadre, no warriors who keep in practice by raiding or feuding—actually no law, it is said, nor customs or duties binding on any who don't choose—"

"Nevertheless," Sidír cut him off, "they've kept civilized settlers out of a huge territory for as long as chronicles remember, and destroyed every army sent to avenge homesteaders they massacred. Whence comes their strength? I called you here this morning, Ponsario, partly to find out where Casiru might be and what he'll do next, partly what to expect from this person we hold."

The merchant smirked. "Traders and peaceful travelers through the Northlands say there is absolutely nothing like the native women." Seriously: "But that's when they are willing. Prisoners are always deadly dangerous. Either they turn into homicidal maniacs, or they lurk for the first chance to pull some treachery—lethal by choice, though it cost their own lives."

"Yes, I've heard. This brach fought fiercely till subdued. But since, they say she's been calm."

"Why does the Captain General ask me about Northfolk? Didn't you have ample experience in the last invasion, ten or eleven years ago?"

"No," Sidír said. "That campaign was an element in a larger effort, to win more farms and pastures for

Rahíd. We also moved northwestward, into Thunwa."
He got a blank look. "The dwellers there live not unlike
Barommians, some yeomen, some herders, spread thinly
through highlands which could be cultivated thickly,
warlike men, who acquired enough knowledge from the
Empire that they stayed it off for centuries. They were
vassals of the Ayan Imperium, though, and we renewed
that claim. I led a brigade of ours. Never have I met
hardier fighters."

"But you broke them, did you not?"

"Yes. Which consoled us for the failure in Rogaviki
country. And advanced my career, until now—" Sidír
sighed. "I've studied everything I could find on the
Northfolk, of course, insofar as time has allowed. But
I've no real sense in my bones of what they are like."

"Well, sir, I have myself had limited contact with
them," Ponsario confessed. "They bring furs to the trading posts for my Guild, which ships fabrics in return.
However, the bulk of that goes through the Metallists,
who do by far the major traffic. Thus I have principally
common knowledge. They live widely spread, chiefly
by hunting, following herds in summer, spending the
winter in houses when they don't gad about over hundreds of miles. Most wives keep two, three, or still more
husbands. Unmarried women . . . seem to have various
possibilities. Wars among Rogaviki groups have never
occurred, they claim, and they exalt the skillful hunter
or craftsman, not the fighting man. Nor have I, myself,
ever heard of a murder or robbery up there, though
doubtless it happens occasionally, inasmuch as our people do report very rare, incidental mention of outcasts.
Rogaviki respect the lands of neighboring folk, both
civilized and primitive. When theirs are encroached on,
they fight with wolverine ferocity. Then, as soon as the
trespassers have left, they are ready to re-establish

friendly relations, as if incapable of holding a grudge no matter what they suffered." Ponsario's cup clacked down, empty. "Yet they are an impossible people really to get to know. They are hospitable to strangers they deem harmless, but visitors have told how they never reveal any depths in themselves. Perhaps they have none. They certainly show little in the way of ceremonies. Their women sometimes bed a guest, but act more like minks—or demons—than human females."

"Is that what you can tell me?" Sidír asked.

"In outline, yes, sir."

"Nothing I had not heard before. You waste my time. Get out. Send me a written report on Casiru and the Rattlebone Brotherhood, everything you know . . . less long-winded than you are."

Ponsario bowed and flourished his way from the chamber. Sidír sat a while gnawing his impatience. So much to do! A civilization to make safe, powerful, stable—thereby assuring the future of Clan Chalif and, before all else, the descendants of his own father—for this, half a continent to vanquish—and how many men whose good faith and good sense he could trust?

Several hundred leathery, hoarse-voiced Barommian sergeants. And their best officers. . . . In the name of the Witch, how long since last I gathered friends for a night's joy? Drinking till heads fly afloat; boasts, memories, bawdy songs; girls for everybody, lavish as the food they bring us; wrestling, gambling, stamping out a ring-dance to a drumbeat like hoofs in gallop; comradeship, comradeship.

He thrust the wish from him. The commander of an Imperial Rahídian army could not well invite his underlings to an orgy, nor accept such an invitation. Not till he was home again beneath the high volcanoes.

At present—The challenge shivered in Sidír like a

harpstring. He rose and departed on rapidly clacking bootheels. Guards at the door slapped breastplates in salute.

The hallway was long, vaulted, set with polished granite and malachite, dimly gas-lit. At its end, an arch gave on a circular staircase. Startled, Sidír halted. Yurussun Soth-Zora was emerging.

Tall in his robe, the Rahídian paused too. For a few pulsebeats both were silent. Then: "Greeting, Captain General" and "Greeting, Imperial Voice."

Gone awkward, Sadír said, "Let me express in person—I meant to later—express the regret my orderly brought you yesterday evening, that I could not dine with you alone as we planned. A task has proved knottier than I foresaw."

Glow from the nearest lamp shimmered off Yurussun's spectacles in such wise that two tiny flames looked at the Barommian. "That is clear. Your courtesy is appreciated. You are still pursuing the matter in question?"

"Yes. And your honorable self is interested likewise? My apologies if you expected notification. It was, is, a piece of nearly routine military business. No direct impact on civil government, except that we arrested a few criminals." *And before we left Naís, I required that police power be the army's.*

"A reasonable judgment. Though, pardon me, not necessarily a correct judgment. When I heard about the major prisoner you took—staff gossip is buzzing—I went to inspect her. Next I was on my way toward you."

"She's a failed spy—better said, a scout—from the barbarians. Nothing else. What do you care?" Sidír realized the Imperial Voice might justifiably take umbrage at his curtness.

But Yurussun grew still more solemn. "You are housing her pleasantly, I see. What are your plans for her?"

Sidír flushed. "I'll keep her about."

"She is . . . handsome. However, you can take your pick of many beautiful girls. You do. Why this risky creature?"

"I don't plan on ravishing her, for ancestors' sake! I'll try to, to get acquainted. I've had no worthwhile experience yet of these people I'm ordered to subjugate. Knowing just a single one could make a big difference."

"Nobody comes to know a Rogaviki, Captain General."

"So I've heard. But *how* are they inscrutable? What does their near company feel like? This sample—a captive, in need of our good will—she can give me a better idea than did what few traders and drifters I've briefly met."

Yurussun stood a while leaning on his staff. "You may learn to your sorrow, Captain General," he said at length. "And that could imperil your followers."

Sidír snorted. "I've been warned, prisoners often are violent. Do you think I, my sentries right outside, I should fear attack by a woman?"

"Perhaps not. But perhaps worse." Yurussun looked down the corridor. Doors reached shut. The ages were gone when Arvanneth needed many palace functionaries. Here was more privacy that he could be sure of in the Moon Chamber or the Arcanum Cubicle itself.

"Harken, I pray you." His white beard swayed as he hunched forward to speak low and earnestly. "When I was young, I traveled far among Northfolk. An Imperial margrave had asked a commission be sent. I was its clerk. Livestock from the south, game from the north were straying across his border and causing damage, dwellers were killing such beasts on sight, an expensive nuisance for both peoples. We negotiated an agreement. Cairns would be raised to define the frontier exactly. From time to time Rahídians and Rogaviki would meet at designated spots, bringing the tails of strays. Whoever had the fewest would pay in proportion to the difference, metal from them or coin from us, according to a formula which assumed the unwanted animals had done more harm than their carcasses were worth. It worked well enough, I believe—was even resumed after our last attempted conquest failed. But the point is, Captain General, there was no king or chief or council or anybody who could speak for that kith as a whole. We must spend months, in winter when they were more or less settled down, going from stead to stead, persuading each separate family. Thus I think I came to know them better than most outsiders."

Sidír waited. He had heard bare mention of this before.

"Their women were often curious about us," Yurussun said in an old man's tone. "They would boldly invite us to their bodies. Some accompanied us a ways, our guides to the next few places."

Sidír mustered scorn: "I've gathered traders' tales. They whisper how the Rogaviki woman is a witch, a nymph, something supernaturally female. The story is she can endlessly satisfy any man she will, without ever satiating him, but the cost is apt to be becoming her helpless slave, who at last cares for nothing else in life but her. Myth! Horse apples! Why don't the factors upriver get ensnared?"

"A short encounter leaves but a sweet, wild memory, I suppose. And I suppose, too, much of the belief about her comes simply because she is as independent as a man, as competent and dangerous. Indeed, her husbands are not subservient. And yet—and yet—did you know that the Wilderwood savages, with whom the eastern Rogaviki have some contact, that they think the plains folk, both sexes, are a kind of elves? I can understand why, and I can understand the Southron superstitions, and I wonder if they are wholly superstitions . . . I, who knew Brusa of Starrok for half a month, and in half a century since have never won free of her."

Yurussun's words faded out. Sidír stood amazed. Not only was self-baring quite unlike a Tolan Philosopher— Rahídian nobles hardly ever fell in love as their peasants or any Barommians might; they kept their women too inferior.

Maybe that tripled the impact of a wholly untamed girl.

"I will, eh, I will respect your confidence," Sidír said finally.

"I put away my pride for you with reluctance," Yurussun mumbled, "however well I know that that youth is dead who bore my name." Then sharply: "Beware. I wish you would have that prisoner killed, or released, or gotten rid of somehow. If you will not, at least watch yourself, always watch. If you feel a spell coming on you, tell me, that I may urge you to break it before too late."

His hand on the staff trembled. Without ceremony, he brushed past and shuffled on down the corridor.

Sidír lingered hesitant. Had he heard truth?

Hah! I'll grant Rogaviki women may be better bedmates than most. Helmeted in skepticism, he proceeded. The stone stairs leading up through the Crow Tower were worn to troughs. Candles guttered feebly in sconces, against chill walls. Echoes rattled like laughter.

But the apartment on top was large, comfortable, well maintained. Four pikemen guarded the landing. They were Rahídians—no sense tying down his élite here—

big, erect in blue jackets and trousers, boots built to march in, brass-stripped leather cuirasses, round casques whereon their regimental insignia were enameled. They saluted smartly. Sidír felt a surge of pride that drove out his last small forebodings. Before the Barommians took over, soldiers had been lower in Rahíd than sidewinders, and deserved it, scarcely more than brigands scouring about through the wreckage of a nation. These might still be derided by scholars; but they stood as the outer wall of civilization.

He passed by and closed the door again behind him.

Donya was on her own feet. He had ordered her issued a robe to replace her harlot's disguise, and the rooms here included a bath. Her right cheek bore a purpling bruise, her left wrist a red slash, and he knew she had taken a battering before his squad got her bound. Her carriage showed no trace. A sunbeam from an ogive window turned fresh-combed hair dull gold and sheened over long roundings beneath black silk.

Suddenly Sidír thought: *If Yurussun came for a look, and saw this she-puma out of the past that has crumbled from him—aye, no wonder he was shaken.*

He himself had barely met her last night, disheveled, filth-smeared, dazed from blows. It would have been useless to interrogate her. Besides, he had at once guessed she might be opportunity for him. He ordered her given treatment and proper quarters, then went back to see how his officers were doing with the servants and the Knife Brothers taken earlier.

Now, when he felt the life radiating from her—

He curbed himself. "Greeting, my lady," he said, and gave his name and rank. "They tell me you hight Donya of Hervar."

She nodded.

"Are you satisfied here?" he persisted. "Do you have

what you want?" He smiled. "Other than your freedom?"

Her amusement startled him. "Fairly spoken," she chuckled.

"Freedom should soon be yours again, my lady, if—"

She lifted a palm. "Stop. Spoil it not by honeymouthing. Yes, I would like a few things more. This is a wearisome place, save for what I can watch of town and birds. Send me playthings."

"Ai—what?"

"If you dare trust me with graving tools, I can ornament a saddle for you. I play the *tano* and—well, if you have none of our in—instruments, let me try if I can teach myself one of yours. I don't suppose you have Rogaviki books, but I might puzzle my way through Arvannethan, if somebody will explain what the letters stand for."

"They have books in Rogavikian?" he asked, hardly believing.

"Yes. Now, for a starter, Sidír of Rahíd, you can sit down and talk." Donya curled her limbs on a couch.

He took a chair. "I came for that," he said. "Do understand, I am sorry about the rough handling you got. But there you were, guest of a criminal chieftain, companion of a foreign spy. You resisted arrest, and I think two men of mine will carry the marks you left to their graves."

"I almost got an eyeball out of another," said Donya, whether genially or wistfully he couldn't be sure.

"You see you left us no choice," he argued. "I hope you will give it today."

"How? I can tell you little more about Josserek than you must already have learned. Hyaah, he is not bad company on an outing. Else . . . he never told me he was anything but a sailor in trouble. He might have later, if you had been less hasty."

"Would you then have told me?"

"No," she said, matter-of-fact. "You are my enemy."

"Are you sure?"

"Will you not soon invade my land?"

"Maybe. That metal is hot, but not yet in the mold. This is why I'm anxious to talk with Rogaviki leaders. You are the first I've found, Donya."

"I am no leader. We have none, the way you mean."

"Still, we can parley, can't we? Like honorable enemies, if nothing better."

She grimaced. "There are no honorable enemies."

"Oh, wait. Opponents can have regard for each other, wish they need not fight, but since they must, abide by decent rules."

"If you do not wish to fight us, stay home," she said coolly. "Isn't that quite simple?"

"The Empire has necessities which drive it. But it can give you far more than ever it takes: security, trade, culture, knowledge, progress, the whole world open to you."

"I have seen tame cattle. Many of them live fat lives too."

Piqued, Sidír snapped, "I am no steer."

"N-no." She regarded him speculatively, her lids half lowered and a finger across her chin. "I didn't mean you are. I keep hounds."

"And I keep you! . . . That was ill put. I'm sorry. Let me try afresh. What I want from you goes far past anything you know about Casiru or the Killimaraichan. I want to learn about your people, their country, ways, wishes, dreams—How else can I deal with them as human beings? And deal I must, whatever shape that takes. You can help me start learning, Donya."

"You will not let me go, then?"

"In due course, I will. Meanwhile ... you came to study us, right? I can teach you, so later you can deal more wisely too. Meanwhile, I promise fair treatment."

She lounged for a space, easy and watchful, until she laughed, well down in her throat. "Yes, why not? If you will keep people from crowding in on me, in flesh and word—let me out of here, even though under guard—"

"Certainly. Would you like to come hunting with me soon?"

"Yes. Very much. Also ... I have been too surrounded for a long while, Sidír. It set me so on edge that I spent all my nights alone. This tower, clean sky everywhere around, is nearly like a hilltop far from any house. Already I feel happier, prison though it be. And you and your Barommians feel more like my kind than do men of Rahíd or Arvanneth. Will you tell me sometime about your homeland?" She sat straight and lifted an arm toward him, gesture of command. "You are in truth a hunter's hound. Come over here."

He did no more work that day or night.

CHAPTER
7

During the month which followed, the last blossoms fell and the last leaves budded out. Word came from northward: the Jugular River was ice-free and roads along its banks dry enough to bear heavy-laden wheels. Meanwhile his reinforcements and supplies reached Sidír. On Kingsday, the seventh of Dou, Year 83 of the Thirty-First Renewal of the Divine Mandate (Imperial calendar) his army set forth.

Behind stayed very modest garrisons, sufficient to maintain order in the city and its satellite towns, villages, countryside, seacoast. For those who departed outnumbered thirty thousand. Most would not go the whole distance. Sidír's plan depended on establishing riparian bases as he went, which in turn would seed strongpoints across the lands. Thus he required abundant matériel at the beginning. Mule trains crowded tradeways. Sidewheeler tugs churned water white;

strings of barges wallowed behind them. In their lead, screw-driven, stately, gilt-laced over pearl-gray hull and superstructure, moved *Weyrin*, Rahídian-built on a Killimaraichan model, transport and office space for the leaders of the host.

This expedition isn't quite like in old days, when Barommian riders whooped merrily down to sack and burn, Josserek had thought after he boarded. *From what I hear of him, Sidír can't wait to found his last fortress and lead his crack cavalry off on summer's last grand foray.*

What he heard had been almost entirely indirect, from Casiru. He saw hardly anybody else while he lay hidden. The Brotherhood vicechief knew ample ratroutes around the city; when he surfaced, he was inconspicuous, a withered native in shabby garments. Josserek was sure to be stopped for questioning, did an Imperial see him before the search died down in favor of preparations for war. Casiru gave him a room with screened balcony in a house near Treasure Notch which he owned through a dummy. None save the master himself and a taciturn manservant who tended Josserek's needs had keys to it. The needs were admitted to include books and exercise equipment, but not a woman. Except for his and Casiru's conversations, that was a dismal month.

Danger? jubilated in him when he felt streets, wharf, gangplank, deck beneath his feet. *Getting out is worth every last drop I may sweat. And if that isn't common sense, then Shark devour common sense!*

"Name and post," demanded the Rahídian boatswain as he trod onto *Weyrin*.

"Seyk Ammar, sir," he answered. "Stoker."

The boatswain peered from him to the register and back again. "Where are you from?"

"Thunwa, sir. Uh, the man they signed on for this post, Lejunun, his name is, he fell sick. Happened I was staying at the same inn. I went to Anchor Hall and put in for the job." In fact, Casiru had handled everything, a bribe to the coal heaver, a blackmail hold on a certain member of the Workbrokers' Guild.

"Aye, here's a scribble about it." The boatswain considered him further. Josserek could remove earrings, trim hair, grow a short beard, tuck a rough Rahídian-style robe above his knees, shoulder a sea bag. He could not change his accent, or the blend of races that made him. "Thunwa, hai? Don't they stay home all their lives?"

"Mainly they do, sir. I ran off when I was a boy." To claim he was born in the Empire's northwestern province, whose mountaineers were unknown along the Dolphin Gulf, had seemed his best bet.

The boatswain shrugged. Others awaited his attention. They were a mixed lot; Imperial citizens had bred fewer sailors than Imperial commerce nowadays demanded. "I see. You can't read or write, can you? Well, they'll have explained our rules at the Hall. Wartime rules, remember. Ink your thumb on this pad. Make your mark here. Get on below, second deck aft, and report to the engineer's mate."

Josserek preferred sail to steam, and aboard power-craft he had always worked topside. The black hole proved hotter, fouler-smelling, dirtier, and noisier, the labor more dull and exhausting, then he had imagined. But on Sidír's own vessel, nobody who counted would give a stoker a second glance, as long as he behaved himself.

Off duty, Josserek explored, perfectly natural for a new hand provided he kept out of officer country. Several times he spied Donya from afar. His chance to get closer didn't come till four days out.

He had scrubbed away soot and coal dust, donned a clean garment, and climbed in search of a breath before his watch ate. Few people were about, none at that part of the main deck where he emerged. Behind him rose the poop, shelter for galley, carpenter shop, and other service cabins. Ahead lifted a three-tiered deckhouse. Its upper front was the bridge, and its top sprouted the stack; but rails and awnings made the flat roofs beneath into galleries for those privileged to bunk there. Josserek sought the starboard bulwark, between two of the small brass guns the boat carried. He leaned outward and inhaled.

The hull throbbed underfoot. A breeze carried smoke away and brought in odors of dampness, silt, reedy growth, wet soil beyond. Though the sun stood at noon, edging with brilliance tall cumulus clouds in the west, that air was cool. Here and there, caught on a snag or sandbar, a last drift of slush melted away in great brown currents. For fear of those obstacles, the fleet kept near mid-channel, and Josserek surveyed widely overstream to shore. He spied fish, herons, dragonflies, early mosquitoes, treetrunks from springtime floods. Banks slanted high and steep, cattails thick at their feet, brush and willow above. Beyond them, the land was no longer flat but starting to rise and roll, intensely emerald green, wildflowers, shrubs, scattered pine and oak groves, no sign of habitation except, afar, a ruined castle. This was not yet Rogaviki territory. Arvanneth had once held and still claimed it; but civil war, then pestilence had anciently gone through here, ambition and strength to resettle had never afterward arisen, the city-state was content with the nominal homage of a few tribes who drifted in from the Wilderwoods. Nonetheless, forest did not flourish. Already this short way north of Gulf, climate felt a breath off the Ice.

A longer way for a march, Josserek reflected. *I daresay the Barommians fume at the pace. But it's incredible what speed Sidír is getting out of infantry, artillery, engineers, quartermasters. I didn't believe his public estimate of twenty days to Fuld. Now I do.*

To check on such things was one reason he had signed himself aboard. He wasn't the sole intelligence collector for the Seafolk, of course. But they were terribly short on data about how formidable the revived Empire was, especially on land. Each bit mattered.

Josserek's vision sought the troops. At their distance they were a mass that rolled above the riverbanks and across the plain like a slow tsunami. He heard wagons rumble and groan, boots thud, hoofs clash, and the drums, bah-DAH-dah-dah, bah-DAH-dah-rah, bah-DAH-dah-*dah*-dah-dah-RRRRP. Banners and pikeheads rippled aloft, as a prairie ripples to the wind. He made out single horsemen in the van or on the flanks, steel agleam, cloaks flying in rainbow hues when they unleashed the full pace of their beasts. Sometimes a rider blew a horn signal. Its wolf-bay laughed through the drums.

He turned from the view, and saw Donya.

She had come around the upper gallery on the deckhouse, to pause at its after rail and herself gaze remotely. A blue Rahídian robe fell from neck to ankles. Had Sidír decided he didn't want his mistress in revealing Arvannethan raiment? Josserek gauged she had lost weight, and her face was empty of expression; but health and pride dwelt there yet.

His heart sprang. *Careful, careful.* On the lower promenade a Barommian officer puffed a pipe. He appeared to young to have been in the former campaign against the Rogaviki. The odds were therefore excellent that he wouldn't recognize that tongue. *Be careful anyhow*. With casualness he hoped wasn't overdone, Josserek sauntered from the bulwark while he broke into song, quiet though carrying as high as he wanted. The melody was from Eoa, the words his . . . Northfolk words.

"Woman, you have a friend. Stand easy; listen in silence."

Had the Barommian understood and inquired, Josserek would have explained he'd learned it from a tavern companion who'd been in the upriver trade. He had composed several additional lines which made the whole thing a banal love lyric. But the fellow gave him an incurious glance and went back to his smoke.

Donya's fingers, clutched the rail. Otherwise she merely watched the stroller, as anybody might. He caroled:

"Remember me, he from the Glimmerwater. We were last together the day they captured you. Can you meet me?" She gave a nod too slight to notice unless a man was alert for it. *"At the front and bottom of this boat is a storage chamber."* Her language had no means he knew of for saying "forward hold." He flipped her a wink. *"Inside the housing over the bows, where I sneaked from below for a forbidden moment, is a bath that must be for your class. Can you go in there alone, unsuspected?"* A nod again. *"A ladder beside the bath compartment leads down, past a space where they keep ropes, to the section I mean. It should be a safe meeting spot. I work at the engine. These are the times I am free."* He named hours, struck by the main gong. *"Which is best for you?"* He repeated them. She signed him that this evening suited. *"Wonderful! If you cannot*

come, or I, we will try tomorrow, agreed? Fare you well."

He drifted off, because his food must be ready and a stoker who missed a meal was preposterous. He scarcely noticed the tired cabbage and fatback. Though he had to fake the customary siesta, he bounced from his hammock and flew through his second watch. Afterward, the stew that was slopped slimily into his bowl tasted good.

Since the army made camp by daylight, the fleet stopped too. Sunset trickled through the ventilation lattices when Josserek hurried off. Tarry odors from the anchor rode locker followed him down to his destination. Walking, he didn't worry about being seen. An engineer could well send a man for something from the miscellaneous stores there. Besides, the chance of such an errand out of any department, at any given time, was slight. But Josserek's heart knocked while he waited in the gloom. When Donya appeared, he jumped to take her hand and guide her behind a concealing pile of crates.

"Eyach, you bearslayer!" She was a wan shadow in his eyes, heat and firmness in his arms, hunger on his mouth. He thought fleetingly he tasted tears, but couldn't be sure, nor quite sure whose they might be.

At last she drew back and whispered: "We mustn't stay long. Why are you here? How?"

"How have you been?" he responded.

"I—" He couldn't follow the rest, and told her.

"Best we speak Arvannethan, then," she agreed, calmer now. "Mine has improved. Sidír and I use it together for practice, save when I instruct him in Rogavikian. He's had little time for that. Yours is not bad. Where did you study it?"

"You first, I said," he insisted. "What happened? How are you treated?"

"Kindly, by Sidír's lights. He's never forced or threatened me, he gives me what freedom he dares, offers me luxuries, is at my side every chance he can make. And a fair lover. I like him, really. I'm sorry that soon I will hate him."

"Why have you stayed? Couldn't you slip off?"

"Yes. Easiest from this vessel, over the side after dark and swim ashore. Hardly a Barommian or Rahídian alive can swim. But I wanted to learn about his forces, his plans. And I have learned, a great deal. I still am learning. That will help us much, I think." Her nails bit his arm. "Your turn! You're an agent from Killimaraich, no? Isn't that why you gained some Rogavikian speech?"

"True. Three or four years ago, before the attack on Arvanneth, we grew convinced it would come, and this march up the Jugular eventually follow. We had spies in Rahíd, you see. My service recruited a language instructor, a man of the Metallists who'd passed his career among Northfolk, traveling as well as trading."

(Josserek omitted the linguistic and anthropological analysis which made his education less garbled than would otherwise have been the case, as well as the psychological techniques which drove it quickly and firmly into his head. Later, maybe, if they both escaped.

(Besides—hard to imagine when this woman stood warm and breathing against him—the degarbling had largely amounted to sifting out what the Guildsman really knew from what he thought he knew. A whole net of assumptions about the Rogaviki underlay his interpretations of every idiom, every construction. Different lines of evidence, scanty though they were, showed those assumptions were not necessarily true, and many of them demonstrably false. The fact was, he taught Josserek a pidgin, fluent, reasonably grammatical, nevertheless a pidgin which left out the most basic concepts.

(It was like being a native of a backward island, who had glimpsed Killmaraichan ships, engines, clocks, sextants, telescopes, compasses, guns, but had only a single word—"windmill," say—for every compound machine, and had never dreamed of mechanics, thermodynamics, or chemistry, let alone free market economics or the evolution of life through geological time.

(Josserek couldn't guess how alien Donya might be to him. Could she?)

"What is your mission?" she asked.

"To observe whatever I can," he said. "Especially about your people, and the possibility of allying against the Empire. Not that it's an immediate menace to the Seafolk. We don't want a war. But if, in some skimpy way, we, I can help you—" He clasped her tighter. "I'd be overjoyed my own self."

"How did you get aboard?"

"Through Casiru. He was absent when the Imperials came."

"Yes, I heard that afterward. But he and you were both hunted. He would hide. How did you find him?"

"Well, of course at the time I didn't know he was loose, but I figured he'd have told what he'd been doing, to associates in the Rattlebone Brotherhood. And probably most Knife Brothers of whatever outfit could locate a member of that gang for me. After dark, I mugged the first man I came on, disarmed him, and put my question. If I'd failed with him, I'd have kept trying; but he proved out. Casiru was informed, and had me brought to him. Naturally, then I admitted I was what he suspected, a foreign agent. He gave me the news, including what soon became general gossip about you. In every way, he was spitefully glad to help me."

He sketched the rest. They went on to a few more words, a bare few, not plans at this stage, but hopes, cautions, arrangements for occasional rendezvous and for emergency communication. He described his times on and off duty, and two ventilators on deck which would carry a loud noise, one to the engine room, one to the black gang's sleepyhole. "If you need me bad, yell down whichever stack is right for that hour, and I'll come boiling up." He touched his sheath knife, and reflected that on watch he could likewise snatch a wrench or crowbar.

"I can do better," she told him. "Sidír frets about my being endangered, like by a lightning guerilla raid. He hung a whistle around my neck. I'll give you three blasts. Right?"

"Right," he said. Kissed her goodbye and went aft surprised at the jealousy of Sidír that seethed in him.

CHAPTER

8

Rains dogged the army till the ninth day. Next evening, stars glintered around a gibbous moon in an ice halo. Its glade shivered over swirling, chuckling darkness. Beyond the riverbanks, land sheened pale: hoarfrost on grass, here and there a diamond twinkle, here and there a murky stand of cottonwood. Campfires and sentinel lanterns spread widely. But they were sparks, lost amidst night and miles, as were fugitive sounds from the host, a man's call, a horse's whinny, a flute's loneliness. Breath smoked in the chill.

Having dismissed the last man who needed conference with him, Sidír climbed a ladder from his office to the upper gallery. For a moment he paused, filled and emptied lungs, tensed and untensed muscles, seeking ease. A day at a desk tied him in knots. Would he ever again have a day in the saddle?

Yes, by the Outlaw God! he thought. *Stay patient. The*

jaguar waiting for prey does no more than switch his tail. His mouth bent wryly. *Trouble is, I have no tail to switch.* In search of calm in eternity, he let his gaze travel above the boat, dappled blotches that were bollards, hatch covers, winches, gleams off guns and guardian pikes, upward among the constellations. He knew them well, the Ocelot, the Swordfish, Baghrol's Lance. . . . But some like the Trumpeter were below his horizon, and others stood strange to him in the north. He found Mars aloft and dwelt on its bluish brilliance until, he didn't know why, a memory swam from the depths of him, a thing he had heard in Naís from an astrologer who sought out forgotten records and pictures in tombs of forgotten kings. That man claimed Mars was formerly red; thus had they seen it who lived before the Ice came.

A sense of measureless antiquity blew through Sidír. *I would truly lead armed men into Unknown Roong, built so long ago that the very heavens have changed?*

He stiffened his shoulders. *The barbarians do, and ransack for metal.*

That brought Donya's image before him, the knowledge she waited in their cabin. Sudden heat awoke. He swung from the rail and strode around the gallery, past a dull-yellow window to his door, and flung it wide.

The room was cramped and austere save for its bed. She sat thereon, long legs crossed, arms folded under breasts, back straight and head high. Despite the cold, she wore merely a beaded headband and his whistle. A chain lamp, feeble, slightly hazing the air with oily smoke, nonetheless brought her forth aglow from shadows she cast on herself and grotesque great blacknesses that wavered in the corners.

Sidír closed the door. His pulse broke into a trot. His mind took firmer hold on reins. *Go slow. Be gentle. Not like last night.*

"I, um, regret I'm late," he said in Arvannethan. A book lay open on the dresser. She had read much in that language, evidently seeking to master its writing, while the expedition crawled along. But the light here was too poor.

She had also practiced much on a kind of lyre he found for her, which she said resembled a little the Rogaviki harp. And she had enjoyed the passing scene, tossed questions at everybody, eaten and drunk lustily, played board games with dash and rising skill, chanted songs of her folk over wine. Once she danced at a palace feast, but that was too inciting; thereafter she danced for him alone. And in this bed—

Till the past two or three days. Then more and more sullen. Or is "sullen" right? She went behind a mask, anyhow, spoke nothing except what she had to, sat moveless hour after hour. Joined, she gave me small response, nothing like formerly. Last night she told me no. Should I have seized her as I did? She endured me. Any slave girl would have been better.

The nearness of her smote him. *No. Never. Not after what we have had. I couldn't help myself. I'll win her back to what she was.*

When she kept mute, he went on, "I was detained by a courier just arrived from Berrydown." That was an Arvannethan translation of the local name for a site where he had left the first of his detachments to establish a base, day before yesterday. "Since we'll plant our second garrison here, naturally I wanted to know what's happened there."

"What has?" Though she spoke leadenly, she did speak. He wished he could give a pleasant reply.

"A patrol ambushed." He grimaced. "Two men lost, three wounded. At dawn, a picket found strangled by a cord."

Did she smile? "Good," she murmured.

"*Krah?*" He checked his outrage. "Already?" he demanded.

"Why not? They are no laggards in the Yair kith."

"But—" Sidír braced legs apart, flung arms wide, sought to make her reasonable. "Donya, it was senseless. Those ambuscaders left four dead behind them. Two were women. The rest must have seen they couldn't win, but kept trying till our men's horns had called in tenfold reinforcements. That was the start of their madness, an attack so near our encampment."

"Well, they got two, and a third later on. They will get more."

"We haven't even invaded! Our location is right on the trade route."

"It's clear aplenty what you intend." She leaned forward. A touch of concern softened her coolness. "Won't you now believe what I've warned you over and over, Sidír? You can't take the Northlands. You can only kill Northlanders. In the end, a part of you will go home— leaving how many brave bones?"

He stood silent a while before he murmured, "Mars was red when the Ice came."

"What do you mean?"

"Nothing endures forever, no life, no shape, no condition." By her response he dared hope he had pierced the flint encasing her. *I'll lead the way from talk of this to talk of us.* He stepped to the dresser. "Do you care for a stoup of wine? I do." She didn't refuse. He gurgled claret from carafe to goblets, gave her one, lifted his in a Barommian gesture, and took a mouthful. It was from the coastal plain of eastern Rahíd, as far north as grapes would ripen, tart on his tongue.

"Donya." He sat down on the mattress edge. His eyes sought hers. His body longed to, but he held his pulse to a canter. "I pray you, listen. I know why you're unhappy. When we crossed the frontier of the southernmost Rogaviki along this river, aye, that started you brooding. Did it start you fully grieving, though? I can't say. I've asked and gotten no answer. Why won't you tell me what you feel and let me try to help?"

Her look might have been a lynx's. "You know why," she said somberly. "Because you make war on my land."

"But I never denied I would. Yet in Arvanneth—yes, and our early days journeying—"

"Your act was in the future. It might not happen. When it did happen, things turned into different things."

"And yet—oh, we've been over this ground often enough—and yet—you admitted yourself, the Rogaviki have no single nation. Here isn't yours. Your home territory is far off."

"That is why I can hold myself quiet, Sidír. But still it hurts to know what the Yair and Leno are suffering today, and the Magla will start suffering tomorrow."

"They need simply acknowledge they're subjects of the Throne, and keep the Imperial peace. Nobody will tyrannize over them."

"The grazers and plowmen will move in."

"Paying them well for land."

"Forced sale, on the pretext it can't really belong to anybody because nobody has a stupid piece of paper calling it his. And what payment can bring back our great game beasts?"

"It'll take long to settle so big a country. You'll have generations to learn new ways. Better ways. Your grandchildren will rejoice that they're civilized."

"Never. Impossible."

Her stubbornness angered him. This was indeed a well-trampled realm between them. He gulped another draught. The wine soothed a trifle. "Why? My own ancestors—But I remind you of what I offered. You, your Hervar, you cooperate. Make no resistance. Give no help to kiths elsewhere, except helping persuade them to accept what must be. Then no soldiers will cross your boundaries without leave, and no settlers ever be let in until your descendants themselves desire."

"Why should I believe that?"

"The Devil Mare kick you! I've *explained*! Sound policy to have native confederates—" He drained his cup.

She took a sip herself. Did her tone milden? "I would have hated you sooner, had you not made that offer. It can't be—I foresee too well how matters would go—but thank you for meaning it honestly, Sidír."

Encouraged, he put his vessel aside and leaned nearer her. The wine glowed through his veins. "Why shouldn't it work?" he urged. "Strong, able folk like yours can rise as high in the Empire as they choose. You and I—fit together like bow and arrow, don't we? The South needs to share more than your land, it needs to share your blood." He dropped his left hand across her right, which rested on the blanket, and smiled. "Who knows? We may be the ancestors of an Imperial dynasty . . . you and I."

She shook her head. The thick locks rippled. She returned his smile, no, grinned, no, showed teeth. "That most surely not," she said, far back in her throat.

Wounded, he swallowed before he protested, "You mean—what people say—Rogaviki can't have children with outsiders? I've never believed it could be true."

"It isn't always." Her voice turned impersonal. "Aye, mules might get born rather often, were many of us not able to will that a seed put in us shall not take root."

He stared. *Ho-ah, what? Mind can make body go strange ways. . . . Shamans I've watched*—He veered to a more immediate ugliness. "Mules?"

"Old stories tell how such crossbreeds, if they lived, were barren. I don't know, myself." Her lips pulled back again as she finished, slowly, like drawing a fishhook across his flesh, "Nowadays their mothers always leave them at birth for the buzzards."

He sprang from her, to his feet. *"Rachan!"* he cursed. "You lie!"

"Did you think I would nurse a whelp of yours?" she jeered. "No, I'd throttle it at its first yell. With glee."

His pulse stampeded. Through smoke-haze and shadow he saw her big tawny form taut on the bed, through thunder he heard, appallingly steady: "Reckon yourself lucky, Sidír, that I haven't yet ripped your maleness off you."

She's as crazy as the rest, rocked in his skull. *She simply hid it better. A race of maniacs*—His palm cracked across her cheek. She hardly moved at the blow; her bosom rose and fell as before.

What she had been to him—pretended she was—
smote him with axes. In his pain he threw her cruelty
for cruelty. "Yaih!" he shouted. "Do you know why
they're done for, your filthy savages? I didn't tell you
this, because—because I hoped—" Air sawed his gullet.
"Well, listen, bitch. If they don't surrender, we'll kill the
game out from under them!"

He half heard a wail. A hand flew to her mouth. She
scuttled to the far bedside and crouched.

He struck harder: "Aye, Bison, moonhorn, bronco,
antelope, deer, wild burro up in the hills, caribou on the
tundra, moose and elk in the woods . . . farmers couldn't
do it, infantry couldn't, but Barommian horse archers
can. Five years, and the last herd rots on the prairie, the
last Rogaviki crawl begging for scraps off our cattle.
Now do you see why they'd better quit their murdering—
while they can?"

She gasped in and out. Abrupt pity washed through
his rage. "Donya," he mumbled, and reached toward
her, "darling, I beg you—"

"Yee-oo-oo," came from her. "Yah-r-r-r."

Hunched on all fours, hands bent into claws, gape
stretched wide, eyes flat green encircled by white and
encircling two tiny pits, she swayed. Inhuman, her noise
ripped down his backbone. He edged away, hand on
dagger hilt. "Donya," he stammered, "what's wrong, be
calm, take care." The cabin bulkhead stopped him.

"Rrra-a-ao-o!" she screamed, and sprang.

He saw her fly at him, crooked fingers, distorted
bleach-white face, teeth ready to be fangs. His knife
jumped forth. Before he could stab, she struck. They
crashed to the deck. She rolled herself on top of his
belly. Her nails raked after his eyes. Blood flowed
loose. He kept his knife, brought its point toward her

ribs. Somehow she sensed that nearness. Weasel-swift
and limber, she writhed about, caught his wrist, turned
his thrust. He clung to the weapon, strained his full
strength inward. His free arm beat around to ward off
hers. She closed jaws on the knife wrist and gnawed.
Her right hand found his throat and started digging. Her
left sought his groin. Her thighs pinioned a leg, held
down his entire threshing body. Her vulnerable breasts
were jammed too close against him to reach. Her back
took the blows of his left fist.

He knew she could kill him.

He yelled. A guard burst in. He choked at what he
saw. He couldn't jab his pike into that embrace without
danger of hitting his chief. He clubbed the butt across
Donya.

She let go, launched her weight, toppled him, and
passed across, out onto the gallery. Those below saw her
soar under the moon to the main deck. Most who made
that leap would have broken their bones. She re-
bounded. Her whistle shrilled. Soldiers tried to box her
in a corner. They couldn't. She flitted, hit, kicked, and
yowled.

A bellow answered. A huge dark man erupted from
below. Sidír lurched outside in time to glimpse the
scrimmage that followed. The dark man sliced one
Rahídian fatally. His fist broke the neck of another. Between them, he and the female left four more hurt. They
reached the port bulwark. They sprang. Water foun-
tained on the river. They were gone.

Lanterns bobbed among shouts and feet, great lunatic
fireflies.

His hurt, shock, horror drowned in Sidír; he knew
only his loss. "Donya," he mourned through the cold.
Blood from his brows dripped to blind him.

Then, a swordthrust: *Why do I call? What is she to me? A witchsprite in truth, and I spellsnared?*

I thought about last night, "I couldn't help myself." *That never happened before, that I could not help myself.*

CHAPTER

9

The sun was well up when Josserek awoke. Memory slammed his dreams out of him. The alarm; the fight; getting to a shore half a mile off in a strong current, his swimmer's muscles aiding Donya; eluding troopers whom horn and light signals had roiled into alertness, her hunter's craft aiding him; trekking death-long hours in a direction she got from the stars, until dawn let them halt by a congealed waterhole without themselves freezing; tumbling into an embrace for warmth alone, and exhausted sleep.... He surged to his haunches.

"May this day gladden you," she greeted him in the soft Rogavikian tongue. When had she come astir? She was using his knife to cut grass.

He stood erect and stared around. Light poured from an unbounded blue. Its warmth soaked through his bare torso, dissolved aches, anointed creaks. To the edge of that sky reached the plain. Waist-high grass covered it, stiffly yielding when brushed against. Like the sea, it showed infinite hues under the sun, deep green close at hand, silvery in the distance. Like the sea too, it ran before the wind in long waves. Wildflowers swam in it like fish, far-scattered stands of elder and giant thistle heaved forth like islets, remotely westward a herd of horned beasts—hundreds upon hundreds, he guessed—moved majestic as whales. Butterflies flitted gaudy. Above went many wings; he could name just a few kinds, meadowlark, thrush, red-winged blackbird, hawk, homebound geese that made a spearhead beyond them. The wind hummed, stroked, streamed smells of growth, loam, animals, sun-scorch.

No humans in sight. Good. He slacked the wariness of the hunted. *Except, of course—*

Donya ceased work and trod closer. Nothing remained of last night's man-eating tigress, nor of the silent, relentlessly loping vixen afterward. A woman flowed toward him, clad in air of early summer, hair aflutter around her smile and above her breasts. *By Dolphin!* he exploded in his loins. I—Common sense closed fingers on him. *She's not inviting me. And she has my knife.*

She gave it back, though. Automatically, he sheathed it. The trousers which his belt upheld were his sole garment, what he happened to be wearing while he diced with his messmates below decks. His feet were cut, bruised, sore. Hers seemed untouched, and she unwearied.

"Are you hale?" she asked.

"I'll live," he grunted. Most of his mind still wrestled most of his body. "You?"

As if released from a trap, joy swooped upward. "*Eyach*, free!" She leaped, raised arms, pirouetted, whirled across yards of rustling stalks which now hid, now showed fleet legs and exultant hips. "Salmon-free, falcon-free, cougar-free," she chanted, "where sun roars, wind shines, earth dances, about and about the heart at peace—" Watching and listening, he forgot himself. A piece of him did wonder whether her song was traditional or sprang straight out of her. It slipped into a dialect he couldn't quite follow, so he guessed the latter.

Weren't the Northfolk said to be an aloof people?

After a few minutes, Donya returned to practicality and him. But she breathed a little harder, and he was acutely aware of how sweat bedewed her skin and strengthened the fragrance of her flesh. As much for distraction as to quench thirst, he drank from the waterhole. It was a depression among grainy gray rocks, filled by rain, muddy, though doubtless cleaner than any well in Arvanneth. When he was through, he saw that Donya, searching, had chosen one of the chunks, a handy size and shape for a missile.

Her words crackled: "While I get food, you build a cookfire and cut more grass. Trim it the way you see I have done."

He bridled art orders from a woman. Again, however, wits prevailed over impulse. She knew this country, he didn't. "What shall I use for fuel?" he inquired. "Green stuff is no good. And why the harvest?"

She kicked at a powdery-white lump. "Gather animal chips like this. Crumble some first, for tinder. As for grass, we need clothes and blankets, against sunburn and flies as well as cold. I can weave them. At that, we'd better walk during the chilliest part of the night, and rest in the height of daywarmth, till we've gotten proper gear at a Station. . . M-m, aye, best I lash together footwear for you also."

She set off. "Wait," he called. "You forgot the knife. And how long might you take?"

Her mirth drifted back. "If I can't fetch a meal with a stone before you have a proper bed of coals ready, don't cast me out for buzzard food. They'd scorn to eat."

Alone, Josserek pondered. His blade would be of huge use. A snapperooll from his pocket helped him equally in starting a fire. The rock she had found on an otherwise boulderless sod was a chance fragment of concrete, maybe from an ancient highway, maybe from before the Ice. Luck, in each case. But he suspected she didn't need luck to survive here.

True to her word, she soon brought a slain rabbit and several quail eggs. "This land really teems, doesn't it?" he remarked.

Cloud-shadow quickly, her mood shifted. She gave him a hard look. "Aye. Because we take care of it. Before all else, we keep our numbers low enough." Wrath spat: "And the Empire's maggots would enter? No!"

"Well," Josserek ventured, "you have an ally of sorts in me."

Her gaze narrowed. "Of sorts," she repeated. "How far can we trust any . . . civilized . . . race?"

"Uh, I swear the Seafolk have no territorial ambitions on Andalin. Think how distant we are. It wouldn't make sense." Perforce he switched to Arvannethan to speak thus: not the antique language of the educated, but the argot of traders and dockwallopers.

She understood nonetheless, and pounced: "Then what is your interest? Why do you care?"

"I told you—"

"Thin is the reason you gave. Our meetings on the boat were too hurried for me to chase down truth. But now—If the Seafolk wanted to observe us, they could have sent somebody openly. He could have named himself a—a seeker of knowledge for its own sake . . . ah, *scientist*, yes, as you told me you have many of, that day we wandered through the city. Why take the risks you did unless something else, urgent, drove you?"

Josserek felt relieved. "Shrewd!" *Too shrewd to be believable in a barbarian?* wondered an undercurrent. "You win. We aren't desperate. But thinking men in Oceania are worried by the sulfur matter."

"Sulfur?" She knitted her brows. "Oh, aye. The yellow burnable stuff. What we call *zhevio*."

"The richest deposits left in the world, that anybody knows of, are along the Dolphin Gulf," he explained. "We got most of our sulfur from Arvanneth, when it controlled those parts. Today the Empire does, and bans export. Sulfur makes gunpowder. Skeyrad styled himself Overmaster of the Barommian clans; but his grandson the Emperor says Worldmaster." He shrugged. "I don't suppose his descendants can ever in fact conquer the whole globe. But you can see why the Seniory and Advisory in Eaching don't like the way things have gone of late."

"Yes. That is sound. We can trust you." Donya dropped the rabbit and clasped his shoulder. Her smile coruscated. "I'm glad."

His temples pounded. He might have grabbed her at once. But she let go, set the eggs down more carefully, and said, "If you will be cook, I will begin on our clothes."

"Well, I am hungry," he confessed. Both hunkered to their tasks. Her fingers sped, fastening stems together.

"Where should we go from here?" he asked. "Or to start with, where *is* here?"

"West of the Jugular and north of the Crabapple River that enters it, by a day's steaming. I watched our progress. The nearest Station is thus at Bullgore, two days' journey afoot. No, I forgot your feet are tender.

Maybe four days. Have a care when you flay yon hopper; he'll be a moccasin. Uncured hide soon stinks and cracks, but should last till we get there. Thence—horses, and home to bear warning."

"Your home is afar, am I right? Do you know the whole Rogaviki territory so closely?"

The fair head nodded. "Stations, wintergarths, and other fixed abodes, yes, of course. From maps if I've never visited them in person. They aren't very many."

His eyes drank immensity. "But how can you find anything? I don't see a single proper landmark."

"Direction from sun and stars, since we have no compass. Distance from heeding how fast we walk, for how long at a stretch. And every Station has a smoky fire throughout the day. In clear, calm weather, you can spot that above the horizon, thirty or forth miles off." She translated the measurement into Arvannethan units. A scowl: "This the keepers must quench if Imperials move toward them, till we have burned those locusts."

Chill touched him through the mild air. *I consider myself tough, I've killed men and lost no sleep afterward, but her tone, her look—Are the Imperials really vermin to her, pests for extermination, no shared humanity whatsoever? How can that square with her society starting no wars and doing no plundering, throughout its history?*

He busied his hands while he gathered resolution. Finally he plunged. "Donya?"

She glanced from her work.

"Donya . . . why did you run wild last night? Didn't we agree we'd spy, collect information, at least to Fuld?"

She dropped the fabric. Her mouth tightened till the thews jumped forth in her neck. He heard a low mewing.

"Forgive me," he whispered, appalled.

She breathed deeply, forced easiness back on herself inch by inch, color back to face and bosom. Her speech remained a croak: "I had to kill Sidír. I failed, the Powers shrivel me. Next time, let me scoop him empty."

"But, but you . . . and he—You told me you like him, sort of—"

"That was before he came north. When he thrust into Yair and Leno, I felt—I no longer awaited, I felt—the earliest piercing of Hervar. Had he brought me thither—But he told me first . . . if we'll not wear his Emperor's collar . . . *he will slaughter the game*—Can't you understand?" Donya yelled. "If I push you off a cliff, what can you do but fall? What could I do but go for his throat?"

She screeched, leaped up, and fled.

Josserek held back. He had seen this before, among certain warlike savages: fury of such typhoon force that she must run it out of her body or else attack him, or an animal, or a house, anything that could be destroyed. Through the high grass she bounded, howling, arms aloft as if to pull down the sun.

Then the Rogaviki are what the Southrons claim, the man from Killimaraich decided shakenly. *At best, barbarians. They've learned a few tricks, but not reason or patience, forethought or self-control.* He wondered why that should sadden him. Disappointment? They'd be valueless as allies—dangerous, even, until they were conquered or wiped out as their weaknesses doomed them to be. *No . . . I didn't expect much from them, politically or militarily. Donya herself, then. She acted so intelligent, aware, knowing, realistic, interested; I'd never met a woman like that before. And it's all ripples on the surface. Her real life is all beneath: more Shark in her than Dolphin.*

He attended to his galley chores. He still needed her help. On the way, he'd continue observing, for whatever that was worth. But as soon as could be, he'd make for a Rahídian west coast port, get passage home, and tell Mulwen Roa that here was no hope for the Seafolk.

Donya ran a three-mile circle. Returning to camp, she flopped down and gasped. Sweat darkened and plastered her hair, dripped off her cheeks, runneled between her breasts. Its odor had a sharpness that gave place quite slowly to the pure scent of woman. But sanity was back in her eyes.

"Do you feel better?" Josserek dared ask.

She nodded. "Yes," she panted. "Much. They won't—kill—the—herds. No, they are what will die."

Presently: "Ung-ng-ng, smells good." Her fit had left no trace in her cheer.

He felt squeamish about embryos from the eggs, which she crunched with pleasure. The rabbit was palatable, given an appetite grown large, but he missed salt as well as spices. "Always drink the blood," Donya advised when he mentioned that. "We'll eat better while we travel."

"Can we kill a grazer?" he wondered skeptically.

"I can, if we wish; or we can take a youngling. Not worth our trouble, though, when we have haste. I'll make a sling for the birds; and there's no lack of small warmbeasts every kind, besides crayfish, mussels, frogs, snakes, snails, herbs, roots, mushrooms. . . . I told you this is a generous land. Soon you will know."

She rose from her meal. Still seated, his gaze climbing the heights, he saw her crowned by radiance, and remembered that "Rogaviki" meant "Children of the Sky." She stretched limb by limb, and laughed into the distances that had wrought her. "Today, we prepare," she said, low and happily, as altogether in this moment as were the dandelions at her feet. "That's no great toil. We will rest as well. And before everything, Josserek, make ourselves one."

She beckoned. Barbarism be damned! He came to her on a torrent.

CHAPTER

10

Five miles out, they met a member of Bullgore Station. Riding a piebald mustang—to inspect a line of wildfowl snares, she related—on spying the strangers she changed course to meet them and accompanied them in.

She was middle-aged, tall and wiry like most Northfolk, her hair in gray braids, her single garment a pair of leather breeches. Brass bracelets, a necklace of bear claws, a pheasant's tail stuck in a headband, and gaudily swirled skin paint were ornaments. Though the saddle on the horse was little better than a pad with stirrup loops, the bridle was intricate. Otherwise her equipment was a bedroll and a knife, the latter clearly meant for tool, not weapon. "Ah-hai!" she cried, reining in. "Welcome, wayfarers. I hight Errody, from yonder."

"And I Donya of Hervar, from Owlhaunt by the Stallion River," said the woman afoot. "My companion has fared farther, Josserek Derrain of a land named Killimaraich, across the Glimmerwater."

"Then thrice welcome," said the rider. "Are you tired? Would either of you borrow my steed?"

Josserek noticed how formal her courtesy was, how slight an outward reaction she showed after that first, surely ritual shout. Not that she was hostile or indifferent; Donya had told him he would fascinate everybody he met. But she held herself back, watchful, cat-private. It fitted the character given her race by every account he knew.

Only it does not fit Donya. Never had he had or heard of a paramour like her. Once, in a moment between kisses, beneath the moon, the night cold forgotten, he had told her this. "I held back with Sidír," she whispered. "Oh, glory to take a friend!" Her hand reached to rumple his hair. It traveled on from there.

Knowledge struck: *She told me hardly a thing else. I said all the self-revealing words. Always, whatever we do, her soul keeps aside.*

If she had a soul, wonderings, yearnings, love that reached beyond the love of life. If she was not simply a healthy animal. *No,* Josserek denied, *she has to be more. When could we have found time for deep talk? We marched, gathered food, camped, ate, played, slept, played, marched. Fear on behalf of her people is hounding her on,* and wished that that might be truth.

He heard her decline the offer of a mount. For pride's sake he did too—*in the teeth of my sore feet,* he tried to jape. Given proper shoes, he could still not have kept her normal pace, His strength and endurance were of a different kind.

After a few trivial exchanges, Errody rode silent. Josserek murmured in Arvannethan, "Isn't she curious about our news?"

"Aye, a-seethe," Donya answered. "The whole Station will be. Why make us repeat?"

He considered that, and the fact that a lone woman, unarmed, set casually forth across uninhabited miles, and the lack of a routine phrase for thanks in Rogavikian. It suggested a people who took patience, peace, and helpfulness for granted. How reconcile the individualism, hard-bargaining acqusitiveness, and sharply defined property rights which Southrons described, or the inmost mind kept secluded which he had observed . . . except when killing rage overwhelmed it? He shook his puzzled head and trudged on through the prairie grass.

The day was bright and windy. Clouds scudded white-sailed, a hawk surfed on the blast, when he came to open fields he saw how crows on the ground flattened their wings and wavelets wandered in battalions on rainpuddles. Hedgerows rustled; trees, hazel, apple, sugar maple, beech, soughed around the buildings. Four young women were out weeding; places like this planted several acres in grain and garden truck, for use and trade. When they saw the newcomers, they quit, and followed the party. Their comrades inside did likewise.

Donya had remarked that a typical Station resembled a typical wintergarth on a larger scale. A partly sunken house filled the east side of a court, glazed windows visible between vegetable beds and steep sod roof. Stables, sheds, workshops defined the rest of the quadrangle. Construction was in timber, locally made brick, and flowering sod, plain and sturdy. A rather lavish use of wood, on this plain where nature sowed hardly any, showed Josserek that the Northfolk must maintain a considerable traffic with the forest dwellers beyond their own lands. Big wagons and sledges, glimpsed through a shed door, suggested the means. A windmill to pump

water stood at the middle of the brick-paved yard, a solar energy collector at the south end of the house, both
Southern-made, crude by Eaching standards but ample
here. Today there was no point in the main chimney
giving off its smoke beacon; but a red banner snapped
atop a very high, guyed staff. Upon this, at eye level,
was fastened the skull of a moonhorn bull, elaborately
enamel-inlaid, monument to whatever incident had
given the site a name.

Personnel numbered about thirty. Three were men,
burlier than common, who did the heaviest manual labor. The majority were women, aged from sixteen or
seventeen onward. They wore a wild variety of garb, or
none; society did not prescribe dress. (Josserek wondered if it prescribed anything.) They didn't crowd or
chatter, but they drew close around, gave greetings, ten-
dered help. No matter how extravagantly well Donya
treated him, the sight of so many lithe bodies was arous-
ing. A young redhead caught his glance, grinned, and
curved him an unmistakable invitation.

Donya saw, grinned back at the girl, and asked
Josserek in Arvannethan, "Would you like to bed her?
She looks good."

"Uh, you?" he replied, taken aback.

"Nobody here for me. Those men have plenty to do.
And I'd not mind a quiet spell for thinking."

Errody, who had dismounted, slipped to Donya's other
side and took her arm in a tentative fashion. Donya returned a slight, amicable headshake. Errody let go,
quirked lips, and gave a subtle shrug, as if to say, Well,
no harm in finding out if you wanted, was there, dear?

Inside, the house differed from travelers' descriptions
of family homes. It held a big common chamber, where
trestle tables were set forth at mealtimes, handsomely
wainscoted and bedraped but with little in the way of

personal items. Those were in the individual rooms of
residents. Elsewhere, aside from utility sections, it was
divided into cubicles for guests. Errody led the way to
a built-in bench. Her associates sat on cushions or
sprawled across a carpet of sewn-together houndskins.
Chairs were not used by the Rogaviki. The red-head settled at Josserek's feet, not at all docilely but staking her
claim.

Donya grew grave. "This evening my friend can tell
about far lands and grand adventures," she said. "Now
I must give you my tidings."

"That the Southrons are coming again?" Errody made
a spitting noise. "We know that."

"Aye, you would. But know you they mean to build
bases the length of the Jugular, and thence harry the
countryside?"

"I thought they might."

"They'll find Bullgore sooner or later. Sooner, I expect. I've watched their horsemen on maneuvers."

"We're readying to leave on short notice. Enough
families, within the Yurik kith alone, have already
promised they'll take two or three of us in, that everyone is sure of shelter." Errody's speech was stoical, and
the whole group calm—resigned—confident of eventual
victory—whatever they were. Josserek noticed, however, that Donya refrained from describing the enemy's
ultimate strategy.

She did briefly recount how he and she came to be
here. The hall buzzed; eyes shone through dimness,
limbs shifted, heads jutted forward. The Rogaviki had a
normal share of curiosity and of relish for a yarn.

"You will need steeds and gear," Errody said.

"First a wash," Donya smiled.

"No, first a drink. We boast of our mead."

The bath proved to be a roomful of showers. Fixtures

were metal, hot water abundant. Squinting at Donya through steam, Josserek said, "That is an attractive wench you bespoke. But I don't believe she could match you."

"No, hardly," was the serene response. "I'm older, and I'm married. Nobody can know men well till she's lived with some of them, year after year in closeness. Yon poor child will never have aught but passing affairs. Unless she turns wholly to women for love, as many do in a Station."

"You don't care if I—?—But honestly, I'd rather have you."

Donya padded over and kissed him. "Gallant you are. Yet we've a long trek after we leave here. Meanwhile I really should use this chance to think." She paused. "Aye, you abide through tomorrow, get well rested, enjoy your lass and whoever else may seek you."

"What will you do?"

"Borrow a horse."

Well, he reflected, *hunters get scant privacy of the skin, unless they go walkabout. How, then, do they develop such privacy of the heart?* Resentment flickered. *And what makes her suppose I have no thoughts in need of marshalling?*

Subsequently they each chose two sets of clothing from a stock kept on hand—undergarments, soft boots, leather trousers whose fringes were a supply of thongs, coarse cloth shirts and bandanas, wide-brimmed felt hats, windbreakers, rain ponchos—plus weapons, tools, bedding, horses. Nobody seemed officially in charge. Errody took over while her associates drifted back to their jobs, apart from the girl who had eyes for Josserek. That one said hers could wait. Her name was Koray.

Errody used a steel pen to write a list of items bought

and their agreed-on value, which Donya signed. "How does this document operate?" Josserek inquired.

"It's an *imak*—" Donya groped after words. She must spend a few minutes clarifying the idea for him, simple though it was.

A Station was set of independent businesses, run by single women and by those rare men who, for miscellaneous reasons, didn't fit into normal Rogaviki life. (Koray later pointed out that the blacksmith was lame. Of his fellows, she imagined the first had left home because of a quarrel in his family, though he didn't say, while the second was a cheerful ne'er-do-well who preferred labor for hire to the rigors and responsibilities outside.) They hailed from everywhere, irrespective of kith origins. Josserek guessed that that was why they could accept the abandonment of this place to the invaders. They had no strong emotional ties to it.

They did have material losses to suffer, of course. A Station sold goods and services which, mostly, required a group sedentary the year around. It was hostel, mart, and specialist factories for an immense area. Travelers in particular—Rogaviki did a lot of individual traveling—could here find what they required en route. A major activity was the swapping of jaded ponies for fresh. Any difference in bargained-out values, or the cost of any outright purchase, might be met with cash; some Imperial and Arvannethan coins circulated. Or it might be paid in kind. Or it might be settled by a note such as Donya had signed, essentially a bill of exchange. Her household would redeem it upon presentation. Probably it would pass through many hands before it reached that goal.

"What if it never does?" Josserek wondered.

"We count not things as narrowly in the Northlands as folk do elsewhere," Errody replied. "We live in too much abundance for a load of goods, either way, to make a difference."

"This Sidír would take from us," Donya hissed.

Koray tugged Josserek's elbow. She had promised to show him around.

For a start, proudly, she led him into her print shop. A flatbed press turned out well-composed pages of flowing alphabet and intricate illustrations. "We can bind books too," she said, "but buyers oftenest do that themselves, in winter."

"Where does the paper come from?" he inquired.

"Most from the South. Happens this is Rogavikian. They've built a mill at Whitewater Station, on the Wilderwoods edge."

This alone, as well as what else he saw that afternoon, told Josserek of a broadly spread and vigorous commerce. Households, self-sufficient as far as their necessities went, bought ample finely made things. Many wares flowed northward in exchange for metal salvaged from ancient ruins; but many, and ever more, were entirely domestic. They were innovative, too. Koray chattered of a newly designed portable loom, or a repeating crossbow which a visitor from the Tantian Hills had described. The pamphlet she was currently printing concerned astronomical observations by a man at Eagles Gather who, besides a Rahídian telescope, owned a Killimaraichan navigator's clock which had somehow found its way to him. Josserek saw a brisk market for the latter item . . . except that the bloody Empire would establish a monopoly.

Apparently all trade, like all manufacturing, was private. No guilds or governments existed to control it, no laws forbade anything—Wait. "Your folk sell furs to the Southrons," he said. "But I hear they never sell meat or hides from big game. Do you exchange those among yourselves?"

"Why, yes," Koray said. "A friend gives a friend a bison robe or a boar ham or, oh, whatever."

"I don't mean gifts. I mean a regular trade. Suppose I offered your horsedealer a hundred bronco hides for a live, well-broken animal."

She stepped back. Her eyes widened. "Nobody would."

"Why not?"

"It would be . . . wrong, wrong. We *live* by the game beasts."

"I see. I'm sorry. Forgive a foreigner's ignorance." Josserek patted her. She relaxed and snuggled.

He was interested in everything he saw, but examined the power systems with most care. The windmill was a conventional skeleton and sails. Alcohol was fuel for blowtorches and a couple of small machine tools. It was distilled on the premises from fermented wild grains and fruits. (Brandymaking was a separate operation.) The main energy source was the solar collector, whose black waterpipes led to a subterranean tank of fired clay. There, under pressure, temperatures rose well above normal boiling point. Simple exchangers tapped the heat for warmth and cookery.

Horses, hounds, and hawks were the only domestic animals, no different from their wild cousins. When Koray cuddled a litter of puppies, and the big lean mother snarled if Josserek got close, he remembered an absence. "Have you no children here?" he asked.

Did she flinch? At least, kneeling over the straw, she turned her face aside, and he could barely hear her. "No. Not on a Station. Nobody marries . . . that I ever heard of."

"But, uh, men do come by and—"

"It would be wrong to, to raise fatherless children. The wives bring forth enough."

"What I mean is—"

"I understand. Did you not know? Many Rogaviki women can will that they not conceive."

Surprised, he thought, *Possible. Psychosomatics; the mind ordering hormonal changes. But what discipline is involved? Our psychologists would certainly like to know.* "Does that always work?"

"No. Then there are other ways." He expected mention of mechanical or chemical contraceptives, however unlikely they seemed in these parts. Instead, as though thrusting wistfulness aside, Koray lifted her gaze to his. "Fear not on my account, Josserek. Unions between us and outsiders . . . seldom bring anything about."

She left the puppies and came to him.

That evening, by lantern light, the company dined well. Mostly it was off assorted meats. Man can stay hale on a carnivorous diet if he eats the whole animal; and, in various preparations, the Northfolk did. But they added fish, fowl, eggs, breads, mare's milk and cheese, fruits, herb teas, beer, wine, mead, liquor, till Josserek's head tolled. Conversation was animated, laced with humor despite the woe moving up the Jugular. Yet it struck him strange, being so much more objective than he was used to. Elsewhere, a strange guest would have gotten at least some leading questions about his experiences, habits, beliefs, prejudices, opinions, hopes, and received similar information about his hosts. At Bullgore they told him of their land, past history, happenings which were common local knowledge; and they left it to him to volunteer what he chose.

Nevertheless, for his entertainment three girls performed a harp dance that began wildly and ended in a way which sent most watchers soon to bed, two by two.

Those were the brackets of the evening. For hours in between, everyone listened avidly to his stories from the Mother Ocean. Queries flew thick and sharp as arrow barrages.

Two additional guests were present, a man and a woman, postal couriers on different routes who had stopped off for the night. From what they told him, Josserek learned that this too was a service performed for gain by individuals, who had no central organization. Evidently it covered the whole domain of the kiths, swiftly and reliably.

—Agile, inventive, Koray proved a joy to him, if not the splendor that Donya was. But long after she slept in the curve of his arm, he lay awake, staring into darkness, trying and failing to understand her people. They weren't barbarians after all—maybe—But then what in the Great Abyss were they?

CHAPTER

11

At the head of navigation, a few miles south of the mighty but treacherous Bison River inflow, lay Fuld, northernmost of the Arvannethan trading posts. Beyond, the Jugular was too heavily gravelled, stones which the Ice gouged forth in its winter advance and washed southward in its summer retreat. Standing on the factor's verandah, Sidír could make out a green and white violence where currents broke on bars. Shallow or not, that was no place for an army few of whose men could swim.

The house occupied the top of a high bluff on the left bank. It was built of wood and brick shipped up from the Southland, in Southern style, a square enclosing a patio. Peaked shingle roofs, necessary to shed heavier snow than the city ever got, looked grotesque on this; the cloister garden was a poor thing; the rooms, however spacious, were chill and gloomy. Sidír had wondered why the makers did not imitate native winter-houses, which visitors reported were snug. Then he let the landscape reach his full consciousness, and felt that probably they wanted every reminder of home they could have.

Below him, along the dock, clustered warehouses, barracks, a tavern. There *Weyrin* was tied. His last barges and their tugs were anchored in the great brown stream. On the far shore, a ferry terminal served Rogaviki who brought goods from the west—had brought goods, until him. A mile outside the settlement, his banners, pickets, dome tents, wagons, corrals, cannon drew diagrams upon wilderness. Those men, whom he had led the entire distance and would lead further, were his crack troops, Barommian cavalry, élite Rahídian infantry, gunners and engineers whose skill was unsurpassed in the world.

Yet they seemed lost in this country. It had changed as he fared, from level to rolling, from long grass to short, from treelessness to scattered coppices. Somehow that deepened distances and alienness. Today was chill, shadowless, wanhued. Black rags of cloud flew beneath a steely overcast. The wind skirled and flung single raindrops. When they hit, they stung.

Inil en-Gula, the factor, pointed. "Yes," he said, "you guess aright, the river does form a boundary. East is the Ulgani kith, west the Hervar."

Hervar. Donya. Sidír locked his teeth together.

"That is exceptional," Inil went on. He was a wrinkled little yellow man, bookish, frankly dismayed at the war, nonetheless unable not to talk with a person fresh from civilization. "As a rule, kith territories have no fixed frontiers."

Surprise jarred through Sidír's rememberings. He had studied what he could about the Northfolk, and asked

Donya about them at length, but always something slipped from him, always he found he had had a wrong idea. And so he was never sure if the idea that replaced it was right. "Why, I thought the tribes were fanatical where their lands are concerned," he said.

"They are, they are, Captain General. Which is why the Empire is making a terrible mistake."

Sidír chopped an impatient gesture. "Fanatics are like dry sticks. They don't bend, but they break, and then they can't spring back."

"The Rogaviki are different. They have no leaders whom you can force to persuade them to make peace."

"I know. The better for us. Isolated individuals lack the mutual support—the web of duty and sanction, the fear of being shamed as coward or punished as traitor— that makes organized groups resist." Sidír recalled incidents downstream, told him by swift-riding messengers while he traveled: bush-whackings, murders by stealth, concealed pits with sharp stakes at the bottom, plugged wells, a clay vessel full of rattlesnakes catapulted into a camp. . . . "I don't deny they're dangerous, treacherous enemies. But dangerous mainly when they get a chance to practice the treachery. I wish they'd be foolish and try some pitched battles. If not, we'll take them piecemeal. We'll make examples that should quell the rest. Meanwhile, Fuld will be adequately guarded."

"I hope you are right, Captain General," Inil sighed. "For both our sakes. But, if you will pardon my rudeness, you show no comprehension of their character."

Sidír forged a smile. "I appreciate rudeness, Guildsman. Lies and flattery are worse than useless." *Did Donya lie, or could I simply not grasp what she tried to tell me? Did her lovemaking flatter me, or did she simply enjoy me for what I was?*

Surely, when she turned on me, it was not in calcu-

lated betrayal but in desperation. What did I do that
was wrong. Donya?

"Explain, then," he requested. "You were saying—
How do tribes define their territories?"

"First, Captain General, they are not tribes," Inil
answered. "Nor clans. Our word 'kith' is a poor approx-
imation of '*rorskay*.' Some claim a common descent,
but as a legend, of no special significance. Families
within one do tend to intermarry, but that's not invaria-
ble; it's just the effect of propinquity. In cross-kith wed-
dings, the husband joins the wife's—no initiation
ceremonies, perhaps no deep feelings about the change,
though God knows what feelings the Rogaviki have
about whatever is important to them. After twenty-five
years in the trade, *I* can't tell."

Sidír rubbed his chin. "And yet that same husband
will defend his adopted soil to the death."

"Yes. Basically, a kith is a set of families who, by tradition, share a certain hunting ground. A huge ground,
to be sure. There are less than a hundred kiths in the entire Northlands, and I believe none has more than two or
three thousand members. The herds they follow define
the regions sufficiently well, being territorial creatures."

Was that why Donya went mad? Because, in her sav-
age way of seeing the world, the herds are her home?
Her gods, her ancestral ghosts?

"Individuals and partner groups travel freely," Inil
continued. "They are welcome guests, for the news and
variety they bring. Nobody minds their hunting as they
go. But serious encroachment, by a large band on another's preserve, is unheard of. I suspect it is unthinkable."

"Even in bad years?"

"They have no bad years. The Rogaviki keep their
population low enough that, no matter how far animal

numbers drop—say during a particularly severe winter—
they always find plenty."

*And that isn't natural either. It's the mark of an effete
and dying people, as in Arvanneth. The strong breed to
capacity, and beyond. That is why the Empire will take
the Northlands.*

But is Donya, then, weak?

"I suppose their religion taboos incursions," Sidír
guessed. "And a deal else."

"I am not sure if they have anything we would understand as a religion," Inil said.

"What?"

"Oh, I have heard some ideas described, that some of
them pursue in a kind of career. But it sounds to me
more like a philosophy than a faith."

*No wars to discipline them. No leaders to guide them.
No belief to sustain them. How have they survived?*

Inil hunched in his robe. "Captain General, it's abomi-
nably cold," he complained. "Shall we go inside?"

"Go if you wish, Guildsman," the Barommian answered. "I'd like to . . . breathe a while longer. I'll join
you shortly."

"The Ice has already touched you, has it?" Inil muttered, and departed.

Sidír stared after him. What the Nine Devils had that
meant?

He swung his attention back outward. There was so
much, too much he must do. Foremost, if not quite
first in time, was the gathering of knowledge. Without
native guides—some natives had always joined the
conquerors!— until now—his scouts must make their
own discoveries and draw their own maps, across vast-
nesses where every rock might hide a sniper, every
grove a deadfall. They could, his lads; they would;
somewhere they would at last find Donya's home, to

keep for a hostage or sack for a lesson. But he must spur them toward getting well secured soon. The summer was brief in this haunted land.

She haunted it.

Why?

He struggled for bluntness. *Good-looking. Exotic. A superb lay. A manlike intelligence and nerve. Most of all, maybe, mystery, the wondering what really dwelt behind her eyes. None of this explains why the loss of her bleeds in me.*

Or why I imagine any mystery. Likeliest she was merely heedless and conscienceless, as ready to let that stoker tumble her as me or anybody, unable to keep up her trickery very long before a chance quarrel set her wits afire. It's not the real Donya I can't forget, it's a dream.

Why should I have the dream?

They call the Rogaviki women witches.

Beneath his Rahídian reason, an old barbarian stirred. He felt the wind's bite, shivered, and followed the factor inside.

CHAPTER

12

Donya and Josserek traveled for several days, north-bound to join her household in Hervar, before they first met a hunter band. He kept no count. In these man-empty reaches, time and space melted together and there were only events—rainsquall, rainbow, chasing down an antelope for food, escaping a houndpack, gaudy sunset through the translucent wings of bats above a lake, hillcock rocketing from berrythicket, butterfly swarm, crossing a knife-cold river, laughter at the antics of fox pups seen from concealment, raid on a beehive in a hollow stump, love made wildly by moonlight, then tenderly again at dawn and once, crazily, while heaven blazed, roared, cataracted with thunderstorm—events like single waves on a endless rhythm of miles. He did observe how the country slowly changed. Low hills and dales became commoner. Trees and mossy meadows appeared oftener; later, heaths did. Nights were colder.

When at last Donya spied a smoke-wisp on her left, she headed for it. "They may have news we've not heard," she explained. "Still more have we need to tell them what we know. As many as can be should gather at this summer's Landmeet."

That's distinct from a Kithmeet, which happens near solstice in each particular territory, Josserek recalled. *The Landmeet is two months afterward, for everybody in the Northlands who cares to come. Shark! Will they take so long to start getting organized? Sidír could be in Roong by then.*

He had learned the futility of argument. "Where are we?" he asked.

"Whose grounds, do you mean? The Ferannian." Donya clicked tongue and thumped heels. Her pony broke into a trot. Josserek's followed, and the two remounts they led.

They came on the camp unobserved, since a ridge lay between. From the top, Josserek saw a dozen circular, cone-roofed pavilions by a stream. Evidently the owners were a Fellowship: an informal association of families who kept winter quarters close together and most of whose members hunted in company. (Some, especially younger ones, adventured elsewhere in any given season.) This day being warm and sunny, full of turf odors, children and oldsters were cooking a mutual supper outdoors: a giant prairie deer roasted in chunks amidst cauldrons suspended over coals. Nearby stood several of the light, high-sprung wagons which carried loads across the plains and floated them across waters. Hobbled draft horses grazed beyond. Riding horses, hounds, hawks were off on the chase. When his gaze swept over billowy greenness toward the eastern horizon, Josserek saw a part of that. Hunters had stampeded a moonhorn herd—surge of russet bodies, earthquake of hoofs—and galloped hairbreadth along the edges, wielding bow and lance.

"Can they eat that much before it spoils?" he wondered aloud. Again and again he had encountered a quasi-religious care for the land and all the life thereon.

"They'll dry and smoke most, then carters will take it to their houses; also hides, bones, sinews, entrails, for every part has a use," Donya said.

"You told me, though, you hunt in winter too."

"Just a bit, and close to the garths. Stored food keeps us—through a blizzard, or while we go visiting afar, or when we practice arts and idleness. Surely you didn't think we spend snowtime like coyotes?" Donya's laugh teased him as she turned downhill.

Josserek was surprised to see the campers go for weapons when they spied the newcomers. Travelers had often remarked on Rogavikian trustfulness. Donya must have noticed their behavior too, for she spread empty hands, and halted at the edge of the site. By then, the folk had put down their arms. A white-haired granny, still erect and supple in the kilt that was her sole garment, took the lead. "Welcome, wayfarers," she declaimed. "We are from Ravens' Rest, and I hight Deraby."

Donya introduced herself and her companion. "Why were you wary of us?" she asked. "Have the Imperials so soon reached Ferannian?"

"No," Deraby said, "though passers-by have told us how they ravage. We feared you might be Outrunners; we found signs of their work a few days ago. In spite of your being well-clad and having a man beside you—*Eyach*, dismount, take refreshment. Avelo, look to our guests' horses, will you?"

"Outrunners," Donya mumbled. She slacked her brief scowl. At Josserek's questioning glance: "I'll explain later, if you wish. Another hazard. Belike no worse than the wild dogs or wilder river we've already met."

The children boiled around the foreigner and insisted on giving him a tour. He learned that the tents were thin-scraped leather, erected on light wooden frames with steel couplings. At the center of each was a hearthpit, a sheet aluminum funnel hung above for a smokehood. Window flaps and entrance were protected by mosquito netting. He noticed a fair abundance of goods, including equipment for sports, games, music, even books. Branded on the walls were symbols he could not read but found pleasing. Wagons were downright gaudy, trimmed in brass and gold.

Among persons present were a couple of mothers who took a turn this day tending and suckling everybody's infants. Their own were two or three years old, long since on solid food but still cuddling up for a draught from a breast every now and then. Lactation reduced fertility, Josserek knew. Likewise did low body weight; and most Rogaviki were lean. Nomadic savages normally had ways, besides acceptance of high infant mortality, to keep fecundity down. There were practical reasons: such as the fact that a woman could not very well carry about more than one baby at a time, while toddlers slowed her nearly as much.

Damnation, though, that doesn't apply here, Josserek thought. *By all accounts, including Donya's when I asked, the Northfolk have good medicine and sanitation; few of their young die. They have horses and wheels for transport. They have what amounts to equality of the sexes; men share in child care, and in a polyandrous household, men will always be around. Motherhood flat-out isn't a handicap, not enough or long enough to matter. So the population growth pattern should be more like the pattern of agricultural peoples. Instead, it's the lowest I've ever heard of—zero, except when heavy losses are being made up.*

That implies regulating mechanisms, religion, law, custom, social pressure, institutions. Except the Rogaviki don't appear to have any such things!

Well, of course their marriage style. A powerful force. What was Donya's estimate when I asked her? Three out of five females never reproduce. How can that have lasted, for centuries or millennia? It's clean against human nature.

By chance, he soon got a partial reply. The earliest who returned to camp were a young and thoroughly pregnant girl, accompanied by a mature woman. Both caught his attention. The first showed marks of tears, though she had won back some calm. That wasn't typical . . . he believed. The second was still more striking. She was perhaps in her late thirties, a tall blonde who must often go nude as she did now, since her skin was everywhere a deep brown against which her hair stood nearly white. She was apparently unwed, for he noticed none of the silvery birth-scars which traced along Donya's thighs. But her walk was deliberate, her countenance grave, in a way he had never before seen hereabouts. Her right arm circled the girl's waist—comfortingly, not erotically—while her left hand swung a staff topped by a sunburst carved in walrus ivory from the Mother Ocean.

"Who are they?" Josserek murmured.

"A Forthguide, plain to see, and a member of the Fellowship whom she's been helping," Donya answered.

"What do you mean?"

"Later."

"The woman gave her name as Krona of Starrok. Far had she wandered, then, from the southern kith wherein she was born. Bidding the youngster a gentle goodbye, she soon fell into talk with the mistress of Owlhaunt. Josserek didn't hear what they said, for hunters were coming back too and eager to meet him.

Some stayed out to guard the kills from scavengers, until morning when butchering could commence. Their fires twinkled through dusk. "Pity you must be off again tomorrow," said a graybeard called Tamaveo. "They'd love to hear you tell of your farings."

"We've time for little more than warnings," the Killimaraichan responded. Though he didn't think it would do much good, he shared Donya's desire to start the tale of the invasion and its uniqueness spreading across the whole Northland.

"We know." Knuckles whited around a haft. "The devourers are back. A new generation of us must die to get rid of them."

"No," Josserek denied. "This is not like any onslaught ever before."

Tamaveo's wife caught her breath and gripped his arm. She was no older than the girl whom Krona had been counseling. In answer to a muffled question, Donya had said, "Aye, it's an easy guess what happened in that family. Its lady died. For the children's sake, her husbands chose to stay together. Doubtless they'd rather have taken a mature mate, but all such in the neighborhood or at the Kithmeet felt they had men enough already, and yon slip was the sole female who'd give them a yes."

"How?" the wife whispered.

Donya threw Josserek a headshake. *Do not madden them with the plan to slay their game.* He could barely see her, seated across the fire beside Krona. The Forthguide had dressed against night in a long gray gown and hooded blue mantle which made her the more enigmatic amidst wool and buckskin elsewhere in the circle. Flames danced tiny on ashes and embers. Faces, hands, meadhorns glimmered from shadow. Supper was past and breezes had borne away odors of meat, soup, loaves, borne in the howls of distant hounds. One by one, stars blinked forth until grandeur wheeled around the north pole of heaven where Vega stood warden.

Josserek nodded slightly. "These are not plowmen or herders moving in for you to massacre," he said, "nor slow fighters afoot and clumsy dragoons, for you to catch unawares, and cut their supply lines in the dry, lean, dusty country above the Khadrahad. The fist and the fangs of this army are the Barommian riders, as swift and hardy as yours, as well able to live off the land, and better equipped, better—" he cold find no word for "disciplined" and must substitute—"prepared to work in teams, than I fear you imagine. The Rahídian infantry will establish stongholds. Out of these the Barommian horse will hunt you down."

Donya had said that the idea of being themselves attacked would not shake them.

"Tell us more," Deraby requested. Her tone was level—though briefly, through the dying firelight, he saw her reach forth and touch the cheek of a granddaughter.

He spoke, and they listened, until long after the late moon had risen. Questions were many and, for the most part, intelligent. But they turned wholly on tactics. How could a daggerman get past a Barommian lance and corselet? Might enemy squadrons be lured into the quicksands common along shallow rivers? What about men in the grass with hamstringing knives? . . . Josserek heard no slightest concept of strategy, or of the possibility of defeat.

In the end, as folk yawned and sought their tents, Tamaveo invited the Killimaraichan to his. Donya and

Krona had gone off into the dark by themselves. Josserek noticed how this man, as senior husband, took leadership in this particular family. His impression was that a wife usually did. However, "leadership" must be a wrong term, in a society where nothing compelled the individual except the individual's own self. "Initiative?" Regardless, Tamaveo's cohabitants were pleased, while members of other households expressed good-natured disappointment.

Within the shelter, by the light of a thin bronze candelabrum, he said, as impulsively as Josserek had heard a Rogaviki speak under normal conditions: "Man from the Glimmerwater, you do us much kindness. May I give you a token in turn?" From a chest he took a cloak, heavy Southland silk embroidered and trimmed in Northland style.

"Why . . . yes, you are good, you gladden me," Josserek answered, the nearest he could come to thanks in the native tongue for something not absolutely extraordinary. He was sincere; the garment was gorgeous. "Uh, what is this white fur? I've never seen a pelt quite like it?"

"Wold cat," Tamaveo said.

"Hm?" Josserek had glimpsed the small wild felines, obviously related to the house pets of Killimaraich. But they were drab-hued for camouflage. "Is it—" Damn, he didn't know how to say "albino."

"Winter phase, of course." Tamaveo's manner suggested pride. Probably the beasts were hard to catch then, hence valuable.

For some reason, Josserek lay long in his bedroll thinking about that. He had met cats around the world. Scientists theorized this was because civilization before the Ice had kept them; certain uniformities in certain fragments suggested it had been global. But he knew of none whose color changed with the seasons, as did the ermine's or an arctic hare's.

Then the wold cat was a new genus. . . . What did "new" mean? In numberless thousands of years, in weathers that shifted decade by decade as the glaciers growled down from the poles, natural selection might well become a whiplash. Genetic drift too, maybe, among populations cut off from their kin. . . . He recalled an island where everybody had six fingers. Or ebon skin, snow hair, and brass eyes on Mulwen Roa of Iki. . . . *Well, I'm no hereditarian savant. I've just read a little, mainly after I went on whale patrol and started wondering how such marvels ever came to be. . . .* Eventually he slept. In his dreams, elephants trumpeted. They were not like those he had seen in tropical Owang or Eflis. They were hairy, and bore immense arches of tusk, and walked a tundra which the Ice cliffs bounded.

—Donya came during the night. At dawn, while a hubbub went through the grayness, she drew Josserek aside and said, "The Forthguide, Krona, is finished here. She's bound next for Dunheath Station. That's on our way—if we'd seed our message widely—so I proposed she join us. Will you agree?"

"I, I suppose so," he hesitated. "What does she do?"

"You do not know? She seeks wisdom. For that, she stays out of any family or Fellowship, travels freely about, repays hospitality by teaching or by helping people like that girl you saw with her yesterday. It's a noble calling, for such as have strength for it."

Well, Josserek thought, *this might make things a little awkward between Donya and me while it lasts. On the other hand, I am interested. And what use if I said no?* "How was she helping?" he asked. "I mean, you two had a long conversation. I'm sure she told you, or you could tell for yourself, what went on. Maybe I should know, lest my tongue blunder."

"Oh, a common matter." The response was indifferent, if not altogether uncompassionate. "The girl has good prospects of marrying. Two of her fathers are in trade, and can dower her well." Since paternity became guesswork after a woman had taken her second husband, the Rogaviki ordinarily made no distinction among the possibilities. "But playing about as lassies do, she had the misfortune that a dart struck home."

Josserek already knew how custom availed itself of the sterility frequent among adolescents. Besides fun and games, many first marriages happened quite soon after puberty. Under parental guidance, a young couple could grow together for a few years before babies started arriving.

"This is a—" He must use Arvannethan. "A disgrace?"

Donya nodded. "If the unwed bore children as wives do, we'd be crowded out of our lives, right?"

"Can she be forced to refrain?"

"No, certainly not. She is human." What notion of subservience that the Rogaviki had came entirely from domestic animals and from what they knew about foreign realms. "But who would take her in, help her in any way, let alone marry her? She'd have to become an Outrunner, or a full-time whore, or something ghastly like that."

"What can she do, then?"

"The usual. It's only that she is still childlike and—sentimental. Well, Krona has spent these past several days heartening her."

"For what?"

"Why, to expose the brat when it's born. What else?" Donya smiled. "And give out the customary story, that she believes it was a mule, from a chance union with a Southron, therefore nothing anybody would want to keep. Everyone will agree." She turned away. "Hoy, we've work, you and I, haven't we?"

Josserek stood still. Noise and movement, waxing light and waning cold, seemed far off.

Why do I care? he thought. *Did I imagine these people have no hypocrisies? And the gods know, whether abortion or infanticide, baby murder is common enough the world around.*

What of it? I must be more of a piece with Killimaraichan civilization than I was aware, if my guts tell me that here too the unborn and the newborn deserve rights, which they've done no crime to forfeit.

The Northfolk feel otherwise. Why am I troubled? What should I expect ... from a race quite strange to me?

Let me continue among them awhile, regardless. If they will fight the Empire to the end, maybe I can help show them how to bring down a maximum number of its men before they must surrender, the last starvelings of them who have not died like unwanted babies of their own.

CHAPTER

13

On their second day as a triad, the Outrunners found them.

Donya saw the band first. She had taken a horse off on a practice which eventually carried them over a hill, beyond view of her companions. This she had done with both her animals since leaving Bullgore, putting them through paces, maneuvers, stunts that would have earned fame in a showtroupe among the Seafolk. "The need may come," she explained to Josserek. By the present time, they were like limbs of her.

He hadn't tried for that, nor had she urged he do so. His horsemanship was merely competent. Krona rode her own beasts in total unity, but denied any necessity for repeated drills; she had raised them from colthood. Thus she and the man jogged side by side and talked. Despite his view of her morals, he came to like her.

Curious about his world, she asked him more than

she answered. However, she was less reticent than most Rogaviki. That did not stem from either egotism or insecurity. He soon decided he had rarely met a person so balanced. Just as she traveled unarmed save for knives, hatchet, and light crossbow, hunting tools only, she felt no threat to her inwardness. In leisure fashion, she described for him what she was.

"Oftenest, unwed women stay on in their Fellowships," she began. "Extra hands are always useful. Still more valued are extra minds."

(He had wondered about the stability of such households. Might a husband not grow tired of sharing his woman, and easily be lured elsewhere? Donya had said no. A wife should have the vigor to keep several men happy; that was one basis on which a girl, counseled by her parents, decided whether or not she really desired to become a wife. Sexual outlets were available for the unplighted: commonly female but not uncommonly male, boys or passing travelers or occasionally a husband. The sole rule was that no children result. Extramarital flings were unimportant in themselves, if the marriage was strong. And it normally was. In theory, a spouse could leave anytime. In practice, a wedding created a "bond of honor," and whoever broke that without mutual consent risked losing the respect of friends.

(Josserek winced at the thought that to her he might be no more than a fling. He dared not ask. Instead, he remarked that in his homeland, two or more women under a single roof guaranteed trouble. Donya had been puzzled. What was there to spat about? In her life, everybody had personal quarters, goods, work, play, enthusiasm, and didn't interfere with anybody else's. Jobs requiring cooperation were organized to finish as quickly and easily as possible. That was plain common sense.

("Then you Rogaviki have a breed of common sense hardier than any I've found before," he joked—and abruptly remembered her amok rage, and much else.)

"But many are not content to abide at home," Krona went on. "They form, or they join, partnerships to trap or trade. They settle at Stations, where they feel the pulse of all the Northlands. They roam abroad, try their hands at different things, come back rich in tales. They adventure as artists, artisans, entertainers, inventors, prospectors, scholars, teachers of booklore, seekers of new knowledge in nature. Some seek knowledge beyond nature, and some of those become Forthguides."

He regarded her with interest and pleasure alike. She was a handsome sight, riding beside him, clad similarly but her shirt half open and hatless flaxen hair tossing free. Her manner was easy, in several ways more cordial than Donya's alternations of brusqueness, carnivore mirth, and wordless passion. Nonetheless, more marked her off than staff secured to saddlegirth, robes rolled in sleeping bag: more, even, than a remembered remark of hers, that lifelong celibacy was her free choice. "I search into the unhuman," she had said. "For this, I must myself, at last, become inhuman—a stone, a star, a river, the Ice."

This day was cloudless, brilliant, but chill, for a north wind blew. Again the country wrinkled treeless, waterholes and rivulets far apart. Grass grew in dry, brownish clumps. Thicker stood heath shrubs, gray-green, which snickered and snapped their twigs around the horses' knees. Occasional elders reared sallow among them. Rabbits sprang aside, grouse and crow fluttered aloft, but there was no big game. "A poor stretch, sandy soil that doesn't hold water well, scant rain in summer. Don't linger; push across to better lands," the Ferannian kithfolk had advised.

How well did its starkness suit Krona?

"I gather your kind keep moving," Josserek said. "You're welcome guests because you counsel the troubled and help train the young—"

"We live for our own enlightenment," she answered. "But this requires, first, oneness of body and mind. Which is not like oneness of horse and rider. Body and mind are not two separate beings. It is oneness like bird and flight. This comes hard, through efforts and austerities. And they can themselves create a barrier. The bird must glide and hover as well as rise and swoop. Possessions, ties to people or home grounds, would add too great a burden.

"The aim is a self-command more powerful than humans can achieve in ordinary life. Having that, how could I refuse to share, through instruction, a little of it with those who ask, when they have given me hospitality? But helpfulness was never my reason for acquiring the control. Nor is this mastery aught save a first step toward the true end: enlightenment."

"I've met ascetics who're after the same goal," Josserek nodded. "Some believe they'll find it when they're received into the presence of—of—*God*, we say, meaning the source of all, supposed to be a person. Others hope to merge their identities with the all itself. I suppose their faith is the closer to yours."

Immediately he wondered if the word he used meant anything like "faith." Had he actually said, oh, "opinion," or maybe "surmise?" Donya had admitted to him that families practiced private rites; but she only knew about hers, which she would not discuss. Clearly the Rogaviki had no set creed, not so much as a mythology. The religions of foreigners amused her.

Krona gave him a steady blue regard. "No," she declared. "Unless I gravely misunderstand you. I've heard rumors about those ideas you mention. They don't make sense to me. Surely reality is—"

She lost him, went beyond his vocabulary and comprehension, saw it, and came back to guide him. He didn't get far. Her concepts were too exotic. He got an impression that, in her view, existence moved toward infinite differentiation. Enlightenment was not the union of the self with a changeless ultimate, but the growth of the self . . . perhaps, metaphorically, its assimilation of everything else into its awareness. At the same time, the self was not a monad. It was dynamically integral with an ever-evolving universe; and in no way was it immortal. Krona made no distinction between knowledge, discovery, intuition, logic, and emotion. They were equally valid, equally essential to insight and completion.

At length he sighed and confessed, "After several years of labor, I might begin to see what you're driving at, not as words but as a reasonable way of describing the cosmos, of living in it. Or I might not. More and more I wonder if I, if any stranger will ever know you folk."

"Well," she smiled, "you're amply puzzling to us. Let's dip pleasure out of that."

They had ridden a short while onward, in amicable silence, when Donya returned. She did it at a gallop, over the hilltop and straight at them. Close by, her pony reared to a halt. The smell of its sweat freighted the wind. Donya's eyes were a slanty green blaze in stiff-held paleness.

Trouble, Josserek knew. His flesh prickled. Krona waited impassive.

"Outrunners," Donya snapped. "Got to be. A dozen or worse. They must have seen me before I did them, because when I did, they were bound full tilt my way."

Krona turned her head from side to side, scanning

emptiness. "Nowhere can we make a stand," she said. "If we try, we're theirs."

"I'd knife myself first, wouldn't you? Best we hold northward. We're near Zelevay territory. Likelier we might find help there, or broken ground where we may shake pursuit, than doubling back though Ferannian." Donya ripped a laugh. "If we can keep in front of the hellhags, that is. Their nags are as scrawny as you'd await, but they've three or four remounts apiece. Come!"

She set off at a smart trot. Animals lasted longest if the pace varied; and she had many miles in mind. Josserek brought his steed next to hers. Through wind, bush-crackle, hoofbeats, squeak and jingle of harness, he asked, "What in the name of everything bad are Outrunners?"

"Those who never get along with their fellows, and turn to preying on them," she replied grimly. "Skullers in wastelands, waylayers, hit-and-run raiders. Nigh all are women, and ill it is to fall into their claws." She bit her lip. "Once I was among those who found the rags of a girl they'd caught. Before she died, she told us a little of what was done to her. It gave me evil dreams for a year afterward. We gathered a band to make an end of them, but they'd scattered and we snagged just three. Left them nailed to trees. Maybe that helped keep the rest from visiting Hervar again."

He recalled what he had heard in camp. Things which followed had nudged it from his mind. "If you knew Outrunners were in these parts—" he began.

She cut his words across: "The odds were long they wouldn't come on us. This is sheer foul luck. Now ride!" While she did, she strung her short, recurved hornbow.

The bandits appeared. They hastened in disorder. Their yells could not reach him through a mile and a half of shrilling air. *Twelve, aye,* he counted. *And plenty spare horses. Ours can't outrun theirs after exhaustion sets in.*

Three of us. Can we do nothing except flee? This damned naked plain! If we could find a defensible spot, we might pick them off with arrows, or sally forth and kill one or two at a time. But surrounded in the open—

Sidír's Barommians wouldn't get netted. Well-armed, armored, trained to fight in units, they'd grind attackers up for dogfood. Then they'd go on and scour the land clean of renegades. Shark! The Rogaviki can't assemble a proper posse, let alone a police force! Resentment that he might die because of this brought acid up to burn his gullet. *Their society is another of history's mistakes. Natural selection is about to act on it.*

"Yow, hoo—oo, rrra-a-ow!" sounded before him.

Around a knoll ahead to the left came two. They had no beasts along save the ragged-shaggy mustangs they rode. These they quirted into a spurt of speed on an intercept course.

Donya nocked an arrow, drew bow, loosed. The string twanged. The missile sped true. But the target was out of its path. She had ducked to the opposite side of her mare, hanging on by a leg. As she bobbed up again, she yammered laughter.

Her comrade pounded nearer still. She too was an archer; the first bore a lance. Her hair streamed in elflocks, so dirty that Josserek couldn't tell if it was blond or brown. Soot, dried blood, grease likewise marked her skin. Breasts flapped above ribs that he could count. She wore leather breeches and several knives. The other one added a plundered cloak.

"Ee-ya-ah!" she howled, and let fly . . . at the horses of her quarry.

A shaft struck home. A remount screamed and

plunged. *This pair of devils will slow us down for the rest,* Josserek knew. He hauled on reins, kicked heels into belly, brought his bronco around and charged.

"You fool—" he heard Donya cry.

Louder sounded the gibing of the Outrunner. Her eyes glistened white above the hollow cheeks, her mouth gaped and drooled. "Aye, come, come, man. Be brave. We'll not kill you fast. We'll stake you down and play—make a steer of you, hai, hai?—Yoo-ee!"

She skirted aside. He couldn't force his animal close in.

As he circled, he glimpsed Donya bound toward them. Behind her, Krona struggled to bring the panicky string under control. The main body of reavers narrowed the distance between.

"Josserek!" Donya called. "Get back there. Help Krona. You're no use here."

She passed in a drumfire of hoofs, leered as she did, and taunted, "Will you play with *me*, you sow?"

The archer screeched, wheeled, gave chase. Likewise did the lancer. *They'd torture me for the sport,* Josserek knew from what he had heard. *The women they'd keep longer.* Almost, he disobeyed Donya. *I should—No. She knows whatever she wants to do. Maybe simply to die fast.*

He returned. The wounded horse still fought to pull free, harder than Krona could match. Josserek lent his strength to the bridle. After a minute, she could soothe them all. The injury wasn't crippling, though it would be if not attended to soon. They continued their trot. The chase had now halved the gap. Josserek's awareness stayed by Donya.

Over the heath she fled. The twain barked and gibbered behind. A high elderbush loomed ahead. Donya whipped her mount around in back of it. For this she had spent those hours of training. The crazies had not. They couldn't stop like that, they plunged on past, right and left, sawing at hackamore lines. Donya's horse sprang after. She guided by her knees. A knife flared in each hand: into the archer's back and upward, into the lancer's side between ribcage and hipbone and across in a slash.

They fell. The archer lay still atop a tussock. The lancer flopped among scratchy shrubs, ululated, spouted impossibly scarlet blood.

In leaps, Donya rejoined her companions. "Here," she said, tossing reins at Josserek. "Lead mine. I'll ride the hurt creature as far as it can go, then we'll cut it loose." She sprang to the bare back. "Gallop!" she shouted.

Long, smooth velocity took hold of the man. Wind hooted in his ears, whipped tears from his eyes. A glance showed how the Outrunners fell behind. They ignored their casualties. But after a while they exchanged yelps, and presently they halted. He saw them dismount, transfer their primitive harness to fresh beasts, take stirrups anew.

Donya's horse bled from the arrow behind her knee. It stumbled. He heard its agonized breath. "They will catch us by tomorrow's nightfall," Krona deemed coolly.

"Josserek we'll hold together, right?" Donya said. "We'll take some of them along to the ants. But swear, if you see me made helpless, you'll kill me. I give you the same promise. Abide no chance of capture. At your first doubt, escape into death."

Krona kept still. He wondered fleetingly if she would do the same, or endure degradation and torment as a final exercise of spirit. *But why must we choose?*

It flared: *We don't have to.*

"Donya!" he shouted in radiance. "Krona! We can win!"

The wife stared, the Forthguide grew expressionless, the hoofs fled onward. "How?" Donya demanded.

"Start a fire. This plain's a tinderbox, and the wind's straight at them. Quick!"

Anguish flitted over her. "I dreaded you'd say that," she uttered, word by saddle-hammered word. "No. Destroy land . . . willingly? No. I'll slay you myself if you try."

His wrath exploded. "You mole!" he roared. "Will you *think*, this single hour in your life? We—we alone—carry the warning. What Sadír plans." To Krona: "Unless the Rogaviki yield, the Barommians will slaughter your game beasts. Every herd, throughout the Northlands. They can do it. Is that news worth a few square miles which'll grow back? Have you slipped the leash on your own mind?"

Donya groaned. Krona covered her face. The fingers on that hand bent until tendons stood forth and nails whitened. When she looked up, her voice barely won through the noise of their haste: "He speaks truth. We must."

It took another minute for Donya to gasp, "Aye, then."

Triumph bugled in Josserek.

He didn't expect either of them could bring herself to the deed. He halted long enough to break several branches off a shrub and collect deadwood. Riding again, with difficulty he made his snapper ignite the leaves. Thereafter the whole bundle soon caught.

Zigzag he went. Now he leaned over left, now right, and swept his torch across bush or grass. Redness cracked aloft. A wavefront of it ran from him, rearward. Flames billowed and brawled, smoke blew off them like black spindrift, ash swirled foam-white over suddenly charred bottom. He barely saw the Outrunners mill away, barely heard their maniac yells.

They might have ridden around the conflagration before it grew too big. But they weren't completely insane. Victims who had nothing to lose could well get them trapped, to roast alive. They fled. The flames hounded them.

Insane? Josserek thought as he stopped. His horse shuddered and panted beneath him, deep racking breaths like Donya's where she wept. The wind from the Ice tossed mane, fanned off sweat agleam on hide, skirled louder than the burning. *If madwomen is what they truly are, it's a Rogavikian madness.*

And . . . maybe what broke their will against us was not caution but horror. Maybe even they find someone who fires the land is a thing too grisly to meet. For they are, after all, Rogaviki themselves.

"It is done." Krona's grief sounded as if from very remotely.

Resolution came. "No," Josserek answered both. "It is begun."

"What mean you?"

He lifted his head on high. "I mean that I'm through with being led. Donya, we should have told them at the Station and in the camp what we know. Never mind if they went wild. The word we bear would not die with us, as it almost did today. And it may be the single thing which can bring them together.

"You don't think like soldiers, you Northfolk. The time is overpast when you'd better learn. The kiths have merely cared about their home territories. At most, when one was invaded, volunteers came from others to help—more for adventure, I'll bet my sword hand, than in forethought.

"You'll change now, or you'll go under. The whole Northfolk, from Wilderwoods to Tantian Hills, have got to bring their force to bear on this enemy. And they can't keep on following the herds till their usual Landmeeting to decide, either. They have got to meet fast.

"Do you hear me, Donya?"

CHAPTER

14

Sidír had lingered three days at Owlhaunt, though he knew his army wondered and whispered, before a courier brought news that hauled him away.

"—yes, sir, a squadron of the Golden Jaguar regiment—"

"Which?" Sidír interrupted.

"Uh, the Khella Spears. They came on a band of natives, bigger than usual. Colonel Felgai thinks the hunters have begun combining their gangs. Like always, these didn't give a chance for parley, they attacked. And they inflicted heavy losses. They had a new weapon, you see, sir. Nests of hornets they'd been transporting around, and slung into the midst of the troop. When horses bolted, they cut out individual soldiers and, three or four against one, women fighting beside men, they killed nearly half. The survivors withdrew, regrouped, sent for reinforcements. The enemy meanwhile took po-

sition on a rock outcrop. The whole regiment has failed
to dislodge them. A winning push would mean awful
casualties. Since the Captain General was nearby, Colonel Felgai sent me to report and ask for orders."

*The Khella Spears—among the finest in my host—
broken by a pack of savages,* twisted through Sidír.

"We can keep them bottled till they die, sir," the
courier volunteered. He was a hardbitten little bowleg-
ged veteran, a Barommian of the old sort who thought
for himself and told his officers straight out. "But
that'll tie us all down. You see, enough men 'ud be
needed to prevent a sally that it'd be too dangerous for
the rest to fare about."

"Aye," Sidír tugged his chin. "A half day's ride from
here? Snatch what rest you can. We leave in an hour."
To his adjutant, a Rahídian: "Arrange for fresh horses
and an escort of, ng-ng, six."

"Sir, no," the man protested. "That few?"

"I'd not counsel the Captain General to it as rule, in
this land o' fiends," the courier said. "But we've cleared
the river road as far as we've gone. I traveled here
alone, didn't I?"

"Six," repeated Sidír. "Now, dismissed. Both of you."

Alone in the main room, he let his heart fly free.
Those were Hervar yonder. Might Donya be among
them? He felt his knees quiver, the tiniest bit. *Foolish,
foolish. The chances are grotesquely against.* His scold-
ing slid off his hope. *Why wouldn't she strike home-
ward? And these are the environs of her winter
dwelling.*

*Here is the dwelling itself. I can show her how care-
fully I've spared it, everything she owns.*

Elsewhere his men were commanded to sack, demol-
ish, and burn. When the cold weather came and they
had no dens, the wolf-people might yield to human wis-

dom, come take what shelter he assigned them; and that example might work on their kindred in regions yet untouched. (Might, might, might!)

But when Inil en-Gula, the factor at Fuld, said he had visited Donya on business occasionally and could guide the Imperials to her garth, Sidír led them in person and decreed nothing be damaged. His explanation was reasonable; solid buildings like these, well out in the wilderness, provided a base of operations. Then by himself after dark, he sought the huge bed where surely she slept. . . .

He padded about the carpet, between racked weapons and eldritch murals, fondling things, books, lamps, vases, bowls, rcmembrances. Sunbeams slanted through the windows high above. The air was warm and smelled faintly, pleasingly, of leather on cushions and ledges. Knowledge that this was hers overwhelmed him. She had revealed him well-nigh nothing of her soul, until that last night when she sought to tear out his throat. How he wished he could read the Rogavikian pages.

I can't stay on, he made himself recall. *I should never have come. The work at headquarters must be finished before I can set forth—before the prairie wind, day after day, can blow this obsession out of me—and if we don't start soon, we'd better not till next year. It'll be hard as is, tracing a way to Roong in summer; and winter rolls early across the Ice.*

He had a hope that that capture would do more than bring the Throne an incomparable booty, more than cut the foe off from their prime source of metal. Could morale outlive such a loss? And on his side, could a renewed will for victory fail to follow such a gain? He had sensed the tiny signs of wavering among his troops, no decay of discipline, no slackness in action, but they laughed less and less, they grew elaborately cautious,

and walking incognito through camp at night he heard
mostly talk about their homes. . . .

Then why do I dawdle here?

*I won't. I'll go to the Jaguars because this is a
chance to deal with a substantial number of Rogaviki
and I may learn something valuable. Thence I'll head
straight back to Fuld.*

Though if Donya is among them—

No! Sidír smacked fist in palm, turned on his heel,
and stalked from the room. Within the hour he was on
his way.

Travel was rapid, for a wide hoof-beaten trail ran
westward along the Stallion River, paralleled by ruts
which centuries of wagon wheels had worn—the Sundog Trace, a major trade route across a land which
dwarfed the Empire. The courier had easily taken it by
starlight. He seemed untired, and the guards rode as
briskly. A prospect of honest combat, not a hidden trap
or a leap from nowhere, heartened them. Likewise did
the morning. Small clouds moved in a dizzingly tall
heaven where larks chanted. The water gleamed, reeds
swayed thick on its banks, fish jumped saber-bright.
Earth reached green, green, grass and strewn trees,
steaming forth its fragrance beneath the sun. Two miles
off, a herd of wild cattle quartered the horizon.

Donya's country.

"Ai-uh," said a man of the escort, when they paused
to rest their steeds. "I'm for a share of this, right hereabouts, when they pay us off. What a ranch!"

"Don't sell whatever you've got in Baromm just yet,
my friend," advised the courier. "No part of the
Northlands'll be fit to settle for ten years, is my guess."

"Why?"

"The natives. What else? Till the last of them is dead,

and I mean right down to babes in arms, we'll have murder to fear each hour we stay."

"Ho, now, listen—"

"You listen." The courier wagged a finger. "No insult meant, but you've mainly drawn garrison duty, true? I've been in the field. I've gotten to know them."

"They'll break," said another man. "I was in the Hozen war. We thought those tribes would never quit either. *Rachan*, you've not seen war till you've stood before a thousand painted devils making a death charge! But three years afterward, I was snugged up with the nicest little brown wench that ever decorated a grass hut. I felt sorry when my tour ended."

"Well, I'll tell you about the women here," the courier retorted. "They'll do for, uh, an example. If you catch any, stand clear and shoot."

"Oh, they're spitfires—"

"Hear me out, will you? I've listened to plenty of men, besides what I witnessed for myself. The local she-cat keeps trying to kill you. Hold a knife at her throat, and she'll drive herself onto the blade, yelling like she's glad to die if she can blind you first. Beat her, cage her—or treat her nice, like a queen—she'll still fight. Tie her down, and when you get on top she'll crash her forehead into your nose and rip out a jawful o' flesh. Only way is to club her unconscious, or fasten her till she can't twitch a toe. And what's the good of that? Too much like a corpse, right? Sir," the courier appealed to Sidír, "couldn't you ship in some decent Arvannethan whores?"

A guard ran fingers through his unhelmeted locks and said, puzzled, "But everybody—traders, everybody—told about native whores, or how the girls would take a man on for sheer fun."

The courier spat. "We're invaders. Makes a difference. You can no more civilize a Northlander than you can tame a scorpion. We'll have to clean them out."

"What does the Captain General say?" asked the corporal.

Sidír had listened through a darkness which deepened behind his face. "They're a fierce lot," he answered slowly. "However, I've seen wars too, and I've studied the past. Nations often swear they'll fight to the last man. They never do. None has ever even talked about fighting to the last woman and child." He rose from his crosslegged seat on the earth. "Come, let's get on."

Toward evening he arrived at the siege, a few miles off the river. On an area the size of a parade ground, a dull-yellow limestone mass reared in blocks above sloping tiers. The bareness around spoke well for the soldiers; they had brought back their dead and wounded from repeated futile charges. Sometimes a head thrust briefly between two monoliths, to peer; sometimes a weapon threw sunlight. But nothing rippled the stillness in which the rock squatted. The sounds of the regiment were themselves nearly lost beneath the sky; metal and banners made infinitesimal splashes on immensity.

"I've offered the best terms the Captain General has authorized," said Felgai. "We'd take them to a reservation, provide them the necessities, leave them a couple of hostages till they trusted us. When my herald finished, they put an arrow through him. Under his flag of truce, sir! If we weren't needed elsewhere, I'd enjoy penning them here till thirst and hunger do for them."

"A different approach might work," Sidír responded. "I sympathize with your anger, Colonel, but we can't waste men on revenge. Truce evidently isn't in their culture. Bargaining is; remember their peacetime trade. I've planned an experiment."

From chopped branches, tight-bundled grass, and

chain mail, engineers improvised a safety shield for a squad to carry before him. He stood under the rock and cried through a megaphone, "Is Donya of Hervar among you?"

For a minute he heard only his heart, and a distant singing of wind. Then a man's voice returned accented Arvannethan: "Who are you that ask?"

"I command this army. I knew her when she was last in the South—I, Sidír of Clan Chalif. Is she there and will she talk to me?"

"She is not and I think she would not."

Sidír drew breath. His pulse slowed. *Well, I go back to headquarters.* "Hearken," he urged. "You know you can't break out. We know you've scant supplies. Your wives, sons, daughters, parents are with you. Must they die amidst barren stones?"

"Better than in a corral."

"Hearken, hearken. Are we beast and butcher, or man and man? Because I am eager to send your people my message, a message of good will, I grant you this: you may go free. Keep your arms, and we will return your animals and gear. Only leave these parts, head west; and tell your fellows when you meet them, Sidír will come to any place they like, if they will talk with him of peace."

Tell Donya.

After a silence, the Rogaviki called, "We must think on this."

The sun had sunken, a last orange streak burned and stars glimmered eastward, when he declared, "We agree. Stand by for us."

Swallows flitted, coyotes yelped, through chilly blue dusk. Sidír made the Rogaviki out as shadows until they entered the glow of lights held on high before soldiers whose lines formed a pair of walls. In their front walked a grizzled man, belike he who had spoken for them, and a big woman, both in buckskins, both with no dread on their faces. Behind came the hunters, young men and women, old men and women, striplings, children led by the hand—some thinly weeping, some big-eyed and silent—and milky babies and those unborn, to the number of about two hundred.

Sidír trod between pikes and corselets. Joy lifted his palm toward the strangers. "Welcome," he said. "I am the master here—"

"Yaaah!" and the leaders sprang for him. Knives flew into their grasp.

Right and left, the Rogaviki attacked.

Surprise lent a terrible power. Sidír barely drew his pistol in time. He shot the man, but the woman might then have gotten him, had an alert halberdier not brained her. Chaos ramped. Hardly a grown Northlander failed to kill or badly hurt an Imperial before he or she died.

Sidír could not blame his troopers, that they slew the little ones as they would have stamped on new-hatched rattlesnakes. Maybe a few natives escaped in the turmoil.

By lantern-dullness among his dead, he wondered sickly, *Are they indeed all born mad? Can we do anything but uproot their race from the world?*

CHAPTER
15

Three days out of Dunheath Station, Josserek and Donya found her Fellowship.

His unwillingness for this moment had come slowly. At first, after he torched the rogue women off their backs, he felt himself less tolerated by his companions than endured. Not since he was a boy brought for sentencing before the deemster in Eaching had he known such withdrawal from him. Hatred would have been better. He closed his lips and did his share. At the Station he could get directions and supplies for his trip home.

On the second evening, though, Krona came out of her thoughts and addressed him gently. Throughout the third and fourth days, she was much in his and Donya's company, separately in the beginning, later as part of a healing friendship. On the fifth day they reached Dunheath, and that night Donya sought him.

On the sixth morning they bade their hostesses farewell, and the Forthguide. Both of them kissed her. That carried more meaning among the Rogaviki than anyplace else where Josserek had been. The moon was now in its third quarter, and there was no darkness on the plains for two people before they slept.

The seventh night she was more slow and tender than had been her wont. Often she chuckled softly, or raised herself on an elbow athwart the stars, smiled down at him, stroked his beard. According to what they heard at Dunheath, on the morrow they should meet the Owlhaunt families. He made a clumsy try at getting her to say something like "I will still care for you, I always will," but she stopped his words in an irresistible way, as she had ever done. He wondered if she, if anyone of her folk was able to look on another human being as he had come to look on her.

From dawn they rode fast, in silence, through blowing cool sunniness swept by cloud shadows. Pine groves darkened ridges, birches danced on hillsides, willows brooded in blueberry bogs, sward ran silvery-green over the curve of the world. Rising warmth upheld an eagle, a lynx basked on a rock, a stallion whose mane tossed like flags led his mares across miles, lesser life swarmed on millionfold ways. *How they glory in their summer,* Josserek thought, *while it lasts.*

Once at a distance he and she spied horsemen. "Lookouts against invaders," Donya judged. Dunheath knew of widespread enemy strikes. Such an expedition had come within a half day, then retreated before a larger force from the camp she sought. She had cursed on learning the Imperials had been too well-organized for destruction, and after a skirmish outrode pursuit on their larger animals.

"Don't you want the latest news?" Josserek asked when she didn't change course.

"Our arrival will be soon enough."

At midafternoon they saw their goal, tents, wagons, beasts, humanity sprawled around a lilypond. "Aye, they've leagued for safety, as we heard," Donya murmured. "Owlhaunt, Wildgate, Dewfall Dale—Hai-ah!" She broke into gallop.

The scene was thronged. Few or no hunters were out today. The gathering was at work on kills lately made, as well as preparations for moving on. Josserek noted that tasks generally belonged to individuals or kin-groups spaced yards apart. He and Donya drew merely brief looks and dignified salutations as they entered, no matter his foreignness and her long absence. Folk assumed that if they wanted help or sociability, they would inform whoever was appropriate; until then, it would be ill-bred to push in on them. This was unlike their reception at the Ravens' Rest Fellowship; but there the whole situation had differed, including the manner of their approach. When Donya had family to meet, she didn't pause for palaver, nor was she expected to.

At her pavilion she drew rein. It was larger and finer than most, of oiled silk rather than leather. A banner flew from the main pole, owl argent on sable. Her kin was busy outside. They flaycd and butchered, scraped hides, cooked over a firepit, refurbished equipment; several boys practiced archery, not with the rider's hornbow but the longbow of war; as many girls drilled with throwing knives and slim sabers; small children cared for infants. Hounds lolled about, hawks glared from perches. It was rather quiet. Nearing, Josserek did observe chat between partners, an occasional grin or lively gesture—but none of the bustle and racket com-

mon to primitives. An aged man, bald and blind, sat on
a folding stool, plucked a snake-carved harp, and sang
for the workers in a voice still powerful.

He stopped when the newcomers did, hearing the
sudden change. For an instant silence spread outward,
like waves when a rock is cast into a pool. Then a tall
man raised himself from his job. It was greasy, so he
went nude. While sorrel hair and beard were gray-shot,
his body could have lived thirty years or less, save for
a puckered scar on the right thigh. "Donya," he said,
low, low.

"Yven," she answered, and left her saddle.

Her first husband, Josserek remembered.

She and Yven joined hands and looked a minute into
each other's eyes. The group made way for the remain-
ing foremost: husband Orovo, sometime metal gatherer
at Roong, stocky and blond; husband Beodan, notably
younger than her, gaunt, dark for a Northlander; husband Kyrian, who wore his ruddy hair in braids and was
a single year senior to her oldest child. Newer offspring
had a right to immediate hugs and kisses: daughters
Valdevanya, four, Lukeva, seven, Gilyeva, eleven. Son
Fiodar could wait a bit, being fifteen, as could son
Zhano and his wife and baby.

When at last Josserek saw them all around her, she in
the pride of her joy, he recalled a myth along the Feline
Ocean, about Ela, the tree whose fruits are the Seven
Worlds. At the end of time, the Hidrun Storm will tear
them from its branches. . . .

He heard Kyrian blurt, "Must we wait on sundown,
till you welcome us home?" He heard her say through
a catch of laughter, "Too slow is the Bright Wheel, aye.
Yet abide a turn and a turn—" He couldn't understand
the rest.

Beodan caressed her from behind, beneath her shirt,

and said something Josserek couldn't follow either, but which made her go "Rrrrrr" like a happy lioness. *Yes, I've read, I've been told,* the man from Killimaraich remembered, *kindred here make their own slang, generation by generation till a private dialect has turned into an entire language never shared with those who are not of the blood.* He had not realized it would hurt this much.

When he wrenched his thoughts to the fact that Donya had been missing from them for a quarter of an evil year, she for her part unaware who of her dear were alive, he admitted how restrained everyone was being. *Because of me?*

Maybe not quite. Others were about too. Closest stood four spinster relatives, members of her household. (No, he conceded, "spinster" was wrong for hopeful maiden, rangy huntress, skilled carpenter, and formidable manager.) Then the companion families gave greetings. As nearly as he could gauge—which seemed more and more remotely—their behavior toward Donya confirmed Josserek's impression that she was their leader. (No, again a false word. No Rogaviki had authority over anybody else. Later he would discover even the parent-child relationship was mutually voluntary, though the diffuseness of interrelationships took the rough edges off that. But Owlhaunt, and a large part of all Hervar, valued Donya's counsel above most, accepted her arbitration, cooperated with her enterprises.) Her return blessed them.

They needed encouragement. Erelong they were telling what had happened of late. Enemy garrisons gripped the length of the Jugular. Soldiers ranged ever further, looted, burned, slew; resistance cost them losses and slowed them down, but could not drive them out and grew steadily costlier as they became wise in its ways. Donya's own wintergarth and its neighbors were in their hands. A few days ago, they had wiped out the conjoined Fellowships of Broken Ax and Firemoor. Information—from Imperial prisoners; from Arvannethan Guildsmen bribed, sympathetic, or in terror of reprisals—was that the invader chieftain planned a dash northeastward across the tundra to capture Unknown Roong.

Poised about her people, who mostly crouched on the earth, Donya nodded. "I awaited no better," she told them, flat-voiced. "Josserek speaks truth." Somewhere in the course of events, he had been introduced. "No single kith can turn enough horns outward against yon wolves. There must be a Landmeet, and not near summer's end, but as soon as messengers can fetch everybody to Thunder Kettle."

"Can this be done?" asked Yven in his soft fashion.

Donya's lips drew taut across her teeth. "The word I shall give you will show that it must be done."

She shook herself, spread her arms high, and cried, "But not yet, for us. Before the horror is spoken, we've earned a day and a night. O fathers of my bairns—" Josserek missed the rest of what she said, and what the company shouted in response. He stood sunk in aloneness.

—While her men collected food, drink, lamps, furs, a tent, a wagon, horses, merrily helped by their friends, Donya played with her children and grandchild. A number of persons sought Josserek, offered him hospitality, made eager but polite conversation such as he had encountered before.

—After she and her consorts departed, people from Wildgate and Dewfall Dale began drifting in to meet the stranger.

—When her hilltop camp was a star-twinkle through

dusk, her half-sister in Owlhaunt, Nikkitay the huntress, drew Josserek aside and murmured, "—she asked me if I would. I am very willing."

"Not this night," he got past his gullet. Mindful of good manners, he would have thanked her; but he could not do that in Rogavikian.

CHAPTER
16

Remembering the effect on Donya of Sidír's plan to exterminate the herds, Josserek feared what the kithfolk might turn into. Reaction at Dunheath had surprised her as much as him. Some personnel there had exploded. But most merely yelled their outrage.

Krona developed an explanation: "I didn't lose myself in fury either, deep though the shock went. Like me, these people do not live by the chase. The hunters do, in spirit still more than in body. For them, when the big grazers go, so does the whole meaning of existence. But a Station is just a clutch of buildings and businesses. If the owners lose it, they can hope to reconstruct elsewhere. It lacks the sanctity of the great ancestral spaces." Did the word that she used quite mean "sanctity"?

Later Donya admitted to Josserek that she wasn't sure the Forthguide had guessed right. "Never would I have thought that words alone could lightning-strike me, the way those did at first. I could bear the threat of invasion—yes, the fact, as long as it had not yet touched Hervar—and stay self-controlled. Was this because I knew we cast back every such venture in the past, and so did not look for any in the future to harm our lands unhealably? I know not. I only know that—this thing about the beasts—I still only keep my calm and have my merriment, by holding fast to a belief that we will stop it from happening. Maybe I'm not able to believe that it can happen." She said no more. It was the nearest she had come to baring her heart to him.

Accordingly, when she addressed the camp from a wagon bed, she insisted that nobody bear arms. Perhaps this was wise. The news did send a minority running and shrieking across the plain as she had done, or tearing the sod with nails and teeth, or off on horses which they flogged to gallop with unwonted brutality. Yet the largest part of them stood their ground and roared; some wept; a third of the whole, especially older people, covered their faces and went off by themselves.

"I don't know why," Donya said in response to a question from Josserek. "Nor do they, I am sure. I might imagine that the very strength of feeling drives them apart, till they can't act on each other as a pack of excited dogs does." She wrinkled her nose. "Aye, the wind reeks from them. Can you really not smell it?"

A race of humans who have no mobs—have no politics? Josserek thought in total bewilderment. *Impossible!*

Donya sprang down to earth. "I will fare off among my men," she said, and left him standing alone.

By evening the households were reassembled. Families went into their pavilions, unwedded individuals made groups that sought into the bush, muted but unmistakable sounds told Josserek how they found comfort, other than in the mead which he glugged. Nobody invited him. He had been given a pup tent, and folk were cordial about sharing food, but they left the alien out of their lives. It wasn't a delicate affront, he knew; the Rogaviki took privacy for granted. The knowledge didn't ease his bitterness.

Nikkitay did, a little, when she sought him anew. She said hardly a word, though she often uttered noises, and left a web of scratches for remembrance. But during that while, he could put Donya out of his mind, almost, and afterward sleep.

Next morning she returned, and suggested a ride. "People will take the rest of this day, and belike tomorrow, deciding what they want to do," she said. "They'll ponder, talk, go walkabout, argue, till the sun grows weary watching them. You and I know already, don't we?"

"I suppose." He looked at her with a flicker of pleasure above his depression such as he felt certain no outland woman could have given him. She was several years younger than her half-sister, lean, long-legged, summer-tinged, blue eyes crinkled from gazing across distances, white-blond hair drawn into a pony tail. Today, besides shirt, trousers, boots much like his, she wore a big silver-and-turquoise necklace, Southland materials but austere Northland workmanship. "Have you any particular place in mind?"

"Aye." She didn't specify, and he had learned that questions harmless elsewhere counted as nosiness here.

They prepared two horses, packed canteens, sausage, bannock, dried apples, weapons, and jogged off. Air lay still, cool, damply odorous, beneath a wan overcast. No big game was visible; herds soon moved on after man tracked them down and took toll, modest though it was in proportion to their multitudes. Songbirds held the scattered trees, rabbits and woodchucks moved in grass. Hoofbeats fell muffled.

After a time he said, "Uh, I can't unravel your meaning, when you told me these Fellowships will be slow in settling what to do. Isn't the sensible thing to go to the Landmeet?"

Nikkitay gave him a surprised regard. " 'They?' What do *you* mean?"

"Why, why, I'd expect them to—" He recalled that he knew no word for "vote," and finished lamely, "Either they come along to the Landmeet or they stay in Hervar. Am I right?"

"The whole of a Fellowship?" Nikkitay frowned, thinking. She lacked Donya's experience of the world beyond the plains. However, she had ample intelligence. "Oh. I see. What happens is simply this. Most persons ask the opinions of others, to help them decide. And in certain cases, of course, because of family ties or the like, they may do what they'd rather not. But I can tell you, it's foregone, few will leave Hervar, whether to go directly with us to Thunder Kettle or as messengers who start the word spreading among other kiths."

"In short," Josserek realized, "each individual chooses."

"What else? Well-nigh all will stand fast. Abandon the land when it's threatened, even for a few weeks? Unthinkable. I'd stay and kill invaders myself—Donya would, everybody would—were it not that the news should be carried, the meeting should be held, and that we know plenty of defenders will remain."

"But . . . if nothing else, won't they want a say at the Landmeet?"

Nikkitay shook her head, half laughing, half exasperated. "There you go again. What could they say? We'll do naught at Thunder Kettle but tell people how things are—you and Donya will, mainly—to help them think." She paused, assembling an explanation. "Naturally, persons will exchange ideas. That's what Landmeets and Kithmeets are for, don't you know? To swap information and thoughts, as well as trade goods, see old friends and make new ones, celebrate, maybe find marriage partners—" Did her voice hold the least wistfulness? Probably not, Josserek concluded. There was no social pressure on a woman to get married, and the unwed state had its advantages.

Dismay surged in him. He smacked fist on saddle and exclaimed, "Have you no idea of . . . of cooperation . . . on any scale larger than a hunting team?"

"What for?"

"To keep from being destroyed. That's what for!"

"Aye, big bands of us have gathered to meet invaders."

"And if you won, it was by sheer numbers, squandering lives of your own like water. If you had your fighters trained, in units operating under orders—"

Nikkitay seemed lost. "How could that be? Are men tame animals? Can they be put in a single harness like a, a team of carriage horses? Do they set the will of other men above their own, as their hounds do for them? If they have been caught and then released, will they return to the hood and jesses like a hawk?"

Yes, yes, and yes, Josserek thought. He closed his jaws till they ached. *Man was the first of animals to be domesticated. You Rogaviki . . . what form has your self-domestication taken? That fanatical, unreasoning, suicidal compulsion to kill interlopers, regardless of prudence or long-range interest or—*

Presently he managed to say, 'The Imperials are just as you describe, my friend. And they're not contempt-

ible on that account. No! In the past, Northfolk made
the cost of entering this country too high. This time, the
enemy can make the cost of resistance too high."

"I doubt that," she responded levelly. "They seldom
fight to the death. After little torture or none, a prisoner
spills everything he knows.... But can you tell me
why, afterward, they complain before we kill them?
What are we supposed to do?"

"You keep no prisoners?" Josserek was appalled.
"Nikkitay, they'll avenge that on every Rogaviki they
catch."

"Civilized soldiers always do. We have records from
former wars. And why not? One of us, captive, is not
just useless to them, like one of them to us, but a downright menace."

"Prisoner exchange—"

"What? How could it ever be bargained about?"

*No parley. No strategy. No army. If they had, if they
had— The Imperials are stretched thin. An organized effort might well cut their lines of communication. Probably Sidír never would have come if he weren't sure
there would be no such hazard.*

*Do I seriously think I can talk these ... these two-
legged panthers into changing ways they may well have
been following since the Ice came? I've seen enough
cultures across my half of the world. Many have died
rather than change. Maybe because change is itself a
death?*

*I'll speak my piece at the Landmeet, and they'll look
at me without understanding, as Nikkitay is looking at
me now, and I'll go home while Donya— O Shark of
Destruction, let her be killed in battle. Let her not be a
survivor, starved, ragged, tubercular, alcoholic, begging, cadging, broken.*

The woman reached across to lay a hand over his.

"You are in pain, Josserek," she said quietly. "Can I help?"

He was moved. Such a gesture was rare among the Rogaviki. He forced a smile. "I fear not. My trouble is for your sake."

Although he used a plural pronoun, she nodded and murmured, "Aye, you must have grown fond of Donya, traveling in her company." After a silence, and with difficulty: "Tales go about, of foreign men who came to care for Rogaviki women. It isn't wise, Josserek. Our kinds are too unlike. She does not suffer for it, but he may." Later on, almost defensively: "Think not we have no loves, we Northfolk. I . . . I should tell you where I'm bound this day. To where those lie who fell in fighting the last troop of invaders, before you reached us. Two brothers of mine are there, a sister, and three lovers who were more to me than partners in sport. Since I may not return here—Will you mind waiting aside, while I seek their graves and remember?"

He couldn't well ask what he was to her. A romp, a curiosity, a favor to Donya? At least she was trying to be kind. Quite likely, for that, she was scaling greater obstacles within herself than he knew of. He owed her much gratitude already, and would doubtless owe her more as they trekked west; for Donya had her own men back, who were sufficient unto her, and Nikkitay could sometimes help him endure this.

—The graves bore no markers, nothing but their newness to find them by on the prairie. If travelers' accounts spoke truly, such mingled burials had no outward rites. If Owlhaunt had any, Nikkitay offered them in the hour she spent by herself. Afterward, rejoining him, she was cheerful.

From the Landmeet I will go home, he repeated, *and be again among my kind of people.*

CHAPTER
17

Four hundred miles down the Sundog Trace lay Thunder Kettle, where the kiths always gathered. Josserek protested the unhurried pace of the score who accompanied Donya there. She replied that haste was useless, for distant groups would need time no matter how hard messengers galloped. "And can you too not muster the strength to enjoy this summer?" she added. "It may be our last."

He saw her before him, her mane aglow in the spilling sunlight, and thought, *Well, I won't escape you any sooner by running away from you.* For a month, then, he fared, hunting, fishing, sporting along the way, doing his camp chores, afterward at the fire drinking dry pungent mead till his blood hummed, swapping tales, songs, jests, ideas—though never any inmost dreams—and at last retiring with Nikkitay to the tent they now shared.

He learned much about the Northfolk, not only jour-

neys east and west from end to end of Andalin, warily
south into civilization and boldly north onto the Ice, not
only wild hunts and mighty feats, but arts which were
often too subtle for a foreigner like him to appreciate,
and social orderings which left him still more bewil-
dered.

As for knowledge and crafts, he had already seen that
most people were literate. Some wrote or published
books. Many corresponded extensively through a mail
service which functioned very well though its carriers
just operated when they felt like it; a person could always be found who did. Simple telescopes, micro-
scopes, compasses, astrogoniometers, timepieces, and
suchlike instruments were in common use, mainly imported though various homemade versions had lately
been appearing. Medical procedures were good, at least
for injuries; in their uncrowded open-air lives, the
Rogaviki seldom contracted diseases. Zoology and bot-
any were sophisticated; Josserek found few if any superstitions about nature, and an eagerness to learn about
evolution when he mentioned it. Metallurgy was excellent, as was the processing of wild substances into fiber
and fabric. This implied a fair variety of chemicals
available, again generally through trade. Besides the
Stations, every wintergarth was a site of sedentary in-
dustries.

Summer was more than the season of roving and the
chase. Then the arts were intensively shared. Almost everybody played a musical instrument or two, out of a
surprisingly large assortment. Line drawing, painting,
carving in wood and bone, ornamentation had, in their
own forms, development equal to any Josserek had encountered elsewhere. Song, dance, drama perhaps went
further. When his party visited a camp on their way, he
saw an hours-long presentation, combining opera and

ballet, which stunned him, little though he grasped of what was going on.

These were not mere nomads. They had a society rich and complex, its traditions unbroken for centuries. Moreover, it was not static like most, it was in a highly inventive, progressive phase.

And yet—and yet—

Coming from an individualistic, increasingly industrialized and capitalistic civilization, he was used to sparse ritual and religious freethinking. But somehow it disturbed him to find the same traits here. Those who sought enlightenment, female, male, Forthguide, solitary thinker, or otherwise ordinary person who spared occasional time for it, were not prophets, mages, or seers. The best name he could find for them was "philosophers," albeit a part of the philosophical quest took place in muscles and viscera rather than brain. Most people were indifferent, agnostics content to inhabit the world of the senses. According to Rogaviki historians, myths and magical practices had existed in the past, but were discarded in favor of a more nearly scientific attitude with an ease that showed how rooted they had been.

Ceremonies, as distinguished from artistic performances, were short and spare: courtesies, not invocations. He was told that families had elaborate ones, evolved through many generations. But as far as he could discover, these amounted simply to communion between members, a means of dissolving an otherwise habitual aloofness. Ancestors might then be lovingly recalled, but there was no idea that they were actually present, nor any supernatural powers. This was as much as Nikkitay was willing to tell him, in her most intimate moods. She gave no logical reason for keeping the details secret. Divulgence just wasn't done.

Damnation, Josserek thought, *these are not Killima-raichan city dwellers! They have an organic society, in the midst of an enormous wilderness. They shouldn't feel so—detached?*

No, wrong word again, and again I don't know what may be a right word. They act like cats. Which must be an illusion of mine. Man is a pack animal, like the dog. He also has the dog's need of mystic bonds to something higher than himself.

His grin traveled ruefully across wind-rippled grasses where a sparrowhawk hunted. *I too, bachelor, soldier of fortune, former outcast and still pretty much outsider, I am not here because it's an adventure; I'm on a mission for my country, which, below my gibes at it, I believe is worth preserving.*

And I'm in love with Donya. . . . Well, she's devoted to her husbands. (In the same way I am to her?) And to her children, friends, home. Isn't she?

He wondered. Did the killing rage that invasion kindled in every Rogaviki breast—every, without exception, though in other respects individuals showed a normal range of diversity—did it really come from love of the land? A Killimaraichan, say, would fight for his nation. He would carry war beyond its borders, for its political interests rather than its naked survival, a thing which had never occurred to the Northfolk. But there were limits to his sacrificial willingness. If his cause grew hopeless, he would accept defeat, even military occupation, and made the best he could of a shrunken existence. Apparently a Rogaviki would not. Paradoxically, however—while the Killimaraichan, given victory or standoff, would be slow to forgive those who had seriously harmed his fellow citizens—throughout history, the moment the last intruder departed, the Rogaviki were prepared to resume relations as if nothing had happened.

Might a key to them lie in their households, the structure and functioning of their families? The business of life is to bring forth life; upon the how of this in any race, everything else turns. But no, here Josserek found himself worse adrift than before. Alone among humans he knew of, maybe alone among animals on earth, the Rogaviki reproduced in such wise as to hold population *far* down.

Now creatures do not raise their numbers forever: just up to the carrying capacity of their territories. Thereafter, either natural limiting mechanisms come into play—for example, difficulty in finding a mate in a polygamous species—or else famine, plague, and internecine fighting trim the swarms. Man is among the beasts that lack a birthrate regulator. Accordingly, from time to time he has suffered the fate of rabbit or lemming. But being intelligent, he can forestall it by various means: widespread celibacy, late marriage, sexual usages which do not impregnate, contraception, abortion, infanticide, gerontocide, emigration. Generally it is the civilized peoples who die from runaway growth. Primitives control their breeding. That the Northfolk did would not have surprised Josserek.

However, in their case, all institutions worked to restrict numbers radically, to a small fraction of what their realm and technology could have supported. Polyandry, illegitimacy as grounds for what amounted to ostracism, and a universal feeling that no wife should bring more than about six children to adulthood: these kept the population at its low level. History said that in times of disaster, when deaths had much exceeded births, a tacit agreement relaxed the rules; but when the norm had been restored, the same unspoken, unenforced consent re-established the status quo.

The genetics of it intrigued Josserek. Superior women attracted the most suitors, or felt able to court the most themselves, and chose the best. But they bore no more young than did less desirable females who merely wed singly or doubly. Husbands of the latter thus passed on a larger proportion of their heredity, some of which was bound to enter later generations of the more prosperous families. Could this leveling effect help explain the fact that no aristocracy had ever arisen here, no government or state, no powerful organizations, no leadership except the most rudimentary kind, acknowledged only to the degree that each individual chose to follow it?

The advantages of being few were obvious. The Northfolk enjoyed a superabundance of game and other natural wealth. This gave them the leisure and economic surplus to create a culture which rivaled those of far harder-working civilized nations. Still more important to them seemed to be open space. They spoke with repugnance or outright horror of the crowded Southlands. Donya had remarked, "I couldn't have stayed in Arvanneth as long as I did, if they there hadn't smelled different enough that it wasn't quite like being among humans." (Diet? Race? The Rogaviki did possess hound-keen noses, though that could be due to trained awareness rather than extraordinary innate capability.)

The problem is, Josserek thought, *long-range public benefit is apt to conflict with immediate private or bureaucratic advantage, and go by the board. That's why common lands get overgrazed, forests recklessly logged off, rivers polluted, useful wildlife exterminated, trade clogged, progress stifled by regulations and taxes— under any system known, tribal, feudal, monarchic, timocratic, democratic, theocratic, capitalist, traditionalist, collectivist, any. And the Rogaviki are anarchs. They make no pretensions to altruism, they haven't even a word for it. A particular Fellowship could gain strength, extra hands, riches by increasing its size. It could scoff at outside disapproval, for it's self-sufficient already and there's no authority to check it. Then soon every kith would have to do likewise, or risk becoming a victim. The process would be more complex than that, of course. Nevertheless—*

What is the factor that keeps their way of living stable? It must have a stronger grip on each and every person of them than a wish for the well-being of their descendants possibly can ... especially since they don't agree what that well-being is; some would like more outland trade, some less, some want a lot of firearms to make hunting easier, some fear getting dependent on the suppliers ... on and on ... and everybody is free to do whatever he or she pleases, short of provoking fatally many kithmates into breaking off relations.

Which hardly ever happens. The sole serious violence I've encountered or heard of among the Northfolk, relates to the Outrunners. And they are pathological cases, who for this reason or that hate the rest. Otherwise—no wars, no feuds, thefts rare, fights confined to barehanded blows—

They're not saints, these people. They're haughty, they're greedy, they'll lie and cheat shamelessly in making a deal, outside their Fellowship they show scant compassion, they've no creed, nothing but a sort of ethic, and it bluntly pragmatic. Furthermore, they're wide open to foreign ideas. Yet they remain true to themselves, century after century. How?

It shouldn't be humanly possible.

Thunder Kettle rose from a ground flat, treeless, billowy with tall green-golden grass, like the land into which Josserek and Donya had escaped from Sidír's riverboat (what years ago that seemed!) except for being drier. A nearby Station, while bigger than usual, still appeared lonesome, huddled between man-planted walls of cottonwoods against wind, rain, hail, snow, drought, brazen summer and iron winter. The rendezvous itself did not loom high, though from edge to edge the view raised awe.

He had met its kind before, scattered around Orenstane, and seen accounts of them in eastern Owang and western Andalin. Something sometime had scooped craters three or four miles wide out of the earth. Digging beneath the soil which had blown in afterward, men discovered fused layers, cracked by the frosts and roots of millennia but not too far gone for the bowls to hold their shapes. Deeper down were, occasionally, relics of ancient cities; or these might occur in mounds on a periphery. This had led scientists in Killimaralch to conjecture that, when the Ice marched from the poles, civilization destroyed itself in struggle for dwindling resources, by unleashing powers which none today had mastery of.

Opposed thinkers derided the theory. More frequently than not, excavation indicated that the catastrophes had happened in uninhabited areas. Who would have bombarded those? Besides, to postulate world-wrecking energies in human hands was baseless sensationalism. Indeed, evidence for substantial advances and retreats of the Ice was new, slight, controversial. It came chiefly from coastal lands, especially the Coral Range, which must formerly have been submerged. Where had the water gone but into glaciers? Well, argued the conservative schools, terrestrial forces might have elevated the continents, or dug pits in the ocean beds, perhaps millions rather than thousands of years in the past. They might also have made the craters. Or perhaps meteorites were responsible for the latter. Since Wicklis Balaloch first proved that shooting stars are stones from outer space, many had been identified, several very large. A rain of huge masses could well have brought down the global society, leaving a remnant of ignorant peasants and savages to start over.

Josserek had gotten fascinated by the issue, after Mulwen Roa lent him books and journals. It was exciting, it was good to live in an era when knowledge exploded outward. But as he rode across the rim of Thunder Kettle, the vision saddened him. Uncountable ages, uncountable deaths, doom that fell upon whole breeds of being, and nothing left save a few shards and bones. . . . Once he had seen the skull of a great reptile, embedded in a crumbling cliff, through whose hollowness the winds of eons must have blown, unheard, unfelt by an unaliveness which time had turned to stone. He saw Donya riding beside him, and thought about her skull.

Oh, I'll try to rally them, try to talk sense into them. What else can I do but try, before I go home?

The sides and floor of the crater were speckled bright with encampments, well apart as always. The Hervar band pitched their own before they went gadding about. Despite the occasion, the atmosphere was genial. People moved briskly over green concavities, chatted, sang, drank, frolicked; kinfolk met and went off in pairs and trios, old friends did, youths and maidens, unwed women and unattached men, those who discovered they had things to dicker about. Josserek would have preferred solitude, but many who had heard of him sought him out and he must needs receive them politely. Then after dark, when he desired company, he was left alone. Nikkitay had found somebody else.

His sleep was haunted.

By morning, word had spread, and a meeting began
not so much to get organized as to crystallize. Donya
and Josserek took a wagon down to the bottom and settled on its bench. She spoke little, and he sat mainly being aware of her profile, warmth, manyfold odors:
smoke, flesh, sunny hair, wind-cleansed sweat, and an
overtone he had no name for because none save
Rogaviki women breathed it from their skins . . . like
sagebrush, like rosemary? By noon she decided the as-
semblage was ready to be addressed.

It was no large audience before a stage. About fifty
from different households, mostly wives, sat or stood in
earshot. The rest were strewn in small groups across the
lower bowl. Strategically placed, persons with strong
lungs and trained voices relayed speech. Nobody ap-
pointed or paid the stentors; they enjoyed the task and
whatever sense of importance it brought them.

"We bear ill tidings," Donya began.

She made no oration. In gatherings like this, Rogaviki
spoke to the point. They kept emotional language for
private use. There it sometimes approached poetry.
(*"Oh, terrible sweetness of stallions, come neighing,
strike lightning from stones and, unmountable, mount,"*
she had whispered to him in an hour when they were
alone beneath the moon; and much else at other times,
though never a simple "I love you.") For fear of unpre-
dictable reactions, her couriers had not bespoken the
ruin which was planned for their country, but had just
emphasized that this invasion was not like any in the
past and that new responses to it must be developed. Today she told them in blunt phrases everything she knew.

They were less maddened than her own camp had
been. Seemingly, the larger the meet, the more inhibited
it became. Besides, the great majority present were from
kiths west of the Jugular Valley. Their lands had not yet

been entered by the enemy, nor would that happen for at least a year. The threat was thus remote enough for them to look upon it with a measure of calm.

They did shout, curse, brandish fists and blades, across the hollow miles. Donya let them have it out for an hour before she turned them over to Josserek.

"Dwellers in the North—" *What can I put before them?* He had had weeks to plan, ask advice, argue, refine, think; and he felt himself no further along. Words dragged out of him: "—joint action, in a single grand scheme—" *What scheme? That they meet Barommian cavalry head-on, a month or two of drill under masters as raw as themselves, against generations of soldierhood?* The relaying criers sounded as far and thin-toned as marmots whistling. "—fight now, not in defense after the foe is across your borders, triumphant in the east, but catch him between two fronts—" *How? Sidír brought well-nigh his whole strength up the river. If superior numbers make him retreat, he need only fall back on his strong points and let attackers ride into the mouths of his cannon. Not that I believe any longer the Rogaviki are capable of a charge en masse.* "—coolness, forethought, instead of blind rage—" *What forethought have I to offer, I who tried to understand them and failed? I'm no use here. Let me go home.*

But can I just leave her to her death?

His speech crawled to an end. He got a courteous buzz of approval. Afterward several persons approached and asked what, specifically, he proposed. Donya replied for him that the main purpose of this Landmeet was to hammer that out. Let folk weigh what had been said, talk it over, ransack their wisdom. Then whoever got an idea could lay it before the whole, tomorrow or the next day or the next.

At the end, beneath a sky where thunderheads towered and a smell of storm blew on a rising cold wind, through brass-colored light, he and she stood alone in the wagon. He turned to her, grabbed her hands, and begged in his pain. "What *can* we do? Anything except die?"

"We?" she asked softly. Her locks tossed around high cheekbones and green eyes.

"I'm minded to stay," he stammered, "if, if you'll have me—"

"Josserek," she said after a while, her grasp and gaze never leaving his, "I've not been kind to you, have I? Come away with me now to my tent."

He stared. His heartbeat answered the drums beyond the horizon.

She smiled. "Do you think about my husbands? They like you too. And we aren't always together, each night. Come." She let go and sprang to earth. When he had followed, dazedly, she took his hand again and led him off.

In the morning he awoke to peace, and to knowledge of what he might do.

CHAPTER

18

The notes he kept as he fared told Sidír it was on Starsday, the eighteenth of Ausha, that he entered Unknown Roong. But this had no meaning, was a mere scribble by a hand which the cold turned stiff and painful, in a book whose pages rattled beneath the wind off the Ice. Time was not here. If ever it had been, it was transformed, congealed into distance, into desolation.

A weary head worked slowly. His first thought was—after a scout cried aloud and pointed, after he lifted his binoculars—*Is that all?* For tiny did the fabled city look below the glacial mountains.

They filled three-quarters of his horizon, left, ahead, right in a monstrous arc; this piece of land across which his horse stumbled was a narrow bay in them. Up and up they climbed, tiers, slopes, scarps, cliffs, toward their full height of a mile that walled in heaven as well as earth. Their foothills lay tumbled and dusty. Further

aloft they shone under a cloudless wan sky, death-pure,
shimmers of green and sapphire, here and there a rainbow glitter, above steely gray. Canyons that clove them
were infinitely blue. Melt water ran down in a thousand
streams which flowed together into roaring torrents.
Several times he had heard an avalanche rumble off
some peak and seen its plume go smoking toward sun
or rain or constellations nameless to him, blanched as if
a ghost volcano erupted in the underworld.

This close, he could feel the chill that poured off the
Ice across his skin, through his garments, into his bones.
But he had scarcely been a day out of Fuld, bound
northeast across the Ulgani kithland, when he met its
workings. Woodlands died away, grass withered, the
prairie became the tundra. Between stiff brown tussocks
grew only moss and lichens. Summer-sodden ground
caught at hoofs, travel slowed to a plopping creep while
strength drained daily from the poor horses, and from
men who never found a dry place to rest. Winds whistled, showers boomed, sleet hissed, hail drew blood
where its skittering bullets struck; but that was better
than clear daylight and the mosquitoes. Sidír was afraid
the mosquito fogs would swirl and whine through his
nightmares till he died. Maybe lying in his grave, he
would still hear them, still wear himself out wildly
swatting, struggle with cloths and plant juices that did
small good, feel the fever from their poison hum weakly
through his brain. Else the waste bore little life. He
glimpsed rare ptarmigan, hare, fox, caribou; waterfowl
might settle on a pool; owls hooted after dark. How his
company would have welcomed a native attack, anything human!

Today they were less plagued. Having found that
downdrafts off the Ice kept most insects away, they followed its border. That lengthened their journey, and to

swampiness added moraine boulders. However, they might well have taken still longer had they continued straight across, without reliable maps or directions or landmarks. The kiths did not forbid Arvannethans to visit Roong, but none had dared the trip in this generation. Sidír's firmest point of knowledge was that the city lay just under the glacier, at the end of a deep notch which somehow remained uncovered.

And now he was *here*. His goal was in sight. He turned attention from the dreariness stretching southward, focused his glasses more sharply, strained to make out the towers of a thousand legends. He saw an irregular dark sprawling which in places thrust forth peaks.

Colonel Develkai edged near. "That must be it, hai?" His voice was dull with exhaustion. "How shall we proceed, sir?"

Sidír gave him a considering glance. The commander of the Barracuda regiment, which had lent a squadron— the Hammers of Besak—to this expedition, was a young man; or he had been. The tundra and the Ice had seemingly laid years upon him. His cheeks were stubbled and fallen in, scarred by welts, his eyes were embers, his shoulders bowed, as if his felt hat and leather jacket weighed too much. The horse he rode was in sorrier case, limping from stone bruises, head a-droop, ribs in ridges beneath dried mud. *Do I look that bad?* Sidír wondered.

"Directly forward," he ordered. "We'll take due precautions, of course. When we get nearer, we'll know better what to watch out for. This night we camp in Roong."

"Is the Captain General certain? I mean, enemy could lurk throughout a warren like that."

"We won't take foolish chances. We should be able to cast back assault wherever we've got room for maneuver and a clear field of fire. Frankly, I doubt if barbarians are present. With their trade routes cut off, why would they be? Roong isn't kith territory, remember. They consider it common property, and therefore won't defend it as fanatically as they do their hunting grounds." Sidír lifted his head, to let the breeze catch the red plume on the helmet he felt he must wear for an emblem of energy. "Colonel, dry shelter is there. Our men shall not sleep longer in the wet. Forward!"

Develkai signaled his bugler. Small, lost, defiant, a call to advance resounded off the steeps.

Soldiers trotted ahead. Banners fluttered, lanceheads gleamed. They were good lads. Besides the Hammers, who were entirely Barommian, they included a company of horsemen largely Rahídian, mounted infantry and engineers, who would form the garrison. Dispersed among them were riflemen, for whom mules carried abundant ammunition.

They and their kind had beaten the Ulgani so terribly that on this trip they saw never a soul. (Skeletons latticed Elk Meadow.) Nor had emptiness daunted them. (The natives were driving game herds away from the river, beyond ready reach of Imperial foragers.) The tundra, its horrors unforeseen, had nonetheless failed before their will. Surely they could lay hand on a pile of ruins.

An hour passed. Shadows of the Ice grew long. And in Sidír awareness waxed of the vastness that was Roong.

Ever oftener he saw mounds where clusters of habitation had collapsed. Finally the entire landscape was an upheaval of them, scores of hundreds. He rode to the top of one for a wide view. In moss and tufts he glimpsed fragments, a broken brick, a ceramic shard, splinters of glass, bits of smooth stuff like hardened resin which men had molded. On the crest, he halted. His breath gusted outward, sharper than the wind that spooked around these barrows.

Elsewhere in the world, remnants of ancient cities were seen above ground, but remnants only, long since mined out by denser populations. Roong was too huge to comprehend. At this nearness, the Ice behind had turned into a setting for it, like earth and sky. Most of its buildings were fallen, even as that which moldered beneath his horse's feet. But they had been so thick that their cemetery became a single undulating elevation.

Brush grew on this, because pieces stood yet to check the wind and trap the warmth. From hill-high rubble piles lifted snags of masonry walls, chimney stumps, eroded pillars drunkenly half-erect. And in a single district, though isolated giants reared elsewhere across more miles than his eyes reached, in a cluster he saw the towers.

Dark athwart Ice and heaven, they bulked, they climbed, they soared. Time had gnawed them also. Windows gaped empty, lost sections of siding opened hollownesses to weather and rats, roofs had come crashing own through floor after floor, entrances were buried in rubbish and drifted soil, lichen had gone up their flanks to their shattered crowns, where hawks and owls now housed. But they were the towers. Such pride and power had raised them that they outlasted nations, empires, histories; before the final one of them toppled, they would have outlasted gods.

Shaken to his heart, Sidír rode downhill and onward.

Scouts reported desertion, everywhere they reconnoitered. While thousands of foemen could lie hidden in these graveyard reaches, Sidír did not believe any were. He led his troopers down overgrown lanes which had been avenues, and heard no challenge except echoes off ramparts. He thought those jeered, faintly, without really caring. A few more dayfly intruders were not worth dropping a cornice upon.

He felt his intuition confirmed when he found signs of the Northfolk. That was at an outlying titan. It fronted on a square otherwise bounded by wreckage; but its shadow had already filled the space with dusk, however much its heights still shone against blueness. Brush had been cleared, firepits dug, débris rearranged into huts across which hide canopies could be stretched. Trample marks and dried dung showed that horses had lately made use of a southbound thoroughfare. Most noticeable was a pile of steel beams, copper wire, aluminum sheet, metals more exotic, stacked inside an entrance which workers had chiseled. The Rogaviki mined Roong in summer. They returned in winter, when the tundra had frozen hard, to fetch their booty. This gang must have abandoned its enterprise to go fight the invaders.

"We'll establish ourselves here," Sidír ordered.

The men dismounted and hustled about, investigating, choosing spots, preparing for night. Their bodies would rest in a bit of comfort such as they had not known throughout the past month. Their souls— They spoke little, in muted tones. Their eyes flickered.

Sidír and Develkai entered the tower for an inspection. The space they found was a trifle brighter than outside, since gaps in the west façade admitted sunbeams. But overhead, everything swiftly vanished into gloom. A few girders barely showed, like tag ends of spiderweb. A chain and hook of modern workmanship dangled groundward. The air was raw; breath steamed, words did not ring as they should. In its odor went a tang of rust.

"They salvage from the top down, eh?" Develkai remarked, jerking a thumb at the hoist. "Makes sense. Wouldn't want to undermine the structure. As is . . . hm, I suppose nothing has kept this from corroding away except what facing is left—curtain walls, interior cement and plaster, resin wrap, that kind of thing. The Rogaviki rip it off and attack the metal with saws and torches."

"Almost a sacrilege," Sidír murmured.

"I don't know, sir. I don't know." Develkai had a good education, but also a full share of Barommian hardheadedness. "I never really appreciated till now . . . what a lot the ancestors grabbed. They left us mighty lean mines and oil wells, didn't they?"

Much of the best we have is along certain coasts, thought Sidír, *which does give weight to the theory that those lands were under water in the days when Roong got built.* He knew little more than that. It was Seafolk, not Rahídians, who read the rocks in search of a past older than mankind. But a sense of ineluctable time tingled along his backbone and out to the tips of his fingers.

"Why shouldn't we reclaim?" Develkai continued. "As is, nobody will ever make anything like this city again—"

Was that why the ancients died? Had they spent so much of the earth that, when the Ice overcrawled a great part of it, not enough remained for them to live in the only way they knew?

"—but we and our children have a right to take what we can, to use how we can, haven't we, sir?"

What can we? Since I have seen the thing itself— Yurussun's shriveled countenance appeared at the back of Sidír's mind. The scholar from Naís had conversed with the scholars of Arvanneth, and later told his colleague from Haamandur: "—Long ago when this society was vigorous, its explorers got as far as Roong. I have found pieces of their descriptions, quoted in later works which the libraries preserve. What they tell suggests that the ancients made a fantastic effort to save the place, digging great channels, erecting great dams. As a result, the glacier advanced around instead of across it. Death struggle of a civilization that owned the entire world. . . . I speculate if destruction came on those people—apparently fast, within centuries—if it came because of something *they* did."

I never understood what Roong is, nor the Ice which dwarfs it, until I saw them.

"And we will. The Captain General was absolutely right about this mission. I admit I had my doubts, but you were right, sir. The barbarians have barely been picking at the treasure. After we install proper management, modern methods—"

He does not yet understand. Sidír looked into the honest visage and said slowly, "We may be here too short a time."

—He refused explanation. A while later, rather recklessly, he took a lantern and climbed alone. Up he went on concrete stairs that were eroded to turtlebacks and slippery with evening's frost—up over gaps where the Rogaviki had fastened ladders—at last onto a platform they had built at the summit. There he stood and shivered. Westward the sun lay below the glacier, which loomed as a barricade of darkness under a bleak green heaven. The moon hung crooked above black humps. Eastward the sky was the hue of clotted blood. A few stars peered forth. Below them, a frozen lake and frozen precipice caught lingering glimmers. Wind had died down and the silence was immense.

I was not right. I was wrong, he confessed to the twilight. *I led my men astray. We cannot use what here we have taken. Maybe we cannot even hold it. I doubt now that we should try to.* He rallied courage. *Eventually—oh, yes, yes, a tamed and settled land, a proper highway laid across the tundra, yes, here will be wealth past guessing. But not for us tonight. For us, the way is too hard, the country too stern, the ruins too big, too many. Meanwhile summer ages, winter comes on apace, hunger lopes close behind.*

I have not proclaimed that. The length of the Jugular River, each outpost supposes its trouble is unique. But I see all their reports. Everywhere the Northfolk are doing better than I would have dreamed at driving the wild cattle of every kind beyond our reach. Well, they're beasts of prey themselves, who know their quarry. . . . Donya is such a wolf, if Donya lives.

He lifted his head. Surely his tired body talked, not his mind. His mind knew that, while he had counted on feeding his army largely from hunting, he was never so rash as to make his plans dependent on this. Soon they might lack fresh meat in his cantonments; but they would have bread, corn, rice, beans, and they could go ice fishing. They might see him crawl back from Roong with his whole band, his venture proven futile; but they would know that was an inconsequential setback, and would come afire at his tale of what riches lay waiting. They might have difficult years ahead, tracking down an elusive, crafty, cruel enemy; but they would complete their task. It was a matter of steadfastness. In the end, they would possess all Andalin, for themselves and their seed.

Then why am I sad? What do I fear?

Donya, where are you, as night closes in on us both?

CHAPTER
19

Restless after several days, the mistress of Owlhaunt joined a hunting party. The Landmeet had dispersed, but that size of gathering inevitably scared away the game it didn't kill, across considerable distances. She expected to be gone awhile. Josserek stayed at Thunder Kettle Station and labored. He declined a couple of offers from girls. To his surprise, everything he needed for his construction was in stock. Here in truth was the principal mart, workshop, hostel of the Northlands. The girls agreed amiably that, since he could, he should devote every waking hour to the task. He didn't tell them that this helped keep him from missing Donya beyond endurance.

She came back in a week. The first he knew was when she entered the room he had made his laboratory. It was large, rammed-earth walls whitewashed, windows full of sun though chill hung in the air. Hand

and power tools cluttered the bench where he stood. A file grated as he trimmed a brass rod to exact size and shape.

He heard the door open behind him, looked about, and there she was. The courtyard at her back lay dazzling bright. For a moment he saw her as a shadow, haloed by stray blond locks of hair. Then he made out the tinge along limbs and throat. She wore merely boots and a brief doeskin tunic. "Josserek," she said. "The stars dance for me." He came to her, borne on the tide of his blood, and their kiss had lasted long when he remembered to shut the door and turn again her way.

She shoved him off, playfully, laughing, "Soon. In a better place." And then, springing straight to seriousness: "How have you fared?"

It isn't me she's asking about, he knew like a knife thrust.

Although—

When she gave him as much time as if he were a husband, he believed her endearments were honest. Yet he dared never hope her feelings came near being like this. That kind of wild captivity should have ended for him before his teen years did; and the Rogaviki didn't seem to recognize it at any age. If they knew an emotion over and above fondness, fidelity, the sharing of fates, they kept it among their household privacies. There was no use in his wondering what kind of gladness she got from her sworn men. And there was no use in being jealous of them. They were fine fellows, who cordially accepted him and his linkage to their wife. Yes, they went out of their way to show him friendship. . . .

But they had ridden off beside her while he must stay behind.

He swallowed, clenched fists, and brought himself

down to calm. "Quite well," he said. 'How was your outflight?"

"Good. Ho, let one tell you how Orovo bulldogged a moonhorn—Later, later." She gripped his arm. He felt her shiver. "Can you at last explain what you're doing?"

This is her country that's endangered. In like circumstances, I'd want the news before I went on to my own affairs. And I haven't her oneness with a homeland.

"I kept pretty noncommittal," he apologized, "because I wasn't sure the scheme would work." *I could have studied the matter more carefully earlier, Donya, but you were here and I would not waste a heartbeat of your company.* "Since, I've become confident it will. In fact, I expect to finish the apparatus in another two or three days."

She let go of him and crossed over to the bench, to see what he had assembled thus far. He snatched the pleasure of pleasing her by demonstrations. Fire crackled between the terminals of his induction coil, gold leaf spread and shut inside a glass electroscope like butterfly wings, a compass needle jumped in response to shifting magnetic fields.

"And ... this will talk ... across a thousand miles?" she marveled. "I've never heard of the like. How could you keep in your head the knowledge of making it?"

"Well, it's not too complicated." *A simple spark gap oscillator and kite-borne antenna.* "The hardest part was collecting what I needed for power." *How do you say "sulfuric acid" in Rogavikian, how test the selection of liquids offered, how check the output of the lead-plate batteries you at length construct?* "Then, certain dimensions must be rather precise, or at least the relationships of their values must be correct." Resistance, capacitance, inductance to generate a wave-length which will activate a shipboard receiver kept turned for this.

Agile, her mind pounced: "How do you measure? Surely our yardsticks don't match yours."

"No," he smiled. "I carry mine around. You see, in my work of intelligence gathering, I might well sometimes have to build assorted devices from scratch. So I know the lengths and thicknesses of different parts of my body. Given those, I can measure out a pretty exact amount of water for weight, or a pendulum for time. If I need better accuracy—" He held out his forearms, whereon anchor, snake, and orca stood tattooed. "If you look closely at these designs, you'll see small markings. They were put in very carefully."

She crowed in delight and clapped hands together. "Then soon you can call the Seafolk?"

"Well, not two-way," he said. "I can tap out a message in dot-dash code which they should hear on their instruments.

"But as I told you, my chiefs didn't throw me into Andalin alone and at random, like a die in a game. We've other agents busy in the Empire. And several 'trade exploration' ships in the Hurricane Sea and Dolphin Gulf are really fighting craft of ours.

"Now—" he found he must shift temporarily to Arvannethan—"for this mission, I've a high brevetcy in my service. If I tell them to send a party to meet me and, more important, to pass on information and proposals of time to our chiefs in Eaching, they will."

In Rogavikian again: "This thing here is a time-saver. Without it, I'd likely have taken months to find my way to our ships, then months yet to get action started, while your people suffered and died. They might be harmed beyond hope. I don't believe Sidír would spend the winter idle, do you? As is . . . by the time I make rendezvous on the Dolphin coast, my fellows ought to be in motion."

Joy brought tears. They clung and sparkled in heavy lashes. "And you'll break him, Josserek, bearslayer, darling, hawk. You'll rid the land of his horde." She embraced him.

He had everything he could do to stand back after a minute, fold his arms, shake his head, and say most softly:

"I? Oh, no, Donya. Not I. Nor some boatloads of sailors. Nor barons from the provinces, theives and assassins from the alleys of Arvanneth. Only you Northfolk can free yourselves. If you are able to."

Hurt, astonished, she protested, "But you said before I left . . . you told me your Seafolk could raise the city . . . cut Sidír's army off—"

"I said maybe that could be," he answered. "He left the Jugular delta lightly defended. Nevertheless, we'll be way too few. We'll need a lot of Rogaviki fighters."

"Yes, yes, I understand that, and you heard at the Landmeet how many shouted they'll come whenever you ask. Their kin who stayed home will too—tenfold."

"Dear, you do *not* understand," he sighed. "I don't know if I can ever show you. Listen, though. We Killimaraichans cannot take an open lead. Our country doesn't want a war with the Empire. We'd be disowned, turned over to Rahíd for punishment . . . unless both powers can keep a pretense that we were nameless freebooters from an unknown part of the Mother Ocean, seeking what loot we could lift if we stirred up trouble." He saw her puzzlement—governments, policies, criminal law, pirates, legal fictions, meaningless, meaningless—

and hurried on: "Well, the Lords in Arvanneth's hinterland can raise their tenant levies, the Knife Brotherhoods know street fighting, the Wise can maybe help make arrangements and intrigues; but we'll still have to have plenty of Northfolk.

"And beyond that—Sidír's army will still be unscathed. He'll not meekly trudge home cross-country, you realize. He'll come back down the Jugular to regain what's been lost.

"Then we'll need *many* Northfolk."

She stood silent, fingers twisting together, before she whispered, "You shall have them. Word is flying from camp to camp."

He nodded. She had done her share of thinking before she left. Much of his, afterward, had drawn on what she told him. The valley kiths would not send warriors at once. They could not. Their grounds were under the sword. But east of them, as far as the Wilderwoods, ought to be a response in territories not yet assaulted. And mainly he could look for volunteers out of the western regions, from the Tantian Hills to the loess plaines of Starrok. Thus had Rogaviki rallied in the past to aid each other against the civilized. This time, the threat to destroy their herds throughout their lands should bring them together by the thousands.

"Only say when and where they shall meet," Donya asked.

"I can't be sure of that now," he replied. "It won't be very soon. I have to get south, meet my countrymen, help them lay the groundwork of revolt. Two months at least, likelier three. Then we'll send for our first contingent of allies. Can you—can somebody—have them standing by, about that time, among households whose wintergarths aren't far from the border?"

"Yes."

"My message will say where they should join us. If luck is kind, they'll give the extra strength to overrun the Imperials down there. The garrisons are undermanned and have little in the way of fortifications.

"But then things get weasel-tricky. Sidír will muster his troops and hurry downriver. We'd not fare well if we met him with our backs to the sea. We'll have to move north. And the second, larger contingent of Rogaviki will have to meet us upstream, at a rather closely figured time. Can they do that?"

"I think so."

"The problem of supply—It'll be winter."

"Each will pack his or her own food. A load of pemmican will keep a person going till there's freedom to hunt—after victory, on the way home."

"If there is victory. . . . Donya, I can't read the future. I've no plan beyond capturing Arvanneth. Not yet. Afterward . . . I don't know." He leaned back against his workbench and gripped its edge hurtfully hard. "You can probably match or outmatch the numbers in Sidír's host. But can you outfight them? They have what's more than their guns and body armor. They have the training of soldiers; they have the spirit. If their lancers charge us, can we make a thousand Rogaviki pikemen stand shoulder to shoulder? I think not. I think they'll complain of the smell, and move apart, and die fighting as individuals—very bravely, yes, but still dying."

"The bravery matters more than the death," she said low.

Anguish took him. "Donya, do you mean to be there?"

"In the second contingent? Of course. What else? That is, if the enemy has left Hervar."

"I don't want you killed! Listen, come south with me."

She gave him a shocked stare. "What?"

"When I leave here, come along. You and ... and whoever you wish. ... It'll be none too safe, but it will be less mortally dangerous than guerrila war and at last a pitched battle against the whole amy, if you've survived that long."

"Josserek, what are you saying? I can't go. I've overstayed myself here as is. Hervar's beset!"

"Yes, yes," he argued quickly, "and I realize you hate to leave your kith there. But you can help them, oh, hugely better if you help me. Think. I—my Seafolk, the Arvannethans—we need someone who understands the Northfolk, really understands them, what they can and cannot do. Someone they look up to, whose counsel they'll follow. And who also has experience with the civilized races. That's you. I doubt if a Rogaviki alive is better qualified for ... for staff and liaison ... than you. And we make a good team, we two. Don't we?" He braced himself. "Donya, you must. It's your duty to Hervar."

He waited for her answer, in a silence which his heart made noisy, while the jade eyes searched him. Was that pain which he saw on her face? When she did speak, her voice was huskier than before and not wholly level.

"I think best we talk about ourselves, dear. Come outside."

The Rogaviki are the Children of the Sky.

She took his hand. Hers was warm and hard. Mutely, they walked forth. The Station trees soughed and cast unrestful shadows, for a wind blew, from the west but touched by cold already moving southward.

Her stride matched his. Soon they were a mile off.

The signs of man became a grove, a few glimpsed buildings, a dusty patch of harvested cropland, huddled in front of Thunder Kettle crater. Everywhere and everything else beneath heaven was the prairie. Waist-high grass billowed from beyond the world's rim. Its myriad greens were paling now, it shone almost silver. The wind smelled of it and of sunlight. Blackbirds in their hundreds rode the booming air. Red patches on their wings and thin sweetness of their cries made on-and-off flashes across distance. High above them, unbelievably white amidst blue, passed a flock of swans.

When Donya finally spoke, Josserek was glad to keep walking. It helped ward off the chill without and within him. She looked straight before her, and he thought he could hear in her voice what will, even courage, the words demanded.

"Darling friend, I feared this would happen. There've been times past when an outlander and a woman of ours grew close . . . had more than a little sport. . . . The ending was never good. Go from me before too late. For now I can only hurt you."

He locked his gaze onto her and forced out: "Are you afraid I resent your husbands, and this might grow worse? No. I would, well, I'd certainly like best to keep you for myself alone. But—" He chuckled harshly. "You give me so much when we're together, I doubt if any single man can give you enough."

She bit her lip. "What have you in mind?"

"Whatever lets me stay with you for always."

"It's impossible."

"Why?"

"Josserek, I do care for you. You've been a gallant comrade, a bewitching talkmate, and, yes, a fine lover. Do you suppose I'd not take you into my family if I could?"

He sighed. "Oh, I know I can't become the perfect plainsman. I'm starting too late in life. But I can learn what I must."

The amber head shook. "You can learn everything, I'm sure, except that. The soul born into you is not Rogaviki. You'll never think as we think, feel as we feel. Nor will we ever sound the mystery in you. It's been tried, I tell you, over and over through centuries, marriage, adoption, joining a kith, settling among foreigners. And it's never worked. It can't. We go crazy, crowded too long. Likeliest we end by murdering somebody. And you, any outlander can't spend more than a year or two with us. His loneliness—his passion growing till he has no wish except for the woman, while she shies off from being hoarded by him—oftenest at the last he kills himself.

"I'll not see that happen to you. Go your way when I go mine, and we'll each bear off a happy memory."

Through a rising tumult, he croaked, "I'm not giving up. And you're not a quitter either. Let's keep trying, anyhow, searching for ways."

Her pace faltered. She cast him an alarmed glance. "Do you mean to come along back to Hervar?"

"No, I can hardly do that, can I? But you've got to come along to Arvanneth. Let me explain in detail, practical piece-by-piece detail, how badly we need you down there. What are you here? An extra fighter. Yonder, though—"

She cut him off by stopping. Awhile she stood, stared down into the grass which streamed around her in the wind, clasped him tight. Then she squared her shoulders, took both his hands in hers, met his look, and spoke steadily:

"This by itself shows what a river sunders us. You

think I can choose what I do. But Josserek, *I cannot.* My kithland is invaded. I must go help defend it.

"You'll say, if I came here, why can't I travel on to where I may be more useful? I can simply reply, first, I've not let on to you how hard this trip was. Without my husbands to strengthen me, and I them, we couldn't have done it. Between us, reason overcame wish. The same is true, in whatever way for each, of those who came with us. We've even kept a layer of mirth. For, after all, we knew this wouldn't last long, just till we'd passed our word, and later given you time to make your preparations, when you said you had a plan. And besides, though this isn't Hervar, it's at least Northland. It's enough like home that the sharpest edge is blunted, of being away from home in a day of danger.

"To go on, into alien country—I can't. None of us can. Kiths whose territories aren't yet profaned, aye, men and women of theirs can join ou. And they will, eagerly, to forestall the violator. I'll find advisors for you among them.

"But myself to leave, no, I cannot, and again, I cannot."

"Why not?" he whispered.

"I don't know," she replied. "What makes us breathe?"

Like a thunderclap, the answer came.

"Josserek!" Concerned, she laid arms about him. "Are you well?"

I'll have to think further. Maybe I'll find I'm wrong. O gentle Dolphin, grant that I'm wrong.

"It's all right," he mumbled.

"You're wan. You feel cold."

He rallied. "I'm disappointed, naturally. Uh, do you, uh, suppose you can stay here till I leave?"

"How long?"

"I ought to finish my farspeaker in two or three days. Then I'd best spend another two or three using it, to make sure the message gets through." *Vary the not-quite-certain frequency. Allow for atmospherics. Stall for time with you, darling; love makes liars of us all.* "Meanwhile, shouldn't we send couriers out, to bring in those companions for me that you mentioned?"

"Right. I can wait . . . maybe a week, though the rest of my party may start back sooner. Hope gives strength." Donya came to him. "And each night will be yours, dear, only yours."

CHAPTER

20

Strange was it to be once more on a ship. When Josserek trod from the stateroom lent him, the salt wind, its skirl through rigging, creak of timbers and tackle, swoosh and smack of waves, deck rolling underfoot, were like a transfiguration of himself.

His half-dozen Rogaviki men scarcely seemed to recognize him, either. He was clean-shaven now, his dark hair bobbed, and had discarded their woolens and leathers for sailor's duck. They had been exchanging smiles and gestures with the crew, but remained uneasy in this environment. Whitecaps ran beneath a murky wrack; spindrift stung; the land from which a whaleboat had fetched them was a smudge on the northern horizon.

"The admiral will see me," Josserek said. "Do you wish to come, Fero?"

"Aye," nodded the trader from Valiki kith who was

his chief guide and counselor. "What about the rest of us?"

"M-m, you know how civilized leaders are. Anyway, lads, most of you'd not follow what was said; and all we're really going to do at this stage is swap reports." As Fero accompanied Josserek in the wake of a cabin boy who had brought the invitation, the Killimaraichan asked, "Are your quarters comfortable?"

"Well, interesting, shall we say," Fero replied. "But road-weary though we are, I doubt we can sleep down below in such clutter of bodies. Can we lay our bags out here?"

Josserek glanced around. The *Pride of Almerik* had a merchantman's capacity, besides guns which were suited to a ship of the line. "I'm sure you can. Plenty of space, and we'll doubtless have you ashore long before any action happens."

Admiral Ronnach received them in his office. He was of the Derrain tribe, like Josserek; but that created no bond between them. What did was the service whose blue jacket and golden flying fish he wore. "Greeting, gentlemen," he said. "Please be seated. Ah ... I suppose Rahídian is our common language? ... Cigars? ... How was your trip from, from the place where you sent us your call?"

"Hard riding," Josserek said. No words could hold the sweep of immensities they had laid under hoof. It had been necessary for them to cross the Jugular, evading patrols from Imperial outposts, and continue east nearly to the Wilderwoods before they dropped south through sandy coastal lowlands. No fixed point of rendezvous would have been safe where Arvannethans dwelt.

"Well, we did grow a bit nervous, sending the boat in

day after day and finding nobody," Ronnach admitted. "Too many unknowns in this business for my taste."

Josserek tautened. "Sir, what's the status of it at present?"

"Embryonic, I'm afraid. Radio messages have been acrackle between here and Eaching. You realize they'd be happy enough there to see Imperial Rahíd racked back a few notches—provided this doesn't cost them a war. Hence everything was to be unofficial, and still the Seniory wants a good deal of information and explanation before it lets us do much. We've gotten some agents ashore, a transmitter secretly assembled in the city, little else."

Josserek nodded. "I expected no better." *I did allow myself to hope, for Donya's sake. But—* "Probably I'll have to be my own field operative, as well as serving on your staff and fighting our superiors at home and the gods know what else."

Fero listened silently. In his cougar eyes was no real comprehension.

Rain raged until torrents down the streets of Arvanneth washed summer's filth and autumn's torn-off leaves into the canals. Casiru's windows showed the Lairs seemingly deserted, each house and inn and hideaway withdrawn behind blankness, Hell Cloister barely a shadow above their roofs. But this room was snug, plum-colored velvety, bright with lamps, crystal, and silver, sweet with incense.

The vicechief of the Rattlebone Brotherhood leaned back, inhaled from a dream weed cigarette, trickled the smoke out slowly across his dried features, and murmured, "Yes, an epic adventure you've had. But I fear I myself am not cut out to be the hero of an epic. Such tend to die young and messily."

Josserek shifted in his own chair. "Would you rather go on as you are, hunted and harassed, till the Empire's constables root out the last of your kind?" he growled. "Coming in on the Newkeep road, I saw scarecrows in the fields that I heard were made from the skins of condemned assassins. It sounded messier to me than sword-death."

"But failed rebels will perish still more inelegantly," Casiru pointed out. "Thus far we haven't suffered past endurance in the Lairs. The occupation forces are too small, too preoccupied elsewhere, for more than sporadic raids on us. They seldom catch anybody worth catching. Our worst problems spring from loss of Guild patronage."

"That alone will strangle you." Josserek leaned forward. "See here, I'm showing you a possibility of the very alliance with Northfolk and Seafolk that you hoped to make. I'm not asking you to commit yourself this day. Obviously you can't. In fact, my side will want a reasonable assurance of success before moving. I'm one of several persons who're opening discussion with the various elements in the city that must reach agreement and coordinate their efforts—else an uprising really would be nonsense. Can't we, you and I, explore these matters together? And then, if you find any promise in them, can't you make further contacts for us?"

"It will take time," Casiru warned.

"I know," Josserek said rather grimly.

"But . . . yes, on those terms you do interest me." Casiru beamed. "You shall be my welcome guest."

Ercer en-Havan, Holy Councilor for the World, set in the robe of his Gray order, upon a marble throne carved so long ago that hollows were worn in back and seat, and fingered the smoke crystal sphere he wore as a pendant, whose engraved map showed coastlines and Ice boundaries strange to the charts today. The chamber around was austere and curtained. Josserek had been led there blindfolded. He knew merely that it was somewhere in the Crown Temple.

"You will understand," rustled the Wiseman's voice, "I receive you for no other reason than that the word you wormed to me through intermediaries merits further inquiry. Perhaps I do but lead you on, drawing forth information, before I have you arrested and turn you over to the Emperor's inquisitors."

"Of course," Josserek answered straight-faced. "And for your part, sir, you understand I'm just a messenger, and those I speak for do not themselves represent the government of Killimaraich. Routine intelligence operations have turned up evidence of, hm, prospective disturbances of the peace in your dominions. Invasion and insurrection are both conceivable. We think Eaching would not disapprove if we lent our good offices toward minimizing the damage. But this is for you to decide."

"I confess to wondering why you do not take your findings to the Imperial Voice."

"Well, your Wisdom, we thought the Council of the Wise could best judge our news and what to do about it. And is not the Council part of the Imperial government of Arvanneth?"

"Yes, thus goes the designation. . . . You hint at a movement to overthrow the Emperor's forces here and proclaim a restored sovereignty: a movement which hopes for aid from Northland barbarians and, ah, Seafolk adventurers."

"That's right, your Wisdom. Whether this succeeds or not is no business of Killimaraich's, directly—though I might remind your Wisdom that it's never recognized Radíd's annexation of Arvanneth. We do believe there's no way to stop the attempt, and your best course is to prepare to exercise some control over events."

"For example, by making preliminary arrangements with other sectors of society to form a—ah—"

"I suggest you might call it a government of national liberation, your Wisdom."

"Perhaps."

"A coalition, at least. Sir, if my principals can help reduce bloodshed by acting as intermediaries between the different factions, they'll be happy to try."

Ercer stroked his fork beard. "More attractive might be an offer to prevent the Imperial Captain General from bringing his army downriver should this coup succeed. Arvanneth has outworn many conquerors. These are no different. A few decades, a few centuries— However, one's personal death is for eternity."

"Well, your Wisdom," Josserek began, "as I told you, it happens we know a little about what the Northfolk are doing."

None had news of Donya for none were from Hervar nor could any be while Sidír kept his headquarters at Fuld. Presently Josserek gave up asking among them. With Fero, he drew aside Targantar of the Luki kith, who was the nearest they had to a leader.

The hunters waited in their tens of hundreds. Few showed to any single eye, for they were widely spread in the Swamps of Unvar. Leafless trees and brush, dry reeds upthrust from frozen meres, still gave concealment, especially on a day like this, when snow tumbled through dim gray light, thick, wet, muffling the land in colorless quiet.

"Are you sure the whole band is collected by now?" Josserek asked.

Targantar shrugged. "No," he answered. "How could I be? But I've ample reason to suppose it."

He described the courier system which had developed among the Rogaviki, rather than having been organized by any particular group, for war purposes. That it had appeared was not remarkable, given the character of that people. It was mainly common-sensical. He had become the person to whom everybody sent information, and from whom at last went the word that set them traveling: simply because Donya had spoken at length with him, his wife, and his co-husbands about this, at Thunder Kettle Landmeet. He knew roughly how many had gone south, converging on this area according to advice which Fero sent. And he knew that several times that number were poised to move into the central Jugular Valley, whenever they heard from their allies. A network of standby messengers and remounting posts waited ready to inform all their camps at gallop speed.

"Can you abide here a few more days, unbeknownst?" Josserek went on.

"I'd guess so," Targantar nodded. "There weren't many farms between the border and these wilds; and be like every party of us that passed near one had the wit to do what we agreed, and take the dwellers prisoner. A swampman or two might carry tales. But everybody who ever learned woodcraft, trading east of the Idis Mountains, ought to be out patrolling against that."

"Good. You see, we've decided it's important to raise the countryside first, especially northward. If the Lords seize control of the provinces overnight, that should slow down news of what's happened, on its way to the main invader army."

"Right thinking. Be quick, though. This place is too wet and glum for us."

"Three or four days at most. Then you'll get your summons."

"What shall we do?"

"Come around the city to the Grand East Highroad. You remember, don't you, the causeway from it is the single footroute across the Lagoon. We've no rafts and boats as the Rahídians did when they stormed."

"Hm. I remember, too, a powerful bastion at the far end."

"That's what the Knife Brotherhoods will do," Fero said, "—attack it from inside, open the gates for you, show you where troops are posted about the place. Cavalry and artillery won't count for much. Those lanes are like upland gorges."

"Ve-ry good." Targantar drew his blade, ran thumb along edge, and smiled.

Through the winter night, from end to end of Arvanneth, Rogaviki were hunting. They had light enough from stars, moon, its ice halo, frosty-brilliant Sky River. When they met any remnant soldiers, it was they whose senses kept sharp among shadows. Afterward they stripped the bodies of weapons, their hounds gave tongue till alleys tolled, and they flitted on in search of their next prey.

Several Imperial squads found shelter in houses, whence their rifle fire cast back assault. No matter. Keep them besieged. Seafolk would soon arrive who knew how to use captured cannon. Word on the radio was that Newkeep had fallen after brief bombardment and tugs would bring a pair of warships upstream.

Dead men sprawled before the Golin Palace. They had defended it with furious valiancy. But Northland archers reaped and, as the early darkness fell, bore steel across their barricades to finish the last of them.

Josserek led the victors on inside. Until then he had kept somewhat back in the battle—the shapeless uncounted little battles which whirled and spat, hour after hour, street after street, passed on or panted to an end, leaving blood for curs to lick from between cobbles and meat for the great city rats. Donya needed him more. But Sidír had had offices and an apartment in this building. He might find a clue to the Barommian, what to plan against him. Eaching would let a few skilled men join his venture northward. Yet those would be few indeed, in a chaos of untrained and untrainable kithfolk. Given superior numbers, help from behind, surprise, a labyrinth to fight in, the Rogaviki could take Arvanneth, if not hold it long. But none of these would be granted them when they met Sidír. . . .

They got no further resistance. Terrified servants scuttled aside while red-stained bisonslayers loped down vaulted corridors, through magnificent rooms. Josserek identified one by his livery as belonging to the majordomo's department. "Halt!" he cried. When the fellow fled on, sobbing his panic, a woman grinned, uncoiled a lasso at her belt, and snaked it out. The crash made a glass chandelier chime.

Josserek pushed knifepoint against neck. "Where's the highest-ranking person here?" he demanded. "Quick!"

"The Im—Im—Imperial Voice—" gibbered back. "Moon Chamber—"

Yurussun Soth-Zora himself? Marvelous! Hold the civil viceroy hostage, oh, most politely, with many protestations about this being for his own protection— "Guide us," Josserek said. He helped the servant up by a hand to the collar and along by a boot to the rear.

Where a single lamp picked out lunar phases upon the walls, an old man sat stern. As the attackers entered, he lifted a pistol. "No," he breathed. "Abide where you are."

Josserek waved his followers back. Belly muscles tightened, aware of sweat and slugging pulse, he said, "You must be he who speaks for the Imperium. Sir, we mean you no harm."

"And you are of the Seafolk," Yurussun responded, calm voiced, almost regretfully. "The wire from Newkeep, before it went dead, related— Ah, well, why should I feel angered that Killimaraich acts as it is in the nature of nation-states to act?"

"That's not true . . . uh, begging your pardon, sir. The situation is complicated, and we—"

Yurussun lifted his thin free hand. "I pray you, insult me not; for I *am* he who spoke for the Glorious Throne, and honor forbids that I let its enemies misuse me."

After a silence, he added in a gentler tone, "If you truly bear no malice, do a kindness ere I depart. Stand aside. Deploy those splendid animals of yours in my sight."

Dumbfounded, Josserek beckoned his Rogaviki through the door. For another while, Yurussun stared at the woman who bore a lasso. Finally he smiled, and in her language he asked, "What is your kith, dear?"

"Why . . . Starrok," she said.

"I thought it was. You have the look. Are you perchance kin to a Brusa who wintered at Pine Lake? She would be my age if she still lives."

"No—"

"Ah, well," Yurussun said. He brought the gun to his brow. Josserek plunged. He was too slow. The shot roared forth.

Snow came again, this time dry and borne in spearlike streaks upon a wind that yelled and hooted.

The day beyond Sidír's inner office was a wild white dusk; panes grew frost flowers, gloom beleaguered hearthfire and lamps.

A sailor on guard duty announced, "Ponsario en-Ostral, sir," and admitted the Guildsman. Josserek glowered from the desk where he was ransacking papers. The Arvannethan simpered, bobbed a precalculated two bows, folded hands over breast, and waited for acknowledgment. Melted flakes glistened in hair, whiskers, fur collar of tunic, where his cloak had not protected.

"Sit down," Josserek said. *From what I've been able to discover, this fat fox needs bullying and cajoling in about equal proportions.*

"Yes, sir." Ponsario chose a chair and lowered paunch onto lap. "Dare I say it was quite a surprise when I was summoned to Captain Josserek Derrain?"

"You expected Admiral Ronnach? He's busy maintaining order—a watch on the Lairs, getting essential work started afresh before people starve—while a dozen stupid factions squabble about how to organize a government."

Ponsario gave him a beady regard. "If the captain will forgive a plain man's bluffness, may I suggest that more able, responsible leadership would manifest itself were the excellent Admiral Ronnach in a position to guarantee its survival? In our present state of uncertainty, none but fanatics, reckless adventurers, and those who hope to escape carrying coffers loaded from the public treasury . . . none but their kinds will come forward."

"The rest are afraid, if they help out, Sidír will return and flense them?"

"Well, Captain, there has been a rebellion against the Empire and there has not, to the best of my poor knowledge, been an offer of protection by, ah, your country."

"Certainly not. It's true that privateers from among the Seafolk have been—are still—involved in a three-cornered contest between Rahíd, Arvanneth, and the Rogaviki. That's outside the jurisdiction of Killimaraich. Learning of the situation, our navy did, by request, send units which happened to be in these parts, to give humanitarian assistance."

Ponsario rolled his eyes, practically saying, Well, if that's the language you prefer, I'll not contradict.

"A few of us plan to accompany the Rogaviki north when they depart shorty," Josserek went on. "As neutral observers, you understand. However, we'll mediate between them and the Imperials if we're asked to."

"I understand perfectly, Captain," Ponsario assured him.

Josserek bridged his fingers and peered across them. "Now, I've learned that you and Sidír cooperated—grew quite intimate, in fact," he said with tiger mildness. "It would be very helpful if we could discuss him ... at length ... you and I. That way I'll get a notion of what to expect—what, for instance, might make him agree to peace terms."

"Nothing will that, sir." Ponsario had begun sweating.

"Well, then, what to expect militarily. . . . Nobody has to know what we two say within these four walls. Correct me if I'm mistaken, but aren't the Guilds in a rather awkward position, after the way they let their interests get identified with the Empire's? If Arvanneth does stay independent, I imagine the Guilds could use, um, influential foreign friends."

Ponsario was cautious but not laggard. "Yes, Captain, your point is well taken. You realize I cannot say anything treasonable. But you merely wish conversation about Sidír, don't you? A fascinating man—"

For the most part, Josserek believed he heard truth.

Everything he could check against different sources rang sound. Ponsario even revealed an excellent grasp of warlike practicalities. As a merchant who had connections up the Jugular, he knew the great river in all its seasons, all its moods. He knew the Imperial host well too; besides his direct relationship with its commander, he had sold it plenty of supplies. And he had considered the logical implications of what he learned.

The army would not reach Arvanneth fast. Sidír would move down from Fuld, bringing in his garrisons as he passed them. Their equipment must come likewise, especially guns and ammunition; for the Rogaviki would surely go through each abandoned stronghold and destroy what they couldn't carry off. Transporting heavy matériel in winter was brutally hard. Doubtless he would use the Jugular itself for a highway, sledding, skidding, and carting stuff over its frozen surface. That would be easier than on rutted, drifted roads, though still difficult. When he got about as far south as the vague frontier, he must go entirely ashore, for the ice would no longer be thick enough. Yet boats couldn't meet him, since floes made navigation too dangerous, nearly down to Arvanneth. By the same token, an expedition moving north to head him off couldn't take along much gear of its own. Captain Josserek—ah, the barbarians among whom Captain Josserek and others would travel as observers—had better not count on artillery for themselves.

"Indeed, sir, my solemn advice to you is that you stay behind," Ponsario lectured. "The Northfolk have no chance, none whatsoever, except for a mercifully quick death from Sidír's gunners and lancers. Nor have the rebels any hope of resisting him when at last he arrives here. The whole affair will have cost him the fruits of a year's campaigning, and he will exact vengeance for that. Yes, none will be left who harbored a subversive thought, by the time he turns his face back northward. Therefore—ah, since the distinguished government of Killimaraich does not wish to maintain a permanent military presence—its best possible deed will be to use its influence to negotiate immediate submission. You, Captain—

"Captain? Captain?"

Josserek shook himself. "Sorry, Guildsman," he said. "My mind wandered."

His mind shouted, louder than the blizzard outside. He thought he saw now how he might go to Donya.

If she lived.

CHAPTER
21

Halfway through the southernmost kithlands, Leno on the east and Yair on the west, the Jugular swung right, then left in a horseshoe bend. Midstream in the lower arm of this lay an island which shifting currents must have cut from a shore not long ago, for it rose almost as high as the banks on either side and even steeper, bedecked with icicle-glittery trees up to a sharp summit. Northfolk named it the Horn of Nezh, and here they gathered to make their stand.

Sidír heard of that days before he got there, when the garrisons he had not yet reached came to join him, reporting that more natives were swarming in than they could stand off by themselves. He reprimanded the officers. The barbarians had no gift for siegecraft or storm. Any stockade defended by firearms ought to cast back any number of them. If they had finally pulled themselves together for a mass hazard against the Imperials when those appeared vulnerable, give thanks to the gods of war.

He did not. Donya of Hervar might be in yonder pack.

His army labored onward. Scouts said the Rogaviki lay quiet, living off supplies, sheltered by tents, covered sleighs, igloos, while daily more of them arrived. No doubt they reckoned on an ally strong and cruel: winter. And in truth it wore down men and beasts, numbed, famished, frostbit, crippled, killed them. Wolves, coyotes, vultures trailed the legions of the Empire.

Yet the march went unhalted. Weariness, pain, loss did not gravely weaken those who had borne their banners from the highlands of Haamandur to the rim of the Ice. Though metal might grow so cold that it peeled away bare skin which it touched, no Barommian took off his Torque of Manhood; he stuffed a rag beneath, and made a coarse joke about being glad he wore it around his neck, not elsewhere. When oxen faltered exhausted, the peasant endurance of Rahídian infantry set men to drawing the wagons till animals had rested. After fuel supplies thinned out, and nobody knew whatever firemaking tricks the plains people did, soldiers ate their scanty rations raw, shared what tea they could brew, slept seated in clusters whose members took turns on the outside. Often in those wretched bivouacs, Barommians stamped through their dances, Rahídians wailed forth their songs.

They would last, Sidír knew. They would soon reach sweeter country, where they could take care of their wants. Then they would regain Arvanneth, wreak justice on traitors, and feast until summer was reborn. And if, first, they met the enemy as a whole, horde against horde, and scrubbed the earth clean of those landloupers—why, next year they would possess the North as a man takes a bride.

He wished his faith had more joy in it.

Before dawn on Dragonsday, the seventeenth of Uhab, he roused to knowledge that this would see the battle. The evening before, he had reached the upper arm of the bend. Riding across the ground between his camp and the foe's he had spied for a while from woods along the riverbank. It had not been especially dangerous for him and his escort. The Rogaviki knew of his arrival, but aside from their scouts had settled entirely on the hardened surface. Tiny fires marked bands of them, spread for miles around the island and downstream. He guessed their numbers might equal his, and that they had some crude idea of using the Horn of Nezh for a stronghold, bringing up reinforcements from the rear as needed. "Meanwhile," Colonel Develkai snickered when Sidír returned, "they've swept the ice clear of snow. Once around the western point of the curve, we've got a paved highway."

The commander scowled. "M-m, they can't be total idiots," he said. "From what little information we have on the fall of Arvanneth—by the Witch, how little!—Northfolk were not mere auxiliaries, they were the very force that took the town."

"Somebody made advance arrangements, sir, pointed them in the right direction, and turned them loose. Nothing more."

"No doubt. However, has that somebody abandoned them since? We'll advance carefully."

Sidír slept ill, as he had done most nights after Donya left him. When he awoke from time to time, though, he found himself fretting about his men. Conscience troubled him, that he should be warm and dry while they lay out beneath a winter-stark Argent Way. It was necessary, of course. Taking more than a few dome tents along would have added an impossible burden, to haul through hill-tall drifts with never a boat for help. And if the Captain General was sandy-brained when they entered combat, there would be extra deaths among them. Nevertheless, his comfort hurt.

An orderly brought him coffee and a lit lantern. Eating before a fight was unwise. He dressed himself, undergarments, heavy shirt, fleece-lined jacket and trousers and boots, spurs, corselet, coif, helmet, sidearm, dirk, sword, gauntlets. Emerging, he found the Barommian garb not quite enough against this cold. Breath stung as it flowed heavily through his nostrils, out again in smoke-puffs. Air lay on his face like liquid. Beneath his tread, snow grated. Otherwise he heard mainly silence. This upper camp lay in shadows beneath the last western stars, the first eastern bleakness. Trees stood skeletal. From a bluff edge he looked down and down to the river. There blurred masses roiled which were his supply train, gun carriages, draft animals, and attendant men. He heard a horse neigh, distant as a dream. Cannon caught sheens along their barrels. They would grow hot today, hurling stones into live bodies. Ice glimmered nearly a mile to the farther shore. Past those ramparts the land rolled hoar till it met the rearguard of night.

Aloneness arose and struck him. High pastures of Haamandur, Zangazeng under the holy volcanoes, Ang the wife of his youth, her six children she bore him, lay beyond the moon. Naís of the gracious mansions, Nedayin the wife of his power, had they ever been?

He called his heart back to him and walked about among officers and ranks, greeting, jesting, ordering, encouraging. Light strengthened till the sun stood forth; then snow glistened clean and softly blue-dappled, ice became diamond and crystal. Bugles rang, drums racketed, voices called, metal clashed, as units assembled and the army got moving.

Sidír was also at the point of departure when a rider addressed his guards, passed by, and drew rein in front of him. "Sir, they seem to want a parley."

"What?" Startled, he remembered, *They never did before.*

"Half a dozen, sir. They left the island area, carrying the green flag, brought their horses up the slopes, and're bound straight our way. No other enemy activity observed, aside from lookouts ashore. Nobody near them, and they don't show anything but hand weapons."

"Hail them," Sidír decided. "If they request a talk, bring them here."

During the half hour's wait that followed, he had trouble staying calm—his blood would not at all—thought he denied himself the right to wonder why. He kept as busy as he was able. His warriors moved off fast. Not many steeds and spears remained when the Rogaviki arrived.

He had placed himself crosslegged on a bench in his tent. Its door stood open southward, showing him treetrunks, trampled snow, a couple of his mounted sentries, flash off a lancehead, scarlet of a pennon which drooped in the frozen air, and then at last the envoys. They came on shaggy ponies which trotted more nimbly over the ground and had lost less weight than the Southron chargers. They themselves were simply clad, fringed, buckskins, hooded capes aflutter from unbowed shoulders. Though leanness, frostbite, sunburn, windchapping had marked their visages, haughtiness helmeted them. They did not deign to slow as they came through the watch.

Their leader carried the flag on a staff. Her cowl had

fallen back from hair which caught the young sunlight
like amber. Long before he could trace the curves and
planes of her face, her name kindled in Sidír, what he
had not dared hope for and now knew he must.
"Donya—" He half sprang to meet her. *No. Not before
my men. Or hers.* He kept steady where he sat. The
cymbals clanged only between his own temples.

She stopped at the tent, cast down her banner to stand
in the snow, followed it herself in a single bound. The
mustang whickered, pawed, and waited. She smiled, she
smiled. "Greeting, Sidír, old strifemate," said the throaty
voice.

"Greeting, Donya of Hervar," replied a different
voice. "If you come in peace, that is well. Enter." *Sit at
my feet, like a dog? I wish this need not be.*

The men followed her. Four were of the same race,
ranging from youth to the border of middle age, Kyrian,
Beodan, Orovo, Yven—her husbands, she said. The fifth
surprised Sidír. At first he thought the fellow was a
Rahídian renegade, then wondered fleetingly if he might
hail from Thunwa, then heard him call Josserek Derrain
and knew he must be of Killimaraich. Yes, he remembered that name!

And the jumbled tales which a trickle of loyal fugi-
tives and subsequent spies had carried north—suchlike
tales bespoke ships— For an instant, Sidír well-nigh
forgot Donya. "Be seated," he snapped. "What have
you to say?"

At his right knee, she looked up with audacity he well
recalled and answered, "If you surrender, you can still
take your people home."

He must search for words until he found: "Donya,
impudence isn't worthy of you."

"No, I'm being honest, Sidír," she said, turning
grave. Her eyes today had the hue of beryl. "We want

to spare our folk, certainly. But we bear you no grievous ill will, now that you're trekking out of our country. Even the Yair and Leno can stay their hands, when they see you bound away. Go. Leave your firearms, for surety to us, and go in peace. Don't die in a strange land, don't make mourning among your kindred." She laid a moth-soft grip over his thigh and let it rest. He felt it like fire. "We were friends of a sort aforetime, Sidír. I wish we could bid each other 'live well,' and mean that."

He knotted fists, mustered will, achieved a laugh. "I've no offer to make you haven't already heard: Come into the peace of the Empire. But since you won't take it, I have this advice for you. Get out of our way. We're on business of the Throne, and if any seek to bar us, we'll drive our highroad through them."

"Wild cattle stampede over cliffs because they don't think," said the husband Yven in a quiet fashion. "You suppose you'll shoot, ride, saber us down. But what if we get at you first? Your cannon need minutes to reload. A cavalry charge can suddenly find itself surrounded by long knives. Hand to hand, man to man or woman to man, a Northlander can usually whip a Southron. Our kind of attack tears at his nerve. . . . All this you know. Worms down the length of the valley know it, from the corpses they ate."

Yes, responded Sidír. *But what you haven't thought is that we might also have taken thought. At Elk Meadow, for example, our horsemen encircled yours and jammed them together for butchering, while afoot your lunatics dashed themselves to flinders against an infantry square. My tactics are forged and tested. Either you break and flee, or our killing machine rolls over you.*

Pain: *Which do I want? I am well aware that if we destroy you completely here, the cost to us will be high.*

Yet if you escape back into your wilderness, we'll spend a decade exterminating you like vermin, and lose no fewer men doing it.

Still Donya's hand rested upon him. Light through the door touched tiny gold hairs on her wrist.

The big swarthy man, Josserek from Killimaraich, stirred. He lacked the feline serenity of his companions; for some unknown reason, bitterness radiated from him. "Keep this in mind, Sidír," he said. "You're off to regain Arvanneth. Supposing you get through us, can you afford the price?"

The Barommian sketched a grin. Sardonicism was a relief: "You demand our guns. What use then our going on?"

Josserek sneered. "The Rogaviki who took the place had none. And they're gone."

"Are the Seafolk?"

"We haven't come to talk politics. I will, though, if you like ... after you've surrendered."

A chance to learn what really happened, what dark thing—No. "If you survive this day, Josserek, I'll ask you again." *I could crook my finger, and my guards would arrest them for questioning under torture.*

No. Not while you are in their midst, Donya.

Her tone lifted uneven. "I don't understand." Those were half-shed tears! "That folk who could be friends make war instead ... yes, outside their borders. ... Who gains, Sidír? Your people at home? Did ever my household threaten yours? Why are you here?"

"For civilization," he said automatically, and heard Josserek snort. The other men seemed as puzzled as Donya, though they did not show her sudden unhappiness.

He wanted beyond measure to stroke her bent head. But his soldiers would see. He sat for a while in his discipline, until he could say: "I'd hate for you to have come for nothing. I did wonder—what made you think you can speak, decide, commit kithfolk in the thousands, not one of whom acknowledges a master? Can you tell me?"

She gulped and gripped him.

After a further time he said, "I thought not. Well, what do you owe them? Why are *you* here? In springtime I made you a promise: Let Hervar help us, and Hervar can stay free of the Empire till it freely asks for acceptance. Now I renew that."

Nobody spoke. Chill seeped inward.

"Well," he finished sadly, "at least you might take this of me: Stay behind. In my tent . . . Donya, whoever else wishes. . . . Keep out of the fight. Keep alive. You can go away whenever you choose. But I, I hope I'll find you here when I return."

Then she raised her face to his, and he saw that the regret had been just a cloud shadow across the pride. "Would you stay too?" she challenged. "I thank you, no."

And at once, like a rainbow called forth in the cloud: "Let us say farewell as friends do."

She waved. Her men nodded, rose, stepped from the tent. She also got up, but to undo the ties that held the doorflap. It dropped with a soft noise, making twilight. She turned back toward him.

Maybe the kiss was brief. He never reckoned its time. Nor did he know how long he stayed watching, after she and her companions were gone from sight.

It was his orderly who had the mettle to recall him, a grizzled Barommian sergeant. "Does the Captain General want his horse? They'll be engaging soon."

Sidír shook his shoulders. "Yes!" He realized he'd yelled. "Yes, let's go. It's fiendish cold."

Waiting, then riding, he wrestled. Was he bewitched? No, civilized men didn't believe in spells and elf-women. Any man who was a man outgrew—before he became a man—this . . . bull-rut craziness . . . no, nothing so simple and decent as that, for a bull never let a single female creature become the sun around which the world went whirling toward springtime. . . . Donya, beautiful hellbeast, what had he let her do to him? Best she die this day. Let her lie slain, by the Devil Mare, by the Outlaw God, or let him, it didn't seem to matter which, let there be an end.

While he could wield a sword, though, he had his duty.

His party reached the riverside. Through a minute's pause to look things over, he won back to a kind of reality.

His host was near the point where the bend swung east. Thus from above he saw both arrays. The shore tumbled downward in bluffs and bedrifted slopes, ruddy earth and icy boughs thrust out of whiteness. About half his cavalry was on top, divided between the two banks, horses murky below hard gleams of metal, a vividness of cloaks and flags. Tiny across the plains, scattered Rogaviki riders resembled beetles.

Hereabouts, snow was mostly shoveled, kicked, or melted off the river ice, which reached scarred gray. On his right came the Imperials, cavalry stamping, infantry tramping, artillery trundling, and steady throughout that noise the drums in their cadence. The army was in close order, each regiment a breath-smoky block nigh to its neighbor. Lances and pikes rose and fell above marching masses, like waves on an inbound tide. *My invincible sons*, passed though Sidír, *and the Empire is their mother*.

More distant on his left, the Horn of Nezh rose high,

a glacier castle whereon grew many-branched spears. These flared and glittered beneath heaven. Enemy clustered along its sides. Behind them was a gap of half a mile downstream to their main body. *But no*, he thought, and contempt scorched through him, *"body" is not right. They've no more formation than so many cats.*

Evidently they had the wit to know their horsemen were helpless against Barommians, for he saw no mounts. Numerous of the hundreds around the island did keep hounds in leash. Beasts of that sort had caused his soldiers losses before now. Like the savagery of their owners, they roused undue fear in civilized breasts. Rogaviki longbows would be troublesome too. But little else was there to fret about. Save for bits of stolen armor, he saw just leather and wool, drab after he had looked upon legionary uniform.

The reserves in the rear, if such they were, appeared still less organized. They stood in separate small gangs, clotted toward either shore. Between them the river lay empty, an open road home.

Develkai, who had stayed by the captain General, cleared his throat. "I believe I see their plan, sir," he ventured. "As we approach, their archers will let fly; then everybody will scramble in among the woods for shelter before we can unlimber our cannon. They'll be hard to dig out, I'm afraid. The land mass will make us split our forces or crowd past on a single side. Depending on which, their rear will take as much advantage of it for a shield against our fire as they can, while they move to engage us."

Sidír nodded. "That's about the limit of their tactical capability," he said. "I'm surprised they've arranged things this well." *The will of Donya? And what about that Killimaraichan?* "We could simply push through, but it'd be slow and expensive." He turned his head toward his chief of couriers. "Bring down the troopers we have ashore—downstream of the island."

"Sir?" Develkai's broad red countenance registered unease. "I thought you didn't want to chance over-commitment."

Sidír's right gauntlet split air. "We'll make an end, I say. Put cavalry to front and rear of their advance corps, and we'll trap it while splitting it off from their main force—then go on and break the remainder to pieces—Make an end!" he shouted.

Develkai pinched off an answer. His thought was clear: If nothing else, having the entire Imperial army on the river meant that when the Northfolk did retreat—no, when they fled in a rout—they would climb the banks faster than horses, and thus get away. Lancers could have hunted them.

Sidír pushed Donya from him and explained, "I've decided they're not worth the cost of annihilation in detail. Not today, when we're needed at Arvanneth. You know how mad-dog dangerous a cornered Rogaviki is. They'd take too many of ours to the buzzards with them. We'll be back next year, and handle them if this defeat hasn't snapped their morale." *I may not be back myself. I may have requested a transfer. I don't know.* "Our present job is to slash through them as fast and cheaply as possible." *To make an end, and get away from Donya.*

"Yes, sir," Develkai said reluctantly. "Have I the Captain General's permission to rejoin my regiment?"

"You do." On impulse, Sidír added, "The gods ride beside you, comrade from Roong."

They embraced and parted.

It was necessary to dismount and lead horses over the descent, slow work that brought sweat forth to freeze on skin. When at last he regained the saddle, Sidír saw that the riders ashore had gotten his orders and were going through the same struggle. Their enemy should have attacked them meanwhile, though the Barommians held higher ground and proceeded three or four at a time, covered by riflemen above and below. But the natives stood as if paralyzed.

Sidír and his guards made haste across the ice. It rang beneath horseshoes. His standard awaited him, gold on scarlet, Imperial Star above the eagle of Clan Chalif. He wished it could have floated at the very head of his troops. Once it would have. But that was when the Barommians themselves were heedless barbarians. Since, they had become civilized, and knew it was bad practice to risk a supreme leader needlessly.

Civilized. . . . Was Naís indeed unreal in this chill waste? Donya had wondered why he fought, and not seen what he meant: law, stateliness, well-being, security, the brotherhood of man under the fatherhood of the Glorious Throne. When one day yonder emptiness was rich fields and happy homes, when the Horn of Nezh bore gardens, for humanity had conquered the inhuman, then would her ghost know peace?

Make an end. "On the double!" Bugle calls went aloft. The Army of the North rolled down upon the Northfolk.

They waited, at bay below the frozen forest. The cavalry at their rear was ready, re-formed, walling off sight of the kiths beyond. The cavalry at their front went from trot to canter. Hoofbeats thundered.

Longbows drew and twanged. Arrows leaped. But every native archer shot for himself. In places a horse screamed, a man toppled from his seat and lay barbed. Yet no single terrible loosing ever came. A trumpet gave command. Upstream and downstream, the lancers couched their shafts and galloped. Behind Sidír, his infantry

uttered a bass cry and followed in quickstep, to right
and left. Thus they cleared a lane for the guns.

His charger sped in such beautiful smooth bounds
that he could use his binoculars. He saw men already
among the trees ahead. They didn't look like Rogaviki.
What were those wires that ran from their positions, to
holes which might have been cut for fishing? *Killimaraich, triple traitor to civilization.* Sidír felt his saber
ache to be at Josserek.

Forward, forward. The foe were making no stand.
They scrambled onto the island, in among woods and
icicles. Their dogs did attack. Frightfulness must be
loose ahead, where the great beasts howled and slashed.
But swords and pistols would end that. . . . The two di-
visions of horse surged around the holm and together.
Here came the foot, pikes and blades, drums and guns,
the banners of the Empire.

It roared.

Sidír felt the blow like a hammer to his skull. White
world and blue heaven spun in a wheel, struck, foun-
tained black.

He was in the river. His horse threshed and shrilled
among broken floes. That sound was lost in the noise of
a drowning army. Water ran unchained, freezing cold,
dark past the snows.

Keep your stirrups, or your steel will pull you under!
Around Sidír, animal head upreared in a steam which
humans churned to foam before they sank. Men grabbed
at pieces of ice, until these turned over upon them.
Close to him, a hand reached from below. A face was
beneath, horribly rippled by the green-black current,
stretched out of shape by terror, but he saw it was a
very young man's, a boy's. He leaned over and tried to
take hold. The gap was too wide. Fingers touched; then
the boy was gone.

The Killimaraichan, smote through Sidír. *He and more like him. They knew we're not swimmers. They brought gunpowder from their ships, mined the ice, placed their barbarians not to fight us but to fool us. . . . Did each single man and woman of those know? It could be. For surely every last Rogaviki can bury a secret as deep as the glaciers buried by the ancients.*

Across wreckage, he saw their rearward thousands move, to the edge of open water and along the riverbanks. What few Imperials crawled forth, they slaughtered.

Why did I not guess?

Did Donya come to me knowing how she could lure me out of my mind? I think so. I am nothing to her but an enemy, and she said that there are no enemies except invaders, and for them there can be no honor. She is not human.

The Horn of Nezh lifted before him, winter-pure save where blood shouted scarlet around slain soldiers. He drew his saber his horse swam toward it. The Rogaviki crouched waiting.

CHAPTER

22

Spring always came shyly to Hervar. But on a morning when Donya rode forth alone from Owlhaunt, the season was fully there.

A rainshower before dawn had left the long low ridges and valleys aglitter; but as warmth grew, the wet rose off in wisps of mist that glimmered and vanished. Hollows kept pools which a breeze ruffled. Grass was still short and tender, intensely green, studded in blue with forget-me-nots. Pine groves towered unchangeable, but willows now shook their blades and newborn leaves danced on birches. Cloudless, the sky was filled with sun, wings, and song. Far off, a moonhorn bull watched over his cows and calves. Their coats were fantastic red. His crown gleamed. Closer by, hares bolted, pheasants left thickets, the earliest bees and dragonflies were questing. The airs eddied about so that sometimes they carried odors of earth, sometimes of the river.

Donya followed the Stallion west until her garth was lost to sight. Finally she found what she wanted, a large flat stone which jutted partly out into the stream. She dismounted, tethered her pony, took her clothes off and stretched happily as light poured into her skin. When she settled on the rock, it glowed against leg, rump, palm of hand. For a while she watched minnows play above the pebbles on the bottom, and let the current lull her. Then she took up the letter she had brought along. It had come the day before, via a postal rider who had stopped at Fuld. She had not shared it with her household, and wasn't sure she wanted to.

The sheets crackled between her fingers. Awkwardly scrawled, frequently misspelled, the Rogaviki language was nonetheless as clear as it could ever be.

In Arvanneth, on the night after equinox, Jossereck Derrian greets Donya, Lady of Owlhaunt in Hervar.

My dear,

By the time this reaches you, two or three months hence, I shall be gone from Andalin. You will not meet me again. That day we said farewell, I thought yet I might return, after I'd brought my shipmates back and finished whatever was left for me to do here. But I've come to see how right you were, and how kind, when you bade me leave you for good.

Your tongue has no word I know of for what I would like to tell you. You remember how I tried, and you tried to understand me, but we both failed. Maybe it is not a thing you can feel, any more than I can feel— Well, I'll come to such questions later.

You care for me, you said. Let that be enough.

Donya put the letter down and sat with eyes turned horizonward. At length she resumed.

* * *

. . . are eager to know what's happened, and what to expect.

Your speech, like mine, has its limitations. I'll borrow Arvannethan terms and hope they carry something across to you. Briefly, though, from your viewpoint the news is fine.

The annihilation of an entire Imperial army was a shattering blow, as you can surely imagine. [Admiral] Ronnach, on my advice, pretended not to know just what had occurred. No doubt some rumor will reach Naís that "observers" were present; but this will be late, vague, and impossible to investigate further. The present implication is that you Northfolk may well be able to do the same, whatever it was, to any future aggressors.

Certainly the Empire cannot spare strength for a second attempt, at least for years. My guess is that it never will. Among deterrents will be the presence of Seafolk in the Dolphin Gulf, with [vested interests] to protect.

You see, by help of farspeakers, a Killimaraichan [diplomatic mission] in Rahíd was able to exert considerable pressure. The Throne had slim choice but to bite the sour apple and sign a [treaty] which, by and large, is pretty much what they desired in Eaching.

Arvanneth is recognized as a [free state], its [independence] guaranteed by both major [powers]. Neither one will furnish it any [armed forces], and both will have trade access. Time will show whether he Empire, developing its [conquests] along the northwestern Gulf littoral, or the Seafolk, developing their commerce and [colonies] in the Hurricane Sea, become the eventual [dominators] of the city. Myself, I suspect neither. Arvanneth has a stable [government] again. In effect, the old order has been restored. It is an order which has outlived many others.

Whatever happens, as far as you Northfolk are concerned, trade will revive immediately. And you will be
left in [peace].

Donya reread this passage twice, pondering in between, before she continued.

Soon a ship will bear me home across the Glimmerwater. From there I'll go to—what? In a way, you will
come along. It will hurt that you do not in your darling
self. Right now it hurts like a new-made wound. But it's
not as bad as it was, and should get better.

Do you remember how, at the last, we stood hand in
hand on the bank of the Jugular, and through a slow
snowfall watched how the ice was healing around the
Horn of Nezh? I feel thus tonight. Afterward, I dare
hope, will come a thaw, and the waters flow free. A
whole world of marvels and adventures is writing,
which I fear you cannot ever know, even in dreams.

She frowned, shook her head, started to read the sen-
tences over, then shrugged and went on forward.

For I think I know what you are; and this whispers to
me a little of what I am.

Do you also remember the day you returned to Thunder Kettle from hunting, and we walked out on the prairie together? You said there had never been and could
never be a whole life shared by Rogaviki and outlander.
Suddenly I saw how this might be—not superstition, not
tradition, not manmade barriers—the very truth.

Since, I've lived in the idea, explored it, tried to deny
it is real, then opened my eyes and seen it everywhere
around me, finally gathered my nerve and set out to
chart it as far as it reaches. I'm not quite the first in the

territory—could scarcely be, after untold centuries—and I've learned a deal from books and from talk with knowledgeable men. (I didn't speak your name!) However, maybe I am by chance the first who came to it knowing something about evolution and used to looking at life that way.

You were so interested when we talked about this—about how whales and dolphins, for instance, are cousins in one household of animals which returned to the sea, while seals and walruses belong to another, and [penguins] are birds which did likewise although the reptile ancestor of birds and mammals must have died eons ago—you were so interested that I'm sure it stayed in your head, whatever else you may have forgotten of what I've been writing about.

Donya nodded to herself. She sent her glance around among the minnows, insects, a frog, a lizard, a robin, her horse; she ran a hand cross her own body.

Man is an animal too. We can see how he and the [monkeys] have a common forebear. And we can see how he has kept on evolving, in his separate homes around the world. Else why would he wear so many hues and faces?

But these things do not go deep in our flesh, no deeper than for different breds of the dog tribe. Like wolf, coyote, and hound, folk of the several races can beget fertile offspring. They can be brought up to any human way of life and thought.

Human way. The races share certain absolutes, which therefore are probably as ancient as the brain or the thumb.

Except for you Rogaviki.

What happened on the plains of Andalin, after the Ice

came, I cannot tell for certain. I suppose a fresh strain appeared by chance, and survived better than the rest, by luck or hardihood, till at last there was an entire new species of mankind.

You haven't recognized your uniqueness, because like us you took yourselves for granted. Yet I believe, now, your stories are right, that Rogaviki and outlander seldom have children together, and when they do, the children are sterile mules. I imagined this was an excuse for getting rid of unwanted babies—and it is that, of course; you cloak your motives the same as we do—but I think it's true as well.

For consider.

Everywhere else, man is a creature of the pack, the herd, whatever you want to call it. Societies like mine, which give the individual a broad freedom, are rare; and both this freedom and the individual himself are defined by the society.

Inevitably, I'm misusing language. To you, "society" means simply "class of foreigners." You know how they vary in, say, Rahíd, Arvanneth, the Wilderwoods, or west of the Mooncastle Mountains; but you make the unspoken assumption that individuals choose individually to live in those styles. "Freedom" is what you might give excess fish caught in a weir, or something like that; if I told you it is a [right] which men have fought and died for, you would stare at me blankly. By "individual" I do not mean "specific person"—But I'm not conveying much, am I?

Perhaps I can't tell you either how absolutely extraordinary the fact is that you Rogaviki have developed a high-level, sophisticated culture as hunters, who have never been farmers and have never known [kings].

Let me try anyhow to describe you from my outsider's viewpoint. The Rogaviki, male or female, is by nature—by birth—emotionally self-sufficient. Apart from capturing an occasional invader (whom he usually kills out of hand for lack of knowing what else he might do) he feels no need to compel others to anything, whether by force or by subtler means such as he uses on his tame animals; nor has he the slightest wish, conscious or unconscious, to be led. Aside from his beasts, I doubt if he is capable of giving or obeying a direct command.

The Rogaviki cannot be domesticated.

Throughout the rest of the world, humans can be, and are. Likeliest man evolved already self-domesticated, a creature not only taught for survival's sake to work within the group and heed its [chief], but bred to this. Those who failed were punished till they learned, while the untrainable perished, by the will of the group.

You Rogaviki cooperate well, as long as you are in small, close-knit bands. But if someone grossly fails to do his share, or badly offends or endangers you, what is your response? You turn your back. You, an individual, will have nothing further to do with him, an individual (Or, oftener, her. The aggressiveness of your women as compared to your men is another curious thing about you, bold though the men are.) When the wrongdoer has been cut off by enough people, we get an Outrunner, or more probably a miserable death.

You have no [laws], just common sense and a limited amount of custom. The strongest bond on you, I'm sure, is the wish to please those persons you care about. You have no [trials] or [judgments], merely arbitrations by mutual consent. You have a high measure of [self-dicipline], and I believe a high average of intelligence, but these come simply from natural selection. They who lack them do not live to bring forth young.

And you have a need for open space which is more

powerful than your wish for life itself. From this, maybe, everything else springs; your marriages, your arts, your feelings about the land, your whole social structure—your souls. (And yet again I use a Rogavikian word without being sure what it means.)

I don't know whence that need arises. "Instinct" begs the question, doesn't it? Many animals exhibit territoriality. My kind of human seems to have a weak form of it. In you it appears overwhelming. That mighty an inborn urge marks you off from me more sharply than could any difference in face or form.

I think your drive to guard your borders originated as nature's response to the necessity of keeping space around you. But where does it come from?

[Pheromones]? A Killimaraichan word this time. It refers to vapors given off by an animal, to influence the behavior of fellow creatures. Musk in breeding season is a rather crude example. I've read how naturalists in my homeland think nowadays that ants and bees work together because of [pheromones]—laying trails to food, for instance. Among humans, who knows?

Maybe you Rogaviki breathe out a substance that, beyond a certain concentration, makes you uneasy. You can't smell the stuff, understand; but maybe, beyond a point, you begin disliking the actual scent of man; and if crowdedness gets worse, your whole world seems wrong.

Donya nodded thoughtfully.

How and why this should be, remains guesswork till we know more. Here's a notion of mine. When Ice came down, at first there was terrible want, until nature adapted to the changed conditions and grew abundant. Meanwhile, a species of human that had no wish to exist in vast, close-huddled numbers could survive better on the plains than the old sort.

I wonder if my hypothetical subtle fluid is the creation of a body chemistry which has effects more strange than this. I don't suppose you ever thought about it, Donya, darling, but you—almost every woman of your people is the youthful sexual dream of every male outlander, made real. Who else could give joy to so many men, and enjoy each of them, and yet have no morbid [compulsion] about it, but rather keep active in all the fields of life? Very few outlander females, or none, I can tell you.

But that alone cannot account for how you draw and hold our men. It's nothing you want, I'm sure. In spite of everything, the [arrogance], the frequent [callousness], the [wantonness], in spite of everything, how [innocent] you Rogaviki women are! You actually warn us. Could it be that that substance which makes you what you are enters us likewise, but we are born without a balancing element? You are no danger to men of your own kind, are you?

Could it even be that this is why you never come to [love] us as we do you—and you, maybe, do them, in your inmost households? There, I've used my mother's tongue.

Donya rested under the sun, beside the stream. The breeze had quickened till it stirred her hair. Out past the shallows, a pike glided by, river wolf.

Well, dearest one, I'm at the finish. "At last," you're likely thinking. But you see, beyond this insight and these questions of mine, which someday may somehow help you, I have no gift to leave. And first I must explain my reasoning, before I could tell you what it's led me to, simple though it is. I may be right, I may be wrong, but here is what I believe.

Everywhere on earth, humans are domestic animals.

Alone in the world and time, Rogaviki are wild animals.

I don't say good, I don't say bad. The future could be yours, or you could be doomed, or both our species could go on for the next million years. We will not live to imagine the end.

Morning is nearly on me, I'm bone-tired, I want to put this in the hands of a man unseasonably bound north today, I have nothing else worth your heed. I only have the hard knowledge that you and I, Donya, can no more be mates in any real way than hawk and sea lion. You told me so on the prairie, and afterward on the snows beside the river. Now I've tried to tell you why.

Fare always well, my lovely hawk.

Your
Josserek

The sun had reached noon when she smiled, more gently than ever he saw. Rising in a single flow, she stood above the stream, tore his letter in shreds, and watched them borne away.

"I will bring my folk your thought," she said half aloud; "but your words want their freedom."

She clad herself, mounted her horse, and rode back home to Owlhaunt.

THE BEST OF
POUL ANDERSON

	51919-1	ARMIES OF ELFLAND	$3.99 Canada $4.99
☐	51919-1	ARMIES OF ELFLAND	$3.99 Canada $4.99
☐	50270-1	BOAT OF A MILLION YEARS	$4.95 Canada $5.95
☐	53088-8	CONFLICT	$2.95 Canada $3.50
☐	51536-6	EXPLORATIONS	$3.99 Canada $4.99
☐	53050-0	THE GODS LAUGHED	$2.95 Canada $3.50
☐	53091-8	GUARDIANS OF TIME	$3.50 Canada $4.50
☐	53068-3	HOKA! with Gordon Dickson	$2.95 Canada $3.50
☐	51814-4	KINSHIP WITH THE STARS	$3.99 Canada $4.99
☐	52225-7	A KNIGHT OF GHOSTS AND SHADOWS	$4.99 Canada $5.99

Buy them at your local bookstore or use this handy coupon:
Clip and mail this page with your order.

Publishers Book and Audio Mailing Service
P.O. Box 120159, Staten Island, NY 10312-0004

Please send me the book(s) I have checked above. I am enclosing $ _____
(Please add $1.25 for the first book, and $.25 for each additional book to cover postage and handling.
Send check or money order only—no CODs.)

Name _____

Address _____

City _____ State/Zip _____

Please allow six weeks for delivery. Prices subject to change without notice.

MORE OF THE BEST OF
POUL ANDERSON

☐	51397-5	MAURAI & KITH	$3.99 Canada $4.99
☐	53079-9	A MIDSUMMER TEMPEST	$2.50 Canada $3.50
☐	53054-3	NEW AMERICA	$2.95 Canada $3.50
☐	53081-0	PAST TIMES	$2.95 Canada $3.50
☐	53059-4	PSYCHOTECHNIC LEAGUE	$2.95 Canada $3.50
☐	51000-3	THE SHIELD OF TIME	$4.99 Canada $5.99
☐	53073-X	TALES OF THE FLYING MOUNTAINS	$2.95 Canada $3.50
☐	51311-8	TIME WARS created by Poul Anderson	$3.95 Canada $4.95

THE BEST IN
SCIENCE FICTION